DEAD ENDERS

ThomasWeasley
to Lois Uhlig
Please Enjoy!

DEAD ENDERS

Thomas Hensley

TATE PUBLISHING
AND ENTERPRISES, LLC

Published by Tate Publishing & Enterprises, LLC
127 E. Trade Center Terrace | Mustang, Oklahoma 73064 USA
1.888.361.9473 | www.tatepublishing.com

Tate Publishing is committed to excellence in the publishing industry. The company reflects the philosophy established by the founders, based on Psalm 68:11,
"The Lord gave the word and great was the company of those who published it."

Book design copyright © 2012 by Tate Publishing, LLC. All rights reserved.
Cover design by Karla Durangparang
Interior design by Ronnel Luspoc

Published in the United States of America

ISBN: 978-1-62024-837-9
1. Fiction / Political
2. Fiction / Fantasy / Contemporary
12.10.29

Chapter 1

The magic was running out. Oh, people had worried about it before. People were always saying the magic was running out. No one listened to them. Or if they did, they stopped listening to them after the magic kept coming and didn't run out after all. But this time the magic really *was* running out. This time there weren't any new secret sources of magic to mine. There wasn't a pocket dimension they could pop and eat the innards of anymore. No miraculous discoveries. Not even a higher magic conversion rate to do things cheaper, faster, longer. All of that had been invented already. Their magic was at the limit set by the laws of physics. Their civilization was old enough and smart enough that all fixable problems were fixed. It was the problems they couldn't fix that kept coming back to haunt them.

The problem was they were all going to die.

"So it's a dead end, isn't it?" Cyan, who had been waiting pensively a few paces away for the results, asked Awesome grimly. *Can he read my face so easily? I guess, living as long as we do, we start knowing what our friends are going to say before they say it—one of the inconveniences of having fixed every fixable problem.*

Awesome tried a one-sided smile and bit his cheek. There was no point trying to hide the results of the study from Cyan now.

"It's a dead end. We're Dead-Enders now. Wyrds are a dead end."

Cyan looked a little sick. Those words weren't thrown around lightly. Calling someone a Dead-Ender was, well, discourteous, to say the least. Of course, Cyan wasn't trying to keep his face straight because of a bad word. *It's for the same reason I can't keep my face straight. It's because we don't want to be Dead-Enders. It's because dead ends are horrible.*

I didn't ask for this, Awesome thought. *I didn't plan on being born in time to see the whole world end. I didn't try to be alive to watch civilization collapse and the future become a flat line leading nowhere. I didn't live or think like a Dead-Ender. But here I am, like some sort of criminal. I guess it's my fault as much as anyone else's. I eat magic too.*

"So now what?" Cyan asked. It's not that Cyan was dumber than Awesome. Cyan just thought best through conversation by prodding and making Awesome keep up and leading him somewhere new. But the whole meaning of *dead end* is that there was no answer to "Now what?" or "What do we do?" Dead ends ended. That's all they did. *We die, and then it's over.*

"Nothing. I told you. My scrying…my scrying says the magic is running out. My scrying says there's nowhere else to find it and no way to make any more. My scrying says we've been so brilliant that we managed to try every trick the universe ever had. My scrying says there's maybe two hundred years left of magic at current consumption. Maybe we could drag it out and go on half rations. Or maybe we could kill each other in a giant war, and a few Wyrds could live much longer. What does it matter? We've done everything we can and invented every invention and done everything there was to do. In the end, no matter how few Wyrds there are, they'll run out of magic and die someday too. It's a dead end. There is no future possibility branch, whichever path I scry."

"There has to be something we can do," Cyan insisted. Cyan wouldn't cry. Cyan wouldn't go into hysterics. Cyan was calm, never feeling something so deeply that it cut to the quick, as if he knew exactly how far he could care about something before there was no recovering from it and pulled away right at the brink. Cyan was taking this better than Awesome. Awesome felt awful. Awesome felt like he may as well faint right here where he stood. Only that might distress Cyan, with Awesome collapsing right in front of him while they were having a conversation. *I can always wail in despair and run in circles after he's gone.*

"I should tell Magnolia," Awesome decided. Cyan had asked what they could do. Well, he could go tell Magnolia that there was nothing they could do anymore. That was something all the Wyrds had a right to know. But Magnolia was his friend. She had a right to know these things first.

"Have you looked for Choice Givers?" Cyan asked.

"Of course I looked for Choice Givers. Look for yourself if you don't believe me."

There was little point in feeling insulted when Awesome had already called himself a Dead-Ender, but how could anyone be such a bungling amateur as to not check for Choice Givers from the very beginning? Wherever there were still Choice Givers, there were still infinite possibilities. A Choice Giver meant the universe still had a choice. A Choice Giver meant Wyrds wouldn't reach any dead ends. Previous Wyrds had scryed before, and there had always been choices as far as they could see. But that just meant the end wasn't close enough, and their scrying wasn't good enough to see that it all led to dead ends.

Once other scryers did see the same thing Awesome did, they would also realize the obvious solution of lowering the total population of Wyrds so that the magic per capita ratio would go up, in which case the lucky winners could essentially maintain the immortality they had become accustomed to. Awesome knew some Wyrds would try it. Wyrds loved to keep their options open. No two Wyrds thought exactly the same. Once the news was out, some Wyrds would start killing, and then other Wyrds would start killing to defend themselves. Then leagues of Wyrds would start killing and defending together. And the magic would dwindle away. *At the least*, Awesome thought, *I can do better than that.*

"What do you think, Cyan?" Awesome asked his friend. "Is there a point to dying morally? Bravely? With dignity? Is it meaningful for Wyrds to keep living the same way as ever, without flinching or deviating to the very end? Would we be proving something? To whom? God? Ourselves?"

"A sort of—Look, our souls, our civilization, couldn't be broken—only our material bodies. We died, but nothing defeated us," Cyan replied, coming out of his trance. "We lived how we pleased until the very end, beholden to no one and afraid of nothing. That does sound better than a civil war followed by some stupid tribe of Wyrds somewhere living it up for another million eons.

"But more importantly, are you sure you looked for Choice Givers?" Cyan asked. Cyan always took Awesome literally. Awesome was the best scryer in the universe, and now Cyan was insulting him again?

"Yes, I'm sure," Awesome said, with the irritation in his voice impossible to restrain.

"Let's go see Magnolia then," Cyan said. "I want to ask her to check for Choice Givers."

"Is this a running joke? Let's all forget we're Dead-Enders and make fun of Awesome?" Awesome guessed it could be something like that. Cyan was so calm that sometimes you couldn't tell he was joking.

Cyan smiled and shook his head. *So. Not a joke, and not an insult.* Well, nothing would change until they saw Magnolia.

Cyan and Awesome got on the starway and whisked along, letting the currents take them.

"Did you catch the Bulls game?" Awesome asked, since the star currents could only go so fast, and they may as well say something.

"Yes." Cyan smiled. "Did you?"

"No." Awesome blushed.

Cyan thought about telling him how the game went. Awesome could tell it from his face. But then Cyan shrugged and looked away. It was the same look as when he had shaken his head earlier.

"Do you really still have hope? I don't think it's possible for anyone to scry something I haven't, you know." Awesome complained.

"Just wait until we see what Magnolia thinks." Cyan smiled cryptically. The time stretched out, and neither of them seemed to want to talk anymore. Awesome sighed and resigned himself to the long wait. *I'll find out his secret when we tell Magnolia.*

"Shiori!" Kotone waved as though Shiori had somehow missed her. Shiori Rin smiled. It felt good to be welcomed so warmly. It felt good that Kotone was so excited to see her that she had to shout and wave.

"Kotone!" Shiori shouted and waved, running the rest of the way, with her school uniform whisking and flapping and her shoes clopping against the cement sidewalk without an ounce of self-dignity. Shiori Rin was thirteen years old, a first-year student in middle school. She didn't need to have any self-dignity. She needed to show Kotone how happy she was to see her.

Kotone Nakano was beautiful. She had pale, unblemished skin. She was tall, and her hands and feet were small and proportionate. Her whole body seemed to fit with itself. She smiled all the time, and the smiles always lit up her eyes. Kotone didn't need any woman's curves or extra flesh to be beautiful. That was inevitable. That was easy. Every girl would get those. She was beautiful because she had what other girls didn't have and never would. She had everything else.

Shiori Rin didn't mind. No one thought she was ugly. She thought she was pretty when she looked in the mirror. There wasn't anything she hated about herself, except maybe her waist. She kept pinching her waist and asking her mother if she should lose weight, but her mother told her a little fat was healthy for a growing girl and to stop worrying and eat whatever she liked. Shiori Rin wasn't fat. She was athletic. She practiced Tae Kwon Do every weekend if not every day. She was in the softball club and was the star of the team. But still, she could pinch her waist. Shiori bet Kotone couldn't pinch *her* waist. Kotone had no flaws.

Kotone Nakano hugged her and then eventually retreated to just holding her hand. "It's been so long! Did you finish your summer homework?"

"Of course. I'm thirteen years old. I know what's expected of me." Shiori couldn't stop smiling though. Kotone, Shiori, and Chiharu had gone swimming together. They'd gone to the beach together. They'd slept in a cabin together and stayed up as late as they could, talking and looking at the stars. Shiori Rin had no idea what they had talked about, maybe softball. Chiharu was on the softball team too. Kotone wasn't. She played the flute. *Kotone's skin is too light to waste playing softball out in the sun, though I'm sure Kotone isn't so vain as think of it that way. It's just that she liked flutes and orchestras and music more than sports. I was not being jealous or envious or sniping at her in my mind. I was not.*

"An entire summer and I only saw you three times." Kotone pouted. "What on earth were we doing this entire vacation? Three times. I got to see my best friend three times. It's like I was working a job overseas or something, but we're just a few blocks away."

"Our families have their own plans." Shiori blushed. "I wanted to see you more too! It's just…I would sleep in or watch TV, and one day just led to another. I wanted to see you."

"That's all over now." Kotone Nakano brushed summer away. "It's the first day of school. From here on, we'll see each other every day. You'll walk to school with me every day. Won't you, Shiori?"

"When I don't have softball practice or sleep in and have to run to school or have class chores. Or when I don't need to ask the teacher something before class. Or it rains."

"Why wouldn't you walk with me when it rains?" Kotone complained.

"Because then I'll be *running* to school. I hate getting wet." Shiori grinned.

"That's right. Chiharu would jump in every puddle. She'd make sure it splashed you too." Kotone smiled, the holder of special inner circle knowledge of her friends. "You'd rather be setting fires."

"Someone had to set the fire that night outside the cabin. It's not like I'm an arsonist in training."

"Hmm? Are you practicing for someone? 'It's not like I like setting fires. It's not like I was doing this for you. It's not like I want you to scrunch closer to the fire where it's warm.'"

"Kotone!" Shiori Rin blushed hotter and hotter.

Kotone laughed. Kotone Nakano watched too much anime. It was corrupting her. *I'm thirteen years old!*

The school came within view as they crossed the last street and made the last turn. The road was swarming with students now. Seating wouldn't change with the new trimester, so Shiori wasn't too nervous. She would see Chiharu when she saw her. Still, her stomach kept fluttering, and she kept standing up on tiptoes to see if that was Chiharu over there. Or maybe it was that girl. Or maybe she had changed her hairstyle and Chiharu was walking over that way. She hadn't seen Chiharu in forever. Maybe she wouldn't even recognize her anymore. Shiori bit her lip. *Three times over the entire summer break. Am I a good friend? I didn't even think of visiting or calling. I was happy watching TV.*

"Chiharu!" Kotone squealed, seeing her. She waved and almost bounced up and down. All the boys stopped to look at her. When she did it, it was cute, endearing, and perfect. *I'm sure it would just be embarrassing and dumb, and the boys would laugh if I was bouncing like a ball.* Kotone didn't care. She had that effortless grace where she did things for her own sake, and others could like watching or not.

"Kotone!" Chiharu Sakai shouted and waved, smiling.

Shiori's stomach got more and more nervous. Would Chiharu be mad? It's not like they had called her, though. *Am I a bad friend?*

"Good morning, Shiori!" Chiharu shouted again, and Shiori's heart floated two meters into the air. She wasn't mad.

"Good morning, Chiharu!" Shiori shouted back.

They raced to walk together into the school grounds. Other friends were meeting too. Other names were being cried out back and forth, and other girls were hugging each other. The first day of school was happiness. The first day of school was everything becoming right with the world again, being able to fall back into the same routines and knowing your parents wouldn't gripe because you were properly working hard and getting to see your friends every day and talk about something new and interesting that happened that day, and it meant getting to play softball again with the whole team. School was happiness. The first day of school was even greater happiness, because the teachers didn't really expect you to work at all that day. It would just be softball and lunch on the roof together and maybe a swimming class, because it was still summer, after all.

Shiori couldn't wait to go home and tell her parents about her day and all the jokes Kotone had made and how Chiharu's catching was so good that a pitcher always knew where to throw. The day hadn't even happened yet, but she was bursting with enjoyment because she knew it would. School was a place of infinite possibilities.

Awesome and Cyan got off the star currents when the chime told them their stop was ahead. It didn't really matter how far across the galaxy or even how far across the universe Wyrds lived. Magic meant everywhere was just a short way away. Once civilization was exploding pocket dimensions for food, interstellar travel just wasn't that exciting anymore.

Magnolia lived in a nice area. She had been famous for raising prize-winning dogs. She gave up after a few decades of not placing highly, when it was clear she couldn't win anymore. But it didn't matter. She was as rich as she'd ever need to be with the trophies she'd already claimed. Awesome wasn't intimidated. He was the best scryer in the universe. No amount of qualifications in any other field could match his. But it was nice to have someone close enough in social status that he was seen for himself instead of his status. If she thought dog breeding was as good a job as scrying, let her cling to her fantasies if it meant they could feel close.

Cyan rang the doorbell, and the two of them waited impatiently. They hadn't said a word in hours.

Magnolia saw who it was and rushed down the stairs to greet them. Okay, maybe she had been as fast as possible. It was a big house, and they had come without warning.

"Cyan, Awesome, how good to see you!" Magnolia smiled. She was beautiful. Everyone knew it. Magnolia knew it, but Awesome couldn't tell her because then she'd deny it and tell him not to flatter her. So Awesome just drank her in with his eyes and let his silence say, "You're beautiful. I love you, Magnolia."

"It's good to see you too, Magnolia." Cyan gave a nod that was halfway down to a bow. "Will you invite us in? We have something important to talk about."

"Don't tell me you two got into trouble?" Magnolia frowned. "Oh, come in, come in. Of course you can come in. You know you can come in without asking and when I'm not here too. Do you want some tea with cookies? I had some down time and was just cooking to keep my hands moving."

"You might say we got into trouble. And yes, please, on the tea." Cyan grinned. Awesome didn't say anything. Cyan had some secret to share with Magnolia, and there was nothing constructive he could put into the conversation until the secret was revealed, but he did take a seat in a nicely cushioned sofa that let him still watch her back as she worked.

Cyan sat quietly, closing his eyes and scrying again. Awesome just waited. *I did not mess up. There were no Choice Givers.* The possibilities ran out. It was all dead ends.

Magnolia finished her cookies and poured the tea and brought the platters over one by one. Then she distributed the plates to each of them, took a cup of tea and a saucer, sipped her tea quietly, set it down, and waited for Cyan to come back to them. Awesome started eating the cookies. It had been a long trip, and that always left him hungry at the end. Magic reserves were depleted; it was time to restock.

This is exactly why we don't have any choices. I can choose to not eat the cookies, but I'm too hungry to listen to such a choice, and so I never had a choice at all. The moment I heard "cookies," I knew I was going to eat them all.

Cyan stopped scrying and looked as confused as last time. Being confused meant being somewhere between hope and despair. *Did I really miss something?*

"Magnolia, before either of us says anything that might taint your opinion, can you scry for some Choice Givers? Any Choice Givers. Look anywhere and everywhere. Try to feel them out. Stretch."

"Of course, if you want me to." Magnolia gave a timid look at Awesome. She knew there was no point using her talent for scrying if Awesome had already tried and failed. He could see further than anyone. Awesome nodded encouragingly, showing he wasn't offended, and he ate another cookie. So Magnolia sat back and closed her eyes, and Cyan and Awesome ate and drank tea, as happy as Dead-Enders could be.

Magnolia opened her eyes. "I keep thinking I've found them, but then I keep thinking I'm wrong, and I'm just imagining things. Why?"

Cyan nodded. "Exactly. I felt the same way. I thought, 'Here's a Choice Giver!' And then I thought, 'Wait, that's not a Choice Giver.' I know what a Choice Giver feels like. I remember meeting Choice Givers before, and this isn't it."

Magnolia nodded.

"But then I thought to myself, 'My first instinct said they were Choice Givers.' Why? I needed to know. I needed to know if I wasn't just seeing what I wanted to see, so I wanted to ask you before you heard the news if you could see them. And you said you could, only they were different."

Magnolia nodded again.

"Then this means I'm right. I'm not just imagining what I want to see. There are still Choice Givers. They're just different. There are infinite possibilities out there, *somewhere*. We just have to find them." Cyan sat back with satisfaction.

"Nonsense!" Awesome protested. "Magnolia only thinks there are Choice Givers because we haven't told her the news yet. She expects there to be Choice Givers, so of course she found something somewhere, eventually. I tell you I saw nothing."

"What's this about?" Magnolia asked.

"Well, this is the bad part of the news." Cyan gave a one-sided smile. "The magic is running out. It's a dead end."

Magnolia gasped. "No!" Magnolia looked at Awesome. Currently only Awesome could scry far enough ahead to see it was all dead ends. The others would still be seeing infinite possibilities. But he knew. Eventually the second-best scryer would know and then so on down the line, with the knowledge cascading to the weakest scryer among all the Wyrds. It's not like he could keep the information hidden.

"It's a dead end," Awesome confirmed. "Wyrds are a dead end. We're all Dead-Enders."

"Don't say that like you like it," Magnolia snapped. Then she blushed to have yelled at him, and she put her hands to her stomach. His words had made her sick.

"Sorry," Awesome said. "I'd feel awful if I were wrong. It's professional pride."

Magnolia scowled. "So you're happy if your pride is retained, regardless of the fate of the universe?"

Awesome held up his hands. "The universe is doomed either way. No point losing my pride too."

"You are insufferable," Magnolia said. But she saw his point. She paused to take a sip of tea. "So? What next?"

Why does everyone keep asking me that? Awesome wondered. *It's a dead end. There is no "next"!*

"What's next is we find these Choice Givers that somehow aren't Choice Givers but are still Choice Givers. And we make sure their choices don't run out. And we preserve our infinite possibilities," Cyan said decisively, as though these Choice Givers were a certainty, a necessity. *But if they aren't our infinite possibilities, what is the point?*

Awesome thought about Choice Givers that weren't Choice Givers. He had only checked all the possibilities of the Wyrd. Cyan was saying something outrageous. Non-Wyrd Choice Givers? That was impossible. The Wyrd were the only sapient species. In all of their travels, they had never met anything else. Space was a void full of magic and Wyrd, and that was it. This was children's talk—stuff and nonsense. But Cyan had asked Magnolia to stretch.

Awesome knew he would have to scry again, if only to squash this hope. The hope had already infected him that somehow he'd been wrong. He couldn't die with dignity while believing fairy tales and children's talk about aliens and God knows what. But suppose he found alien Choice Givers. *What could we do for them? We're just a bunch of Dead-Enders.*

"*We can do whatever we can.*" A voice came back to him.

And why should I care if they have any choices? Why should they have any when we don't? Why should we help them? We're the ones in need. They're better off than we are. Why won't someone come save us? Why should only they have infinite possibilities?

"*Because infinite possibilities are beautiful,*" a voice responded quietly.

"What's the point of Choice Givers who aren't Choice Givers, who aren't Wyrd, and we've never met before!" Awesome yelled at Cyan, at himself, and at God. He stood up and started pacing, wanting to throw something. "You're telling me to find them and, and—what?—scry out their best path, the path that keeps going on and on, like a flower that just blooms and blooms? As a service? As a 'Hey, guess what, we're super-sentient aliens, and we know how to scry, and, just so you know, if you don't follow or emulate this Choice Giver, it's the end of the line. We're going to die in a couple hundred years though, so it's not like we can prove any of this to you. Take us on faith. Have a nice life'?"

Cyan nodded. Magnolia smiled. Even though he was still protesting, they simply waited with patient, knowing grins for him to give in. This was stupid. This was ridiculous. He had chosen to die with dignity. He was going to be the better Wyrd. He wasn't going to go around killing people so he could live longer. Wasn't that noble enough?

"Choice Givers are the noblest souls. Those who follow or emulate the Choice Givers are noble. Those who don't

are nothing but Dead-Enders. You know this." The quiet voice wouldn't stop.

"Okay, but I'm only checking once. If I don't see these Choice Givers, they aren't there. It's ridiculous for me to be checking twice in the first place." Awesome sat down. Cyan and Magnolia nodded. They knew he'd find them. Awesome closed his eyes and scryed. *Stretch. Search anywhere. Feel it out.* Infinite possibilities were still out there, somewhere. Where?

Shiori sneezed. Someone was talking about her.

"Don't mind!" Chiharu called out then threw the softball back to her. Shiori sighed and caught it. She wished people wouldn't talk about her behind her back while she was pitching. It caused foul balls and made her look stupid.

Shiori Rin watched the signal. Two fingers meant a fastball right down the middle. Something she couldn't possibly foul ball, which would restore her confidence. Chiharu was so sweet, always thinking about her and trying to find a way to help.

Shiori took her pose then wind-milled her arm, stepped up, and threw as fast as she could. There was a satisfying *thwunk* into the mitt. The batter hadn't even tried to swing. Shiori smiled as she caught the ball and turned around. *How's that? Who's stupid now?*

Softball was finally back. The national tournament would start in just a couple weeks. There were just a couple weeks to work off the rust and get the team ready to play. The coach was running them like mad to get them back in shape. Of course, their team wouldn't make it to nationals or even district play. She was a good pitcher, but she had no illusions she was the best in Japan or anything. Still, she promised herself the team would win before it lost. *Take your Viking's due. If we're going out, we're going to take some other team down with us.* That was all any one could ask of them. They were just thirteen-year-old girls. Well, except for the fourteen- and fifteen-year-old girls on her team. She was in the first year among middle schoolers but still the fastest runner on the team. There were only so many starter slots, but if you had the ability, you could be a starter at thirteen or even twelve. Third years, second years, and first years alike had to earn their spots via nothing but merit.

Shiori nodded at the call, another fastball down the middle. If the batter wouldn't even swing, there was no point trying harder. She took her pose, wind-milled, and threw. *Thwunk.* Strike two. The batter still hadn't swung. It's not that the batter wasn't trying. It's just that Shiori's opponent probably hadn't played all summer, and the ball was faster than she remembered it. *Maybe those few months helped me grow my arms, and I'm stronger now,* Shiori mused. *One more.*

Chiharu signaled a changeup with one more ball down the center but at half the speed of the previous two. Shiori grinned. She took her pose and wind-milled but held on to the ball until half the momentum was already gone, releasing at the last second. The batter swung—too early! *Pwunsh.* The ball was snug in Chiharu's glove.

"Strike three, you're out!" Chiharu intoned. Practice didn't have umpires making the calls for them. The batter sighed and gave her bat to the next hitter. She would have to run a lap around the field for failing. Of course, Coach just wanted them to run laps around the field regardless. But this way everyone was trying their best to somehow not run, even though everyone would end up running anyway. Such an evil coach.

Shiori was about to take a drink before the next batter was up when she fell down. Something touched her. No, it disoriented her. No, it just ruined her balance. A few people started toward her in concern, and she waved them away. She tried to stand up and show them she was all right, but she couldn't. The world was spinning. No, it was like it wasn't this world at all. Heatstroke? Her parents would throw a fit. She'd be taken off the team. She wouldn't compete in the tournament. *Get up! Get up!*

Shiori stood up. She laughed and kicked the dirt as though there had been a hump that tripped her. She waved everyone away and stuck out her tongue, holding her hand in front of her face for apology. Everyone was relieved. *What on earth? Never mind. Throw this pitch and show them you're fine.*

Thwunk. Strike.

"So now we have a problem," Awesome concluded in his report to the government. "All choices for Wyrds end at some point in the future, currently estimated at two hundred years from now. But all choices for life don't end. There are still Choice Givers out there somewhere, trying their best, transforming the future. But as far as I could tell, they are very few. The odds of their success, well, who can tell? But those odds would be much higher if we lent them our aid. A Wyrd's life is meaningless as a Dead-Ender. We can hop, skip, or jump, but we're all heading to the same place, and soon. But for a Wyrd's life, every day would be precious if we lived with them. We could be part of saving their world and saving life itself. If we could feed the power we use into the hands of their Choice Givers, they would have a decisive advantage over the technological level of their own civilization. It appears they never even discovered magic, nor are they a life form dependent upon it. That's their strength, but it means we can tip the scale by giving magic to whomever we please. Should we intervene? Should we help? For our sake? For their sake?"

Awesome looked around the walls of the capitol building and met the eyes of each of the legislators in turn. "If we do determine to help this alien civilization, we must also find out a way to fold our bodies into the tightly restricted dimensions of Earth and take on a physical form while still somehow being spread out enough in the etheric dimensions to have access to magic we can feed on. I have no idea how this could be done. My specialty is scrying. But I hope the government could devote itself to answering this question as quickly as possible. Once the process is finished, I would like to be the first to volunteer and test its safety. I want to be with them. I want to be where the choices are."

The legislature waited for Awesome to make any more bombshell announcements. Starting a speech with "We're all doomed. It's the end of the world," and then following this up with, "I have made first contact with the first-known sapient alien species outside our own," and then transitioning over to a budget request to "go where we're needed and do what we can for our cousins who share everything important about what makes a Wyrd good, no matter how strange or backward they seem"—well, it was probably the strangest speech ever made to this body. But they were old, wise Wyrds. They had ruled well—as well as could be expected.

Wyrd civilization had long since fixed everything in government it was possible to fix. They had figured out what worked and what didn't, and government had pretty much been on autopilot ever since then. *It's not their fault magic is running out. We didn't do anything worse than our ancestors. It was just time. Who could imagine that in the lower dimensions, there were forces like chemical energy and electricity—such weak power sources?*

It was being released everywhere, all across the universe. Energy Wyrds couldn't access and had never really noticed or seen because it had so little to do with the real world. It was like looking through a microscope at a village of little people. The quantum forces at work down there must seem enormous to the people down there, but it was a meaningless grain of dust, the entire system, from up here. Even if Wyrds could find a way to extract the energy from those levels to feed themselves, it would probably feed one Wyrd for one microsecond or so before the whole thing was exhausted and the universe of the little people destroyed. It was amazing that such small beings could still reach sentience. Perhaps matter down there was more dense. Or perhaps the universe was a fractal, and size had no relation to complexity.

Awesome wasn't a scientist. *I'm sure there's some explanation. It doesn't matter. What matters is how the government will respond, because I need their folding device if I'm going to go live among the living instead of just the walking dead.*

"Awesome, you are our best scryer. I gather that no other scryer can see any of the dead ends you speak of yet?"

"Correct."

"There's no chance that you've made a mistake?"

"No chance, sir. I've checked and rechecked."

"Awesome has never lied to us about his scrying before. Nor does he show any signs of insanity. I move that we take his testimony at face value and discuss the option he's laid before us."

Awesome breathed a sigh of relief. Thank goodness Wyrds had good rulers.

"We have to be prepared for when this reaches the public. There could be a war."

"There *will* be a war, I fear. The logic is too simple to refute. Fewer Wyrds means more to go around for whoever is left. The fewer Wyrds, the better."

"Then we have to be prepared to win that war. Raise the strongest army and kill anyone who tries to disturb the peace by eliminating the competition. We aren't animals who think with our stomachs anymore."

"Could we trust that army once raised? It could turn and kill all the civilians, achieving the exact same goal."

The legislature came to a glum silence. Who could they trust?

"Awesome, could you scry out a way to avoid war between Wyrds?"

"Sorry, sir. It doesn't work that way. All my scrying shows is Dead-Enders and Choice Givers. Since all Wyrds are equally Dead-Enders now, I can't tell you anything about any of them. Good and bad decisions look the same to me. It all leads to the same dead end either way."

"So…" A legislator tapped on his desk, trying to grasp the idea of despair, of futility. "So none of our decisions matter except whether we will build this folding device or not?"

"Correct," Awesome said.

"I think Awesome has made an indisputable argument. If there is life somewhere out there that needs our help, that's at risk of becoming Dead-Enders like us, it is our duty as fellow living beings and agents of choice to help them. Their values and ours are the same. Their good and ours is the same. If Wyrds are no longer viable as a life form, we have to make sure life goes on, somewhere, and lives in our place."

"If we did find a way to fold Wyrds into this lower dimension, could they live any longer there than they do here?"

"No, sir. Folded or not, Wyrds would be consuming the same amount of magic, probably more than usual, if we want to help the Choice Givers down there. If there's no more magic moving down the funnel, we'll still die just like if we stay here."

"So we can't even live to see if our help was of any use or made any difference."

"That's not true, sir." Awesome hastily corrected. "We can scry to make sure they're on the right track and that their future is branching out healthily, filling up the infinite channels of possibility. I think we would know what we had achieved by the end. If we achieve anything, it will be apparent. It will be fulfilling."

"Does anyone know if this folding device is technically possible within the laws of physics?"

"I think it is. My physics isn't fresh, but nothing in my memory screams 'impossible' out to me."

"Then the next step is to take this to our most trusted scientists and let them get to work. I assume everyone is in favor of creating a folding device?"

The Wyrds supported the bill unanimously.

"Look, look." Shiori grabbed Kotone's arm and pointed. "They're selling ice cream at that stand. Let's go!" Softball practice in the summer was exhausting, even when you weren't getting heat stroke and falling over like an idiot in the middle of practice. This was exactly what she needed. She could eat Mother's dinner too, so it wasn't like she was spoiling her appetite.

"If you want." Kotone let Shiori drag her along, smiling. Chiharu agreed heartily, since she'd been running in the sun this whole time too, and the three of them set off.

"What do you think? What do you think?" Shiori asked excitedly. Chiharu looked at all the flavors. "Tea? Blueberry?"

Kotone Nakano got out her wallet and ordered a scoop of vanilla.

"What do you two think? Should I get chocolate almond surprise? It sounds tasty. What could the surprise be?"

Chiharu Sakai got out her wallet and ordered a scoop of vanilla.

"Neh, neh." Shiori grabbed Chiharu's arm to make her look at the flavor. "What do you think the surprise is?"

Chiharu laughed. "If you don't hurry up we'll finish without you."

"Unfair! I was the one who suggested!" Shiori rushed to the ice cream clerk and slapped her money down. "Three scoops of chocolate almond surprise!"

"Three scoops?" The boy blinked, looking at her friends.

Shiori Rin blushed. "Two then." She almost mumbled. The clerk seemed more satisfied and bent down to work. He seemed to be giving extra-large scoops though. A girl's outrageous demands had a magic of their own.

"Do you think we'll get to go swimming tomorrow?" Shiori asked her friends once her ice cream was in hand. "School is for swimming. Why go through all that to build a pool and not swim in the summer?"

"I think they wanted to make sure everyone had their swimsuit ready," Chiharu offered. "It would have been embarrassing if some people weren't prepared. They'd be left out and look like show animals at the zoo."

"So that means they'll let us swim tomorrow right?" Shiori asked.

Kotone picked at her ice cream, taking microscopically small spoonfuls. "I'm so busy. There's a recital coming up, and we have to learn all new songs. I hope I fit into my old swimsuit."

"Did you grow so much over the summer?" Chiharu asked, trying to look her over head to toe again.

"Yes and no. I'm worried because I barely fit already. I just keep getting taller." Kotone fretted.

"Don't worry. You won't be taller than the boys at fifteen." Shiori squeezed her hand. Even Kotone could feel insecure. *And here I was making snide comments about her skin this morning in my head.*

"But…who can say?" Kotone picked at her ice cream. Shiori was already well into her second giant scoop. She was so distracted by swimming that she hadn't even tasted what chocolate almond surprise was supposed to be. *Sigh. Mother will be mad if I can't eat all my dinner.*

"The softball national tournament starts in two weeks. Shiori is terrible too." Chiharu made a face.

"I'm not terrible! I just fell down!" Shiori raised her voice. *Traitor!*

"You fell down?" Kotone instantly looked worried.

"I'm not an invalid!" Shiori yelled, flapping her arms.

"Of course not. You're just terrible," Chiharu Sakai said soothingly.

"I'm not terrible either!" Shiori protested.

"Of course not. You're just awful," Chiharu compromised. Kotone burst into laughter. Eventually all three of them were laughing as hard as they could.

Somewhere in there, Shiori had finished off her chocolate almond surprise. *I guess the surprise is that the whole scoop is tasteless.*

Kotone stood up and threw the rest of her ice cream away. *Gosh, what a sweet girl.* Shiori marvelled to herself in appreciation. *She only bought ice cream so we wouldn't feel like we were leaving her out or think she wasn't enjoying it as much as we were. Will I ever be that considerate?*

"Then see you tomorrow?" Kotone asked Chiharu and Shiori.

"Yes!" Shiori smiled. It was so good to be with her friends again. "See you tomorrow!"

"See you tomorrow!" Chiharu chimed in.

And the group broke apart, heading home to their families. Shiori Rin was an only child, but Chiharu had two younger sisters, and Kotone had an older brother. They'd all be getting home from school about now too. Then they could all tell each other about their day over dinner. She wasn't jealous. She loved her mother and father and Melody, and that was that. Besides, it meant less competition for the bathroom and easier laundry days—and being able to stretch out on the entire sofa to watch TV. *I'm not jealous at all.*

Chapter 2

There had been a leak. How? Did some scientist somewhere blab something to all of his assistants? It was impossible. But the alternative was that a politician had hidden all of his thinking and all of his motives all of this time and then immediately leaked the knowledge behind their backs. Who had it been? Or could some other scryer have found the same truth, realized the same solution, and started upon the exact same invention as the government had? Were there no leaks, just a giant coincidence? Absurd. There had been a leak, which meant someone didn't like what they were doing and wanted to break it up.

Why? Awesome didn't understand. Why, when the reasons were so obvious, so natural, to carry out this task? Why were there still people who disagreed, who wanted to do something else, who got in the way? This was so obviously clear-cut. Were they insane?

The leak was twofold. One, everyone knew the world was coming to an end. Two, everyone knew about the new aliens and the folding device. Thank God not everyone *owned* a folding device. It was complicated and expensive enough that, as far as the government knew, they had the only working prototype. But Wyrds were smart. Anything that could be made could be replicated. Were there Wyrd scientists right now getting classified information, building things in remote corners of etheric space, smuggling parts across the star-

THOMAS HENSLEY

ways? To do what? Invade? Or maybe to live as tourists because it was fun? Or maybe they were so anxious to help out that they wanted to cut in line. Motives could range across whole spectrums of good to silly and stupid to evil.

Awesome got out his phone and called Cyan.

"Hello?" Cyan answered.

"It's Awesome," he said into the phone briskly. "I messed up. I thought if Wyrds got involved, because we were so advanced and wise, blah, blah, we'd be a blessing to these aliens. But what if we're a curse? They were doing just fine without us. I mean, not really. They barely had any Choice Givers left, and almost all their paths led to dead ends. But compared to us, they were doing just fine. And I just unleashed the whirlwind on them. I have to get down there. No one knows who is capable of what. I have to clean up my own mess."

"Just one magic user in the wrong hands could do incalculable damage," Cyan agreed. "But what can we do about it now? The moment we told them about your definitive discovery of the alien Choice Givers, it's been the government's responsibility, not ours."

"I only trust two other people to carry out this mission—you and Magnolia. Anyone else could be folding into the alien dimension for any reason at all. But they keep sending other people down instead, fobbing me off with excuses like, 'We only have a prototype, and we have to see if it's safe,' or 'There are veterans, soldiers, who would be much better suited to this task.' They even mentioned sending anthropologists! Somehow we have to convince the government that the three of us merit a place down there."

"Hold that thought. Awesome, you'll want to see this. Turn your phone to channel five," Cyan said.

"Okay, but this had better not be a Bulls game." Awesome sighed and let his phone project a viewing screen.

It was live. A giant horde of journalists were waiting for a spokesman to come out from the capitol building. The tension was obvious. Everyone knew the world was ending, but did that mean someone would resort to violence? They still had two hundred years left. Could everyone ignore the future and let things return to normal? Or was this just the calm before the storm? No one knew, just like no one knew how a leak had occurred, who did it, or why someone else wanted a folding device.

A spokesman strode forward, smiling and confident. "Greetings, greetings. Everyone take a seat." He waited for pictures to be taken and the journalists to settle down.

"As you know, it has come to the government's attention that the magic is running out. This is a grim, sad fate. But we all knew it was coming, someday. It just happened to be us. I've been advised that there are no good choices, but that doesn't mean we have to make evil ones. Violence is wrong. Murder is wrong. Greed is wrong. Hoarding is wrong. Magic was meant for all of us. No one has more right to it than anyone else. When the magic runs out, it runs out. I utterly abhor and I utterly reject any logic that says we should ration or restrict magic to any smaller segment of the population. The government will do everything in its power to keep non-state actors in their place. If they think reaching a dead end is a license for murder and mayhem, they will be corrected. We stand ready to enforce the peace wherever violence breaks out." The spokesman let his grim glare fade and tried to relax a bit, to relax his audience a bit.

"But this isn't why we assembled you here today." The spokesman reassured the public. "We are here today to celebrate, to discuss a new hope. There are rumors, reports, of a project our government has embarked upon. Some parts of them were true. We have found a new, fragile, weak, small, sapient alien species. They don't feed on magic like we do, which means they could continue living and thriving forever. There are no technical barriers to their universe brimming over with possibilities. But if we don't help them when we have the chance, those possibilities might come to an end. Though they don't realize it yet, they are in grave danger of flat-lining. A handful of Choice Givers live within their society, a society of billions of Dead-Enders. Almost every line the future can take leads to extinction or stagnation and to nothing ever changing again. Their society hasn't learned the lessons we have. They are young and silly, like children. They haven't fixed everything they could fix. They haven't invented everything their laws of physics allow them to invent. They don't even know how to scry.

"We must give them these gifts. We need to teach them the importance of choice and of possibility. We must show them that the true value of the world is truth, beauty, and love. We must scry for them and tell them when they are going astray and what the consequences of their actions will be before they so foolishly embark upon them. They are blind children who don't know where to go or what to do. And we must protect their remaining Choice Givers, by force if necessary, with all the power we have. Maybe in the next two hundred years, we can set them on the right course. By then, we should be able to see the fruits of our intervention.

"But this isn't just pure charity. They offer us something in return—they can promise us that when we die, nothing vital dies with us. That some part of us lives on in their souls and their memories. That our civilization and our culture will have meant something to someone. They can offer us an amazing gift—a chance to stand proudly when the magic runs out, when we all leave this place and meet our Creator. He will ask us, 'I gave you these gifts, this long life, this power, and what did you do with it?'

"It's important that we answer him with something positive, not 'We killed each other so that we could hoard magic a bit longer for ourselves,' and not 'We slept in because there was no point doing anything anymore.' What if we all went before God, every one of us, and with a clean heart said, 'We made sure that God's will suffused an entire new universe of possibilities out of nothing but love. Have we not done well?'

"Our government wanted a chance to tell God something like that. And so, we built the folding device. Today we are happy to announce our first pioneer to an alien world. Obviously, he's not here today. The mission and the device must be kept secret for reasons of public safety. But I *can* announce that we succeeded. The Wyrd known as Xanadu is safely living among the aliens. Magic is funneling through his conduit from our world into theirs, so we know Xanadu must be alive and active. However, we have found no way to communicate, or, for that matter, to bring Xanadu back to the etheric plane. His life is with them now. Our scryers can detect the growth and paring of their world's branches. Whether the Choice Givers or the Dead-Enders are winning, we will know if Xanadu has done his job without any reports from him.

But naturally, we don't expect a single Wyrd to move mountains. We will be sending down more, one Wyrd for every Choice Giver. The best Wyrds we have. And if any of those funnels stop, and we have reason to believe a Wyrd has died, we'll send in another. We won't let this world fail, not when the hopes and prayers of the entire universe rest upon it. Updates on how the work is proceeding can be expected regularly. That is all."

The spokesman gathered up his papers, waited for a few more pictures, refused to answer questions, and walked back into the capitol building. Awesome released the breath he had been holding. So it had started. It worked. One Wyrd for every Choice Giver and maybe fifty Choice Givers in the world. *Me, Cyan, and Magnolia. Somehow, all three of us have to be among those fifty—those forty-nine.* Some stupid "expert" was already down there taking up a slot. How could he convince them to give up three of just forty-nine remaining slots? This was terrible.

"What do you think?" Cyan asked him over the phone.

Awesome sighed."I think it was a good speech."

"Do you think they'll give us three open slots?" Cyan asked.

"I don't know." Awesome sighed again. "I hope so."

"There isn't much time to wait and hope. Forty-nine open slots. Those could all be filled tomorrow. They could all be filled tonight, for all we know. Now that they know the folding device works, there's nothing stopping them."

Awesome's stomach felt sick again. "I know."

"So when are we sneaking in to the capitol building?" Cyan asked nonchalantly.

"What?"

"When? Tonight or tomorrow? And are you calling Magnolia, or am I?" Cyan followed up.

"I don't remember agreeing to sneak into the capitol building."

"You just did. Now are you going to call Magnolia, or am I?"

"The capitol building will be full of security. The folding device may not be operable without enormous numbers of technicians. It could need a week to recharge and be useless even when we got there. Any number of things could go wrong!"

Cyan just waited silently on the phone. He had an unnerving ability to know when he'd already won an argument, which seemed to be every single time. Awesome sat there, petulant, trying to outwait his friend.

"All right. I'll call Magnolia. Let's get together this evening and find a way in. I hope you're secretly a spy or something, because I have no idea how to break in to the most secure building in the universe."

"Oh, we're not breaking in. We'll be invited in. You're their top scryer. Get us in, and then we bolt for the folding device room and flip a switch, and we're gone for life before they can say 'Jack Sesame.' Easy, really."

"Of course." Awesome piled as much sarcasm as he could on the line. "I guess I can ask them to at least let us see the device being used, since I came up with the idea. They'll probably compromise that far. Then we just break the glass window or whatever and jump. Stupidly enough, it sounds like it will work."

"Now you're talking. Call Magnolia."

"Right. And, Cyan, we don't move until we get that invitation and that tour, even if it takes me a week." Awesome put his foot down.

"Roger that, Captain." Cyan hung up.

Cyan was a genius. Hope was rushing through his blood again. These were his aliens, and he was going to save them.

Shiori Rin ran the rest of the way home. She needed to run more because the softball tournament was coming up. And she needed to get home in time to eat dinner before Tae Kwon Do practice. It wasn't too far a walk from home to school, so she got back in a flash. She opened the door just by turning the knob, and she crashed in to the foyer; her family never bothered to keep it locked because there hadn't been a theft in the neighborhood in living memory.

She kicked off her outdoor shoes and slid into her indoor slippers, not wanting to pollute her home with anything from outside, and she announced, "I'm home!" between deep breaths from all her running.

"Welcome home," she heard from upstairs. Her mother must have been on the computer upstairs. "Dinner's ready, but just take a snack or something until Father gets back from work."

"That's okay!" Shiori shouted up the stairs. "I had ice cream with Kotone and Chiharu on the way back. I'll hold until dinner."

"Oh? How are those two?" Mother called back down. "They were so sweet when we went to the beach together."

"They're fine, Mother. I had so much fun today. We ate lunch together on the roof and walked to school together, and everyone hugged me."

"Well I hope you hugged them back." Mother 's voice chided her humorously.

"Of course! Twice as hard." Shiori bragged. "Do you know when Daddy's coming home? I have Tae Kwon Do practice in thirty minutes."

"Oh, that's right. I don't even have a car to drive you there until Father gets home." Mother sounded worried.

"That's okay! I can run there. My softball coach told us all to run everywhere until the nationals."

"Oh, please come upstairs and stop yelling up at your mother like we're in a fight, Shiori. When is the national tournament starting?"

"Two weeks!" Shiori shouted up the stairs. "I have to go change. This is awful. Softball and Tae Kwon Do in the summer sun, and all this running, and I can't take a bath until tonight."

"You could take a bath now," Mother reminded her.

"And then run to Tae Kwon Do and back? What's the use?" Shiori griped.

"My poor Shiori. Every day is so full of problems."

"I really have to get changed and go. I love you, Mom. Tell Dad I love him when he gets back and to eat dinner without me!"

Shiori Rin rushed into her room and took off her school uniform, hanging it up carefully on her closet door where it wouldn't get wrinkled. Then she grabbed her Tae Kwon Do uniform and pads and mouth guard and stuffed it into her duffel bag. She checked the mirror. She had short hair because she was too busy with sports to let it get in her eyes, and she had no figure at all. But she was definitely pretty, with nothing to worry about. Then she struggled into some loose street clothes she could run in, a T-shirt with frills at the bottom and shorts, got out her street shoes, and carried them to the foyer in one hand and her duffel bag in the other. Her arm hurt from all those throws, and it was pathetic how hard it was to hold her bag with just her arm muscles. But in a few seconds, she had struggled into her shoes and properly secured the bundle across her back with tightened straps so it wouldn't bounce when she ran.

"I'm off!" Shiori called upstairs to her mom again.

"Have a safe trip," Mother replied.

Shiori opened the door and started to bolt away when she practically bulled into her father.

"Daddy!" Shiori's face lit up. "I had the most amazing day. I'm off to Tae Kwon Do. Enjoy dinner."

"I can give you a ride." Her father was still trying to recover from the collision, much less the machine gun of sentences.

"No need! Love you!" Shiori dashed off before he could give any reply. He would be tired and hungry from work; he hadn't eaten two jumbo scoops of chocolate almond surprise like she had, and the meal was already ready. She bet Mom had been waiting hungrily too. Plus, running was fun. Exercise was fun in general.

Shiori paced herself once she was outside the sight of her house, and occasionally she had to come to a complete stop to wait for a light to signal "Walk" across the streets. She wasn't tired at all by the time she got to the dojo, where she went to another changing room and got into her Tae Kwon Do gi. It was red, her favorite color. The belt was black. Becoming an ace pitcher and a black belt wasn't that hard. All were just manifestations of the same body—motor control, reflexes, speed, and strength. There were girls with black belts younger than her. But she knew all the skill in the world couldn't beat an adult. Her elbows and fists and kicks didn't have any weight behind them. Oh, she could break plywood boards, but it's not like muggers just sat there waiting for you to hit them, and their reach was so much farther than hers that they'd probably just pick her up and dangle her by her legs the first kick she threw.

Shiori didn't train in Tae Kwon Do to avoid muggings. There had never been any muggings in Inazumu. She didn't like hurting people either. It's just that it felt good to have such perfect control of your own body. She wasn't super bright, and she didn't want to study all day every day. So she practiced Tae Kwon Do and asked Chiharu for help before tests. Chiharu Sakai was the smart one. She was always up at the top of the class rankings. She was also the one who chose what pitches Shiori should throw and where. It all worked out. She'd rather be pretty like Kotone than smart like Chiharu, but she had earned this black belt herself, with her own skill. This ability was hers alone. It was important that she was the best at something among her friends, or she'd start to feel like she didn't belong. She didn't want her friends to put up with her out of pity.

"Rin! Demonstrate the form at the front of the class."

"Yes, Teacher!" Shiori rose from sitting on her heels. *Here we go.* "K*yaa!*" Side kick. Step forward. Elbow. Punch, punch, punch. "K*yaa!*" Front kick. Axe kick. Left roundhouse. Reverse roundhouse. Jumping reverse roundhouse. Shiori smiled, still perfectly balanced and in the place from which she had launched herself. She took a guard stance and then left it, turning and bowing to her master.

"Good. You may sit."

"Yes, Teacher." Shiori bowed again and walked back around the mat, trying to keep out of the limelight. But she couldn't stop smiling at how cool she must have looked.

Once lessons were done, she was putting her shoes back on and strapping her duffel bag on her back. She was sweating horribly, and it was still hot outside, even with the sun down. Her casual clothes would be drenched. At least her school uniform would be clean in the morning. Mother would have seen to that or replaced it with another set. The uniform was cute. The dress shirt was white while the skirt was plaid, with red-and-brown-and-green checkered squares, and it hung below the knees. There was a little shield on her right breast with the initials of her school, and it was colored blue for her first year. They had a white beret, like the French wore, to cover their hair on the way to school, but you had to take it off once you actually arrived. High schoolers got much cuter uniforms, with overcoats and a ribbon tie on the front. But that was ages away.

"See you again, Rin!" Futabe said as dusk fell and she got into her parent's car.

"See you again, Futabe!" Shiori waved.

"Bye-bye, Rin. See you again." Her other classmates vanished into the night. She waved and told them all good-bye. Then she started to jog home. A bath would feel so good.

I've got to get a more sane schedule. Staying late for club practice with softball and attending Tae Kwon Do classes and having homework would be impossible. She had been lucky that it was the first day and the teachers hadn't assigned anything. *I'll ask Mom to reassign my schedule to just the weekends now that school has begun.* Shiori should have done this before summer break ended, but it never occurred to her. She just slipped into vacations like a glove and never woke up until they were over.

The night was gorgeous. The city had lights everywhere, with billboards and store windows advertising everything. The streets were still pretty crowded with people trying to get back home. Vending machines were still offering cool drinks, in season for the summer, and various snacks. If she ate another snack without touching any of Mother's dinner, Mother would kill her. She passed a few barking dogs out on walks, and she paused to pet them all until they stopped barking and started liking her.

"Hi, Mrs. Aede!" Shiori waved to her neighbor, who was watering her flower garden.

"Why hello, Rin. First day back from school?"

"No, now I'm coming back from Tae Kwon Do practice." Shiori ran in place, because she'd never brush off an adult who was talking to her.

"Well, hurry back to your parents. I'm sure they're worrying." Aede smiled at her.

"They won't worry. This neighborhood is completely safe," Shiori argued.

"Streets are *never* safe at night. And parents are *always* worried." Mrs. Aede took an extremely stern pose with her arms crossed. "If those two lost their only child, a tiny little daughter, what would become of them?"

Shiori felt a little awkward. She knew how fragile her parent's happiness was. Being an only daughter meant she couldn't mess up at anything. If she started using drugs or failing school or getting in fights, they couldn't rely on any other child to make them proud. It was all on her. If she hurt herself in any way, she'd ruin the entire meaning of their lives. They had spent their lives making her, so she had to make sure she didn't break. She always looked both ways before crossing a street, avoided anything that would catch a cold—like Chiharu's puddle jumping!—and stayed kilometers away from any bad influences.

I'm their entire life, the pillar of their happiness. I know I have to be strong all the way until they're eighty and I'm sixty, and I'm taking care of them every day. But I don't want to think about all that work at once. I just have to be strong one day at a time and do what's expected of me that day. If I tried to think about all the work I have to do for the rest of my life to not hurt them, I'd go crazy.

"I'll be careful, Mrs. Aede. See you next time."

"See you next time, Rin, dear." Mrs. Aede relaxed, the child properly lectured.

Shiori finally made it back home, unstrapping her duffel bag and kicking off her shoes and breathing heavily through her mouth. "I'm home," she called out.

"Welcome home," her mother replied again, this time from the kitchen. "Come fetch your dinner before I put away all the plates."

Shiori put her indoor slippers on. "Yes, Mother. Is the bath ready?"

"Yes, but your father's using it right now, so you may as well come eat."

"Fine." She had so wanted to take a bath.

"Do you have any homework?" her mother asked as Shiori fetched herself a cup of tea, a bowl of rice, and a bowl of soup full of tofu, vegetables, seaweed, and pork or maybe beef. It looked delicious.

"Nothing, thank goodness. Mother, could you reschedule my Tae Kwon Do to just Sunday? I can't possibly juggle all these activities at once."

"Of course, dear. I'll call your instructor tomorrow and explain."

"Thanks. *Itadakimasu*," Shiori Rin properly recited before she took her first bite of food. She could snack on some ice cream without saying it in front of her friends, but she couldn't imagine eating dinner at a table in front of her mother without showing any manners. She'd kill her.

Once dinner was over, Shiori got up to help with the dishes, but there weren't many left to do anymore, and Mother shooed her away. "Go take your bath. Tell Father to get out if he hasn't already."

"Okay." Shiori walked to the bathroom and knocked politely on the door. "Daddy. Mother says to get out already."

"I'm already out. Just give me a chance to dress," Father reported with a sense of being unjustly accused.

Shiori Rin stepped back into the living room and turned on the TV, politely waiting her turn. It was a news item on a guy supposedly performing miracles, such as healing the sick and summoning fishes and loaves of bread—straight out of the Good Book. No one had figured out his trick. Some people thought he should be put in jail, but no one could point to any harm he was doing. He was just a really, really good magician—a new Houdini.

"This again?" Shiori's father walked up behind her. "The office won't stop talking about it. The explosions, flashes of light. There have been videos of people flying in midair and now miracles from the Bible. It's the same nonsense all over the world."

Shiori watched intently. "They must have been on wires or something. Or the tapes were doctored. It must be like some giant hacker worldwide project that they decided to do together for fun."

"Even so, it's strange. No one has figured out how they're doing it. People have been hurt. I don't like it." Her father sighed as a journalist dug into the fish and showed it was real genuine food, not rubber or papier-mâché or something.

"Surely no one's been hurt by this one. He's healing the sick," Shiori said.

"He's *pretending* to heal the sick. And no, not this one. Others. A new one seems to show up every day." Father was patient, but he never let a mistake go uncorrected. He was very good at looking over her homework.

"I have to take a bath. Anyway, it's all very far away from here. This is like the safest city on Earth. No thieves in living memory," Shiori Rin reminded Daddy, because he seemed to genuinely be worrying.

"That's right. That's why we moved here, so our precious Shiori could grow up safe and sound. Nothing will happen here. It's probably just doctored footage anyway. Probably nothing has happened anywhere."

Shiori went to take her bath. *Father didn't sound convinced. Father was trying to reassure himself. That is really strange.*

Shiori undressed yet again then showered down. Mother would want to use the tub after her, so she couldn't take too long. But she wanted a long time because today had been exhausting. Plus, she had had that heatstroke she wasn't about to tell her parents about. Relaxing in the bathtub was the best solution she had come up with. She hadn't felt thirsty at all, though she'd forced herself to drink a lot of water afterward. Shiori rubbed her arms with a sponge until all the pain in her muscles was gone; then she got up, turned off the shower, and settled into the bathtub's warm water. There was no time to daydream. She just had to relax and soak as fast as possible. She wasn't sure how to relax quickly, but she was sure she could get the hang of it.

Ten minutes or so had passed, and she wondered if she'd dozed off when her mother knocked on the door and asked how she was doing.

"Five more minutes." Shiori raised her voice to reach beyond the door. She sat in the tub as long as she dared then realized she hadn't shampooed her hair yet and got to work. She was still dressing when her mother knocked on the door again.

"Almost out! I promise!" Shiori jumped on one foot, trying to put her sock on. Her hair could dry instantly because it was short. She checked for anything left over in the bathroom and then walked out in a stately manner.

"I swear, you certainly enjoy your baths." Mother had her arms crossed.

Shiori thought about saying something snide like, "Better than not taking any," but it wasn't ladylike, and it was rude to her mother, who just wanted to take a bath like anyone else on Earth after a long day.

"I'm sorry, I think I dozed off." Shiori placed her hand in front vertically in front of her face and gave a little bow, closing her eyes. She'd stick her tongue out and bite it, but that was more for friends and less for dignified parents.

"It's okay, dear. Go on to bed then." Mother closed the bathroom door behind her, and Shiori was left to herself again. *You see? Just be honest and thoughtful, and I'll never have to get into any fights. I'm glad I didn't give the glib response.*

Shiori was tired. She brushed her teeth in the bathroom upstairs that just had a toilet and sink. Then she stared into the mirror, wondering what she was supposed to do next. *Have I packed my school swimsuit? I did that yesterday. It's still in my bag since I thought we would be swimming today.* Shiori walked into her room and checked to see if her school uniform was clean. Then she checked to see if her alarm was set. She sat on her bed wondering what she'd forgotten, but she was simply too tired to guess. Maybe nothing. So she got back up, turned off the lights, and got into bed. She was so tired.

Chapter 3

Shiori woke up to a strange red glow in the room. She tried to turn over and go back to sleep, but the dumb light wouldn't turn off. Then she thought some sort of construction vehicle must have had its lights parked directly across from her room and be shining into it. She didn't understand it since she was on the second floor, but oh well.

But then she noticed the light was in her room. And it was making a strange humming sound, too.

Shiori sat up, rubbing her eyes. Could she be having some sort of stroke, an after effect of the heat stroke? *Maybe blood is pouring into my brain, and all my brain can make of it is to create a floating red light and a humming sound. I should call out for help. But what if this is a dream, or I'm crazy, or…* She didn't think her parents could help with this anyway.

The red light seemed to orient on her. Then it spoke. "Hello." Oh great, now it could speak to her.

"It's like four in the morning. Why did a red light decide to bash through my window and tell me hello?" Shiori asked it, politely, all things considered.

"I'm not red. I'm Awesome," the red light replied.

"I'm sure you're super amazing." Shiori yawned. "When you're done shining and humming, just go back out the window and leave me alone."

"No, I mean, I'm the color Awesome, not red. There's a difference."

"There's a color called Awesome?" Shiori was so confused.

"Yes. And Wyrds identify themselves by their colors. So I'm Awesome. Please, tell me your name."

"Shiori Rin," Shiori said reflexively.

"Hello, Shiori Rin," Awesome said.

"Don't call me Shiori. Only my friends and family can call me Shiori. It's Rin to you." Shiori said. What were you supposed to do when a red light started talking to you? Scream? Hit it with a pillow?

"Hello, Rin. I'm an alien from another world. I've come here to help you and maybe protect you. You're a very important person."

"What?" Shiori asked. Then it all started making sense. This was one of those hacker pranks. For years now, all sorts of odd things had been witnessed or caught on tape that science simply couldn't explain. Apparently some group of computer graphics savvy kids were having a real bang at tricking the world with their holographic special effects, though they'd never actually come forward and taken credit for their work. And now these very people were somehow recording her, projecting a holographic image, and teasing her, and they were probably putting it on the Internet. "Go away! I'm going to call the cops."

Awesome looked perturbed. It turned back and forth, blinked a few times, and then just sat there floating. "I can't go away. But if I disturbed your sleep, I'm sorry. I'll wait for you outside in the morning then."

"You do that, and I'll call the cops. I'll call the neighbors. I don't know how you're doing it, but someone is going to catch you hackers. Now if you're leaving, leave. I'll see how far I can trust you by what you do right now." Shiori was furious. *This is so utterly illegal.*

Awesome blinked and then floated to the window, undid the latch, pushed it open—all apparently without any hands to do it—and flew away.

Could a hologram open a window? Shiori stood up to look out the window and check where it went. She gathered her sheet around her chest and kept it close, suddenly afraid of cameras trained at every angle to her window. The window was open. It had been closed seconds before. She leaned out of the window to see if someone on a ladder had been pulling a prank or something. No. And there was the stupid light waiting beneath the bush.

"If you're going to sit out there, at least turn off your light so no one else will see you!" Shiori whispered loudly at it.

"Sorry." Awesome bobbed and then turned off.

You've got to be kidding me. I can't figure this one out. The window was opened and closed by that red gem. Wait, not red, that Awesome gem. It could talk. It could fly. What hacker could do all of that? She couldn't make any sense of it. So she closed the window, went back to bed, and hoped it was all a dream.

Awesome was waiting for her in the morning. Shiori gave an agonized groan and glared at it.

"I'm sorry if I offended you. Like I said, I'm new to this world. I'm an alien, a Wyrd, so I don't know if what

I say or do is offensive to folded-dimension dwellers."
Awesome started floating beside her as she walked
to school.

Shiori Rin sighed. "First off, we're not 'folded
dimension dwellers.' This is Earth. Japan. Inazumu,
really. I'm a human being—a girl, to be precise. But anyway, I'm a girl. I'm a Japanese middle-school girl. And
in Japan, nobody floats around or shines for no reason. So stop acting like an alien super technology and
start acting like a piece of jewelry. Here, get in my bag."
Shiori held it out, and Awesome hopped in. She knew
she shouldn't be encouraging it, but if she was going to
be haunted by aliens, at least she could keep it from the
neighborhood and not be any more embarrassed.

"The first thing you will learn about being a
Japanese middle-school girl is that we *aren't* 'important,' if I remember what you said last night and
wasn't dreaming."

"What's important about you isn't your educational
status. You're a Choice Giver," Awesome replied.

"Okay, this is another rule: Aliens don't get to use
special phrases that don't mean anything like they're
standard Japanese. I'm just me, Shiori Rin. I'm not some
alien queen who descended from the heavens and ended
up on Earth. I have pictures of when I was born, and
I have eyewitnesses. I'm not what you think. Actually,
I have no idea how you're even speaking Japanese with
me. But you should go back home and let me pretend I
never met a floating alien in the first place."

"I'm speaking Japanese—and floating and shining—with magic. A Choice Giver is what it sounds

like. It means through you, the world still has choices. If the world follows you or emulates you, the future opens up into infinite possibilities. That's extremely important. Choice Givers transcend species lines. You aren't a Wyrd. You're an Earth-human-Japanese-female-schoolgirl Choice Giver."

"Pick one designation and stick with it," Shiori snapped. "I'm just a kid. I'm not…a prophet or cultist or whatever. I don't preach to anyone. And don't tell me I should start preaching now. I won't. That's not me at all, and I wouldn't be any good at it. I just want to live out my life the way I think I should."

"You're not a prophet, not a cultist, not a preacher, but a Choice Giver—someone who contains infinite possibilities," Awesome corrected.

"I can't tell them apart," Shiori Rin patiently replied.

"Okay. I'll see if I can explain it to you better later. Let's set that debate aside for the moment," Awesome offered.

"Sure," Shiori Rin agreed. "But look, that's Kotone Nakano ahead, or Nakano to you. Don't say anything, and don't flash or float or anything. I'm going to talk you out of bothering me, and you're going back to outerspace. But until then, stay in my bag, and let me have fun at school."

"Nakano is also a Choice Giver. It's okay if she knows about me," Awesome said.

"How convenient." Shiori rolled her eyes. "Now hush." Awesome hushed. Her respect for him went up again. He had obeyed last night and this morning. He didn't seem malevolent, just extremely pushy and sure he was right about everything. As far as alien encounters went, she supposed this wasn't bad. *But why me? This is absurd. Because I'm a Choice Giver? What does that even mean? There's nothing unique about me. Chiharu's way smarter than me, and Kotone's way nicer than me. All I can do is sports. And any boy could play sports better than me. Why doesn't Awesome go chase down a pro baseball player and leave me alone?*

"Good morning, Kotone." Shiori tried to put an especially cheerful voice on, but it sounded absolutely artificial.

"Good morning, Shiori." Kotone looked like she'd seen a ghost.

"What's wrong?" Shiori touched her arm. The two of them fell into the same pace, walking to school together.

"Nothing. Is there something wrong?" Kotone pretended to smile.

"Yes. There's something wrong, and you're going to tell me about it on the way to school, or I'll sick Chiharu on you." Shiori had a vague pit of dread in her stomach.

"I…I saw a ghost last night. It was white and shining and started trying to talk to me. I screamed. My parents rushed in, but the ghost ran away. I couldn't sleep all night. Occasionally the ghost would come back to the window, and I would scream again. My parents spent the rest of the night with me. They think I've gone crazy. But I'm not crazy. Over half the world believes in ghosts. I looked it up online. It's not crazy to see a ghost and then believe in ghosts." Kotone rushed the words out.

"It's not crazy," Shiori agreed, sighing. "Kotone, you're not crazy. Promise not to scream or call me a plant-monster body snatcher or anything, okay?"

"Why? Are you a b-b-body snatcher? Did you kill Shiori?" Kotone's eyes were getting wider and wider.

"No! Calm down! They aren't ghosts. They're aliens. If you spent all morning talking to one, like I had, you would have seen they aren't ghostlike at all." Shiori held Kotone's hands to show her she was still flesh and blood and to keep her calm. Had Shiori been this scared when she saw Awesome? She didn't think so. *Was I supposed to be? How many thirteen-year-old girls meet aliens in the night so that we could draw a valid statistical comparison and grade where I am on the courage curve? Maybe that's why I'm a Choice Giver. I wasn't scared at all.*

Don't get a big head just because an alien starts flattering you. You're not important. You aren't even brave. You were probably just too stupid to notice you were in danger.

"You talked to one?" Kotone's voice was so high that it almost popped.

"Yes. It's sitting quietly in my bag right now. Now, Awesome, listen carefully. One of your alien friends has scared my best friend and ruined her sleep last night. I want you to very carefully say, 'Hi, Nakano,' float a few meters up into the air, and then go back into my bag and be quiet, so you don't scare her. And move slowly too."

"Hi, Nakano," Awesome said, quietly floating.

"You see? They're respectful aliens. They aren't trying to hurt us. So it's okay. That white alien just wanted to talk to you." Shiori smiled. The situation was rather hilarious, with her comforting Kotone like she was a pro at alien-human relations and had done this all her life.

"Just to talk to me?" Kotone repeated to herself. Then she straightened her legs, and the hunted look went away. She still looked tired though.

I'm clearly the strange one. How on Earth did I meet an alien, tell it to leave, and then go back to bed? Shiori laughed, thinking back.

"I'm glad you saw one, Kotone. I was still wondering if I had gone insane or had permanent brain damage or something. But now it's settled. There are nice aliens that want to meddle in our lives and call us princesses and the like, and besides that, we're the exact same. Our lives are the exact same. I guess it's an overall plus," Shiori said.

"What if it wants to talk to me again?" Kotone looked distressed.

"Then we'll talk to it. They're nice, really. And cute. They're harmless."

"I want to tell Chiharu about it. I don't want to keep it from her. The three of us shouldn't be divided like this." Kotone became more confident.

"Okay. We'll tell her at lunch." Shiori Rin hugged her. She really was relieved Kotone had seen one too. Now she just had to figure out how to make the aliens go home.

When lunchtime came, Shiori was bursting with the need to talk. They had gone swimming that morning, but that no longer mattered. Describing encounters with aliens was just way more fun. It was more fun than she had ever dreamed of having. *I'm one of the most special people in the world, and so is Kotone. Awesome told me she was a Choice Giver, but I didn't believe him. But the aliens contacted her too. He was telling me the truth. He may have been telling me the truth this entire time. I wish I remembered what he had said right when he introduced himself.* She couldn't think back beyond their conversation this morning.

Shiori practically dragged Chiharu up the stairs until they were up at the roof. Kotone walked up the stairs after them, like she was heading to an execution.

Shiori twirled in a circle and then held an impish grin on her face, watching Chiharu. "Promise not to scream or call me a witch or anything," Shiori said, excited.

"I promise," Chiharu said, setting down her tea and opening her bento, sitting down as calmly as ever.

"I met an alien last night. Kotone did too. The alien's name is Awesome. Awesome, say hi to Chiharu Sakai. But call her Sakai."

"Hello, Sakai." Awesome floated out of her bag again.

"Hello, Awesome." Chiharu smiled and took a sip of tea.

"No, I mean, really. Chiharu, this isn't some prank. I'm not using a wire. This is an *alien*. Kotone saw one too." Shiori gave a pleading look to Kotone.

"It's true. I met an alien, Chiharu."

"Me too." Chiharu said. "His name is Cyan. Cyan, say hello to Rin and Nakano."

Cyan floated out of her bag, glowing blue. "Hello, Rin. Hello, Nakano."

Kotone looked sick. Shiori just started laughing.

"Okay, you got us." Shiori sat down and started unpacking her lunch. "*Itadakimasu*." She started eating, staring at the new alien.

"You visited every single person on Earth, and you called them all Choice Givers, and now you want to be our alien symbiotes or something and give you food," Shiori accused.

Awesome rose out of her bag. "No. Sakai is a Choice Giver."

"Right, like everyone. We're all just full of choices," Shiori explained.

"You won't listen to me." Awesome sounded angry. "You are a Choice Giver. Nakano is a Choice Giver. Sakai is a Choice Giver. And maybe fifty other people in the whole world. The three of us decided to synchronize to the three of you because we're friends, and we wanted to stay together, and you were all nearby to each other. I didn't know the three of you were friends, though it makes sense, since all three of you are so different from Dead-Enders that you'd naturally be drawn to each other. But all three of you are incredibly special. To be precise, each of you is one in 140 million."

Awesome continued. "Furthermore, we aren't *aliens*. We're Wyrds. You told me to pick one—a term you gave. So I'm following your wishes and calling you by the right names and as girls and all that. But you just keep calling us aliens."

"Hey now!" Shiori raised her voice. "I didn't ask you to jump into my bedroom window. Nor did I come to your universe to start telling you what to do. It's completely different when I ask for simple courtesy from you and when you ask it from me."

"I didn't say I came here to ask for favors or tell you what to do. I came here to help you and protect you and save your entire world! Why don't I deserve simple courtesy?" Awesome glowed with righteous wrath.

"Because I'm a real person, and you're just a floating blob, idiot!" Shiori yelled.

"Now, now." Chiharu touched her arm.

"I…sorry. I didn't mean it…and I'll call you a Wyrd from now on." Shiori blushed. So much for her professional human-alien relations. She should let the UN take over from here. *I'll probably start an interstellar war like this.*

"Last night, Cyan told me the same thing—That he was here to protect the Choice Givers. He seemed earnest and serious, but I don't understand why they came here. Japan is peaceful, and Inazumu is safe. We shouldn't need any protection." Chiharu acted like the conversation had finally gotten through introductions, and they were ready to talk about serious matters.

"I… Am I the only one who doesn't sit down and chat with glowing lights in the night?" Kotone asked, bewildered. "Did I…drive my alien away? Is it going to report me or something?"

"Your Wyrd." Chiharu touched Kotone's arm, just like she had Shiori's.

"I'm sorry. My Wyrd." She half bowed to the floating gems.

It was Cyan who talked this time. "The Wyrd you're referring to is Magnolia. She's our friend and wants to be your friend, Nakano. She's completely harmless, I promise. She raised *kfelshew* in our world. She bakes *itzur.*"

"Okay, Cyan. Hello. I gave a rule to Awesome, and I'm extending it to you. Don't use alien gibberish and pretend it's normal Japanese," Shiori spoke up.

Cyan blinked and flashed a few times. "She bred and showed dogs. She's great at baking cookies."

"Much better." Shiori nodded.

"We need to protect you for two reasons. We are scryers. And don't raise your voice, Rin. *Scryer* is a real term in your language," Cyan continued.

Shiori closed her mouth, her cheeks heated.

"We can see the future, but not in the terms you're used to. We only see the possibilities. Possibilities that flatline…errr…possibilities that stop branching, are called dead ends. People who stick to those tracks are Dead-Enders. They're scum. The worst. Trash. We don't know what happens on those possibilities. We just know the *nature* of that possibility. It's a flat line. It never changes. Nothing happens ever again.

"Scryers can see the other side of the coin too. We can see Choice Givers. These are the people who, by following or emulating them, allow for infinite possibilities. They're people who are not only *not* Dead-Enders, but they have overcome the very possibility of dead ends themselves. Wherever they go, the dead ends disappear. They are like dragon slayers—heroes. There's a miraculous power in them to keep the universe alive. It is changing, growing, branching. When a scryer sees a Choice Giver, it's like the most beautiful field of flowers you've ever seen. It makes you want to cry."

Cyan was interrupted. "Except for one particular Choice Giver who—" Awesome started.

"Hush, Awesome." Cyan broke in. "She apologized, but you haven't."

"What should I apologize for?" Awesome groused.

"For trespassing, apparently." Cyan said jocundly.

"I'm sorry, I didn't mean to." Awesome sighed.

"I know." Shiori blushed. "Let's just move on."

Cyan took that as a chance to continue. "So as long as there are Choice Givers, your universe will never reach a dead end. Nor can it ever totally be dominated by Dead-Enders. But when we reached your planet, there were only *fifty* Choice Givers left in the world. If anything happened to you, and if all of you should die of an illness or an accident or anything, your entire world would flatline. It would stagnate or just go extinct, since a flatline can't tell the two states apart since they're the same essence; they never change. Any Choice Giver is precious. The last fifty Choice Givers among all known life, among all known creation…how unbelievably precious can you be?"

"What do you mean, among all life? Are you guys robots or something?" Shiori asked.

Why is it always me or Awesome interrupting? Don't tell me we're similar. Oh no. My favorite color is red! At this rate, Shiori would be stuck with Awesome for keeps. Shiori would rather have Cyan. Cyan was calm and smart, just like Chiharu. But that meant Cyan would rather have Chiharu. Of course, everyone would rather have Chiharu, except Magnolia wanted Kotone, and Awesome wanted her. Perfect.

"No, we're alive. Besides, sentient robots are also alive, if they existed. Which as far as I know, they don't," Cyan replied.

"Then," Kotone broke in, "then Wyrds don't have any Choice Givers anymore."

"Correct. We're a dead end." Cyan sounded sad.

"That's horrible. I'm so sorry," Kotone said.

"If you understand that, you understand why we can't let the same thing happen to you," Cyan said.

"But the same thing won't happen here," Chiharu said.

"Like I said, Japan is at peace, and Inazumu is safe. We don't have any bad habits, and we look both ways before we cross the street. We're as safe as humanly possible without just sticking us in a cushioned room. It's nice that you came all this way to protect us though.

"By the way, how do Wyrds protect humans? I don't mean to offend, but all you can do is float and blink. In any case, it's nice that you came all this way. But you may as well go back. We promise to stay safe. I intended to live in a safe manner anyway. You can go tell your other Wyrd friends that we're all safe, and everything will be fine."

"That…isn't exactly true," Awesome said.

And then the lunch bell rang. No one had eaten much. But then, this was more fun than eating. Kotone,

Chiharu, and Shiori all looked shocked that they were even at school, on the school roof, and that they were supposed to be attending class right now. For a second, it was like they had been living entirely different lives.

"We have to go," Kotone said nervously.

Awesome blinked for a bit. "I'm going to go find Magnolia. Can I tell her you'll talk to her now, Nakano? She just wants to help you like us, only she's more compatible with you. She"—Awesome blinked a bright red—"she thought you were the most beautiful, and so…"

"I'll talk to her with everyone else. We'll work this out," Kotone promised. And then she was flying down the stairs. Shiori got up and ran too. Chiharu just gathered her stuff and walked, but she didn't care about regular things like being late or getting punished or looking stupid. She was calm. And she was one of the top-ranked students, so the teachers would give her a pass anyway. Stupid Chiharu. It was just like her to take Cyan for herself.

Chapter 4

George Flint was an environmentalist. He lived on a commune and lived frugally. He didn't eat meat, and he hated everyone who did. He wrote newsletters about all sorts of pollution and letters to the editor about whatever laws were being debated in Congress. He even attended a few protests, for the whales, for the owls, and for the minks that were being caught and skinned in Russia. No one listened. It was all so meaningless. No one cared. Oh, a few people cared. But no one cared as much as he did. And because he didn't have any power, there was nothing he could do. The animals were defenseless. The trees were defenseless. The rivers were defenseless. The air was defenseless. Even the mountains were getting their caps blown off and mined away. Even the earth was defenseless. Soon enough humans would find a way to pollute space.

He hated them. He hated the polluters. He hated everyone who benefited from pollution. And he hated everyone for not caring. He tried to distract himself and to do other things. He took a lot of drugs. He hooked up with girls who felt the same way. But after every distraction, he could read in the news some new atrocity, such as there being more CO_2 in the air, underground water supplies running out, erosion of the topsoil, depleted uranium poisoning, and shark fin soup. It was like the entire world had gone crazy, or it was just intent on making him feel bad by doing every single thing wrong, writing up an article about their heinous deeds in the paper and then delivering it to his door.

He tried gardening. He tried bonsai tree pruning. He tried lecturing public school kids on how they needed to recycle. Nothing helped.

I mean, give me a break. Recycling? There was a giant patch of pollution in the Pacific Ocean as large as several states. The horse was already out of the barn. The pollution was already here, *everywhere*. Recycling new pollution changed nothing. And nobody recycled anyway. He would lecture the kids and then watch them go throw something in the trash that was recyclable two seconds later. Those dumb kids probably knew he was watching and were laughing about it too. They were exactly what was wrong with this world.

At age forty-five, George Flint realized he had done every possible thing, and the environment had gotten worse every year in his life. It was hopeless. It was like fighting the tides. Then he read a book, *The World without Us,* by Alan Weisman. The book talked about how the world would look if suddenly, overnight, mankind disappeared. If humans just went away, how the animals and plants would flourish. There were pretty pictures of green things overgrowing cities.

George Flint finally got it. Environmentalism wasn't hopelessly trying to minimize the harm humanity did to the environment. Environmentalism meant wiping humanity off the face of the Earth. Weisman understood. He was talking in code to people like George Flint. Stop beating around the bush. Stop pretending you don't know what the problem is. The problem is people. The solution is mass murder. If we environmentalists would just rise up and kill everyone, then it would all be over. The pollution would end, the Earth would recover, and the birds would sing. Balance would be restored to the ecosystem.

There was only one problem: George Flint was just one man. When he mentioned his theory to a few people, they disagreed with him. Some disagreed with him vehemently, even though they were environmentalists and knew all the same facts he did, and even though they knew the pollution would never end until the source was eradicated. They were such hypocrites. He was surrounded by worthless hypocrites.

George Flint left the commune. He started wandering around the country in a truck, trying out his message in city after city, hoping to find one clear-thinking group that would see the obvious logic of it all. The problem was people. The solution was mass murder. Some organizations were more sensible than others. They talked about reducing the human population down to a billion or half a billion, or a million or half a million. But then they would stop. They would stubbornly refuse to admit that if you left even two humans alive, they'd eventually reproduce, and you would be exactly back up to seven billion or seven quadrillion, for all humanity cared.

Humans kept reproducing so long as there was any nature left to rape. If they ever got out into space, they would keep reproducing until they had raped every last environment in the entire universe. They had to be stopped here, now, while environmentalists still could.

Stopped meant *killed*. The universe had to be made safe from the polluters who would never stop once they got started. It would be pollution from Rigel to Vega; landfills and skinned minks from Betelgeuse to Orion; bratty kids who wouldn't recycle; and meat-eaters who didn't mind torturing and killing animals from Algol to Altaire.

Environmentalists kept talking in code. They kept talking about birthrates and about letting the population fall "naturally." Population didn't fall naturally. Population grew naturally. Across all human history, population has always grown, and still they talked about population falling "naturally" and "voluntarily." Population didn't fall voluntarily. Or to be more precise, when population falls voluntarily in one human community, another human community just moves in whose population did *not* fall voluntarily, and you are back to square one. The whole world's population has never fallen voluntarily, not once, and it was still rising. The environmentalists were just cowards. They were whistling by the graveyard, pretending they couldn't see the most obvious logic on Earth. People weren't going to volunteer to cease to exist. They could only be forced. George Flint stopped riding around in his truck. He couldn't convince anyone. They didn't want to be convinced. His arguments were flawless. His logic was crystal. They just refused to see. They believed what they wanted to believe. He built a cabin and started gardening again. There was nothing he could do. Even if he went on a killing spree, humans would just reproduce and fill up the space. That had been his point—

that if you left the job unfinished, it was like not doing the job at all. Killing two people wasn't going to cleanse the world of mankind. He couldn't raise an army to work alongside him at the mass murder project, so it was over. He just wanted to farm and forget. Hopefully he'd die of cancer sooner or later, and then he wouldn't have to read any more news stories about the world becoming any more polluted—polluted with humans. *Pollution* meant *people*.

That was when the Wyrd appeared. Its name was Green, like the environment. Green understood him. Green agreed with him. Green said it only made sense. Green wanted to protect the animals and plants and rivers and air too. George Flint could talk to someone like Green. It was a pleasure to garden and say what you thought, and to be told "That's brilliant," instead of being jeered at or glared at or ignored. So when Green said he might be able to do something about it, George was all ears. George knew Green was an alien. But since Green always agreed about how bad pollution was, it was obvious Wyrds weren't like people. They were like the plants and animals, at harmony with nature. Green was the right type of alien. A man could work with Green. Aliens could have any sort of technology, any kind of bizarre power. If Green thought he could help eradicate mankind, well, then maybe he could. Maybe Green and George Flint could be like Butch Cassidy and the Sundance Kid.

"I can't kill everyone," Green said. And George sighed. He had hoped. That stupid feeling of hope had invaded him again, and now it would take forever to stamp it back down. "But there is a way to kill mankind. Kill the Choice Givers. Kill the Choice Givers; kill the world."

"Who are they? Really big polluters? I told you, if even two people live on, it doesn't matter." George sighed. Maybe Green was like all the rest, always talking about limited action, morality, and all that nonsense.

"Choice Givers are like mankind's engines. They keep the engine going. Stop providing fuel to the engine, and the engine turns off. Mankind turns off. It reaches a dead end. That's when humanity will die."

"I don't get it. People live off of food. Their fuel is plants and animals, or, if you want, fossil fuels, sunlight, wind power, uranium, etc., not choices." George liked Green. At least he had his heart in the right place.

"They die in their souls. They give up hope. They turn to stupid beliefs. And then they rot away on the vine. The stupid beliefs and stupid feelings choke them to death. They dwindle, they decay, and then they disappear. Only Choice Givers keep the cycle going. Everyone else is a Dead-Ender. The Dead-Enders are everywhere. If Choice Givers didn't keep inspiring them, they would just properly flow into a dead end and die. Kill the Choice Givers, kill the world." Green encouraged him. It had a pretty good ring to it, that slogan.

"How do I know if it works? I mean, you're saying this will take a long time. I'm forty-eight years old. What if I kill them all, and nothing happens?" George complained. Pollution meant people.

"I told you before, didn't I?" Green was always patient. "I can scry the possibilities. After the Choice Givers die, the world always flatlines sooner or later. It has to. It's the rules. I don't know how long it will take, but I can promise you it really will happen. Trust me," Green said.

"Why should I just trust you?" George complained.

"Because I believed in you," Green said, blinking green lights and acting hurt.

George blinked back tears. Green was his only friend. He was the only one who got it, who didn't give him mean looks. Green was right. He had to trust him and kill the Choice Givers, kill the world.

"Okay, Green. Sign me up." George Flint grinned.

Chiharu Sakai wanted to restart the conversation as soon as they found Magnolia, but she had softball practice with Shiori after school, and Kotone had flute practice, and Awesome hadn't found Magnolia by the time they were done. Awesome went off to try and find Magnolia again, and all three of the girls went back home after telling each other, "See you tomorrow!"

Chiharu had a lot of homework to do. She was smart, but she was also thorough. Homework took time. Getting perfect grades on everything took even more time. When she got home, she carefully took off her shoes and aligned them in their proper place for when she wanted to leave again. She was tired from softball practice, and she was even more exhausted from staying up last night talking to Cyan, when he suddenly appeared at 4 a.m. She needed a bath and then to go to sleep. But if she went to sleep now, it would ruin her sleep schedule. She had to go to sleep around ten so she woke up refreshed and ready for school by six or seven. That meant staying awake, which meant doing homework.

Choice Giver? I've never had any choices. Logic always dictates my next choice—logic and reason. If there's a winning move in a game, there's no choice but to take it. The whole point is to win the game, which means if there is a move before that winning move that gets you to the winning move, there's no choice but to take that move too. If the game was easy enough, you could see the logical necessity behind every move because it inevitably led to the winning move at the end. Computers could do that with chess. But I can't. Chess is hard. It's life that's easy. I could tell the winning moves since I was five. I could tell the moves that led to the winning moves, and the moves that led to the moves that led to the moves, by age ten. After that it was all downhill.

Work hard. Study. Get along. Be nice. Be honest. Keep quiet. Get good grades. Dress properly. Behave properly. Stay calm. Don't say anything you'd regret later. Obey those who are placed in authority above you. Get a good college-entrance exam grade. Get a degree. Leverage it into a graduate degree. Leverage that into a secure, high-paying but not particularly difficult job. Find another graduate degree holder with a good job who has done all the same things. Marry him and have smart, well-behaved kids. If they make you happy, have more until they stop making you happy. Teach your kids everything you know about the game of life by age ten, so they don't make any mistakes either.

I already won this game at age ten. I won this game when I saw all the moves that by necessity lead to victory. Life has been boring ever since but not bad. The moves were right, which meant they couldn't possibly lead her astray. Life was just boring. She had to focus all of her attention during softball and exert all of her effort during test taking. But she never had to work hard to know what to do, to know what to say or not say, to know who she should be. Softball was fun. Being herself was boring. Only suddenly, apparently, it wasn't boring anymore.

I'm a Choice Giver. I'm not sure how to leverage that. I don't know where that falls into the plan. I don't understand the rules of this game. I don't get how to incorporate it into the game of life. Maybe the Wyrds would explain it to her fully, and then it would become obvious and then boring again. But Chiharu had rarely had so much fun in her life. Yesterday had been great, making fun of Shiori and hugging Kotone, who was so happy to see Chiharu that she had shouted over the heads of a huge crowd of boys and jumped up and down to get my attention. *Was anyone that nice and that self-effacing just to make a point? Kotone would do anything for me. That's what she was saying. Kotone's my best friend in the world—only so is Shiori. I'm not going to separate them out in my mind. They're both my best friends, hopefully for life.* People usually grew apart, but Chiharu knew she wouldn't. She would be the same person her entire life. This was because she had already started life's chess match, and now she was committed to playing the game out to the end. *I can't change my strategy midstream. So I'm me, and I love my friends, so I'm not going to stop loving my friends, ever.*

Today had been even better. Today had started at 4 a.m. when she was contacted by an alien. It was obviously an alien. It said it was an alien, and there was no other explanation. So Cyan was an alien. He was not from outer space but from dimensional space—from hyperspace or from somewhere above. Cyan called it the "etheric plane." *No matter where we pointed our telescopes or flew our spaceships, we never would have found the Wyrds. We were only looking sideways, but space is a manifold that stretches out in every direction. I always wondered why we hadn't met aliens yet. It was obvious they would have to exist, by just the laws of averages. X stars have planets. X of those planets are in the habitable region for life to emerge. X of those planets develop life. X of those life forms become multicellular. X of those life forms become sentient. X of those life forms visit the Earth. Since the number of stars in the universe was some inconceivable amount, no matter how low you set X each time, unless it was zero, someone should have visited by now.*

She couldn't see any reasonable place to put a zero. None of those steps were that hard. As proof, mankind had done it. Anything that could be done could be replicated. But now there was another explanation. X of those life forms don't realize that moving sideways is a waste of time and fold up or down instead. *Maybe any alien that was sophisticated enough to reach the Earth was sophisticated enough to find a universe of their own, with-*

out any obnoxious neighbors, and were just as happy that we never found them. I don't know. It's just a theory. But it could be the answer.

Then she had talked with Cyan more on the roof. Even better, her friends had been Choice Givers too. She couldn't have predicted that. Cyan said there were only fifty Choice Givers in the whole world. Chiharu had thought she would be alone in this making-choices thing or whatever she was supposed to do—go on a quest to find the Holy Grail and bring back choices to the people. But she could go on this adventure and stay with her friends too. The flood of happiness when she had realized that during lunch was only barely corralled by a calm, deliberate sip of tea.

Obviously, I won't let the Wyrds interfere with my life game. If I deviate from the winning moves, who knows where I'll end up? It's the winning move. It was irrational to stray from it. Whether there were Wyrds or not, she'd already won. She didn't need their help for anything. But if she could win at life *and* have fun with the Wyrds and her friends, then that was even better.

Just talking to the Wyrds was fun. Cyan was smart—really smart. He had a lot to say about an entirely different world. Obviously she'd eventually squeeze him dry like a sponge, until every day he would just be repeating himself. That would be sad. But that's what happened whenever you met a new person. They would be new for a bit, but then they would be old. New people are exciting, but they're like coal. You burn through the fuel, and then it's out. Old friends were higher grade. They were a renewable resource. They made you happy because they loved you. She didn't know if Cyan could be an old friend. He was an alien, after all. Maybe they'd get bored with each other, have nothing in common, and go their own way. But for now it was fun. Coal was there to be burnt; like not using coal, not using new people was just wasteful.

Chiharu yawned, going over her kanji, her math, her science, and her history, and filling out all the appropriate worksheets. Her eyes were watering because they weren't blinking enough, because she was too tired. *I'm not going to make it to 10 p.m. like this. I need to mix things up and go take a bath.*

Chiharu looked at Cyan just sitting on the counter. She couldn't decide whether he looked like a marble, a glass orb, or a really expensive gem. Could she just leave Cyan out as a paperweight or some silly curiosity she felt like collecting? Cyan wouldn't betray her intentionally. *If Mother came into the room, he would just sit there, blue and lifeless.* But she was still worried. Suppose someone stole Cyan or broke him. He wasn't exactly a strong creature. He's just a floating, blinking, talking gem. She needed to make a necklace and wear Cyan as a pendant. That way she could keep Cyan with her at all times. She could just imagine one of her little sisters picking up Cyan to play with and bashing him against a counter until he broke and died. *Then she'd come crying to me with the broken pieces, and I would have to forgive her yet again, like I forgive them every time they break something of mine.* Getting along and being nice were cardinal rules.

Chiharu got up then wondered if she was supposed to be taking a bath or making a necklace. Ugh. She was too tired. *Bath first. It's a cardinal rule to bathe every day.*

Chiharu undressed and started the shower. She kept her hair a medium length because it blended in, not too short or too long. It was also perfect for their trio. Kotone's was long and beautiful, and she wore it to be as beautiful as it could be, with ribbons or hair clips or twin tails or whatever occurred to her for that day. Shiori's was short like a boy's. Her face was shaped like a girl's though, heart-shaped and wide-eyed. No one mistook her for a boy, thank goodness. *So I obviously have to have medium-length hair to complete the symmetry.*

She was starting early so the bathtub was empty, so she started filling the tub up too. With five people to bathe, she wasn't really starting that early. It was baths as soon as everyone got home until bedtime, really, in the Sakai family.

Soaking in the tub, she thought about Cyan. She was already attracted to his mind. But that could just be the novelty of him having an entire new world to describe. It could also be how calmly he lays things out. He's just so reasonable. It was easy talking to him. She didn't have to force herself to get along with Cyan. They got along from the very start.

Her stomach growled and reminded her dinner was probably being served, so she got out and got dressed, sighing at her ordinary body. That was okay. She was smart. Someone would be attracted to her remaining good points, somewhere down the line.

When she arrived at the dinner table behind everyone else, she ate mechanically, saying, "*Itadakimasu*" first, telling her parents an edited version of her day. "We went swimming. Shiori was showing everyone she could do every stroke, only she couldn't do the butterfly at all, and I kept calling her a terrible butterfly. It was great."

"Someday you'll tease Rin too much," Father warned her.

"No I won't, because I can tell when her face is laughing and when it's crying. I pull back if I think she'll cry. I push home when it starts to laugh." Chiharu smiled. Shiori was so transparent, like a perfectly shined crystal. Those wide eyes transmitted all of her emotions instantly and without fail.

"Someday." Father shook his head and continued with his meal. Chiharu smiled. Father just wanted her to mess up at something. That was okay. Maybe she should, just to please him—something small. It must be tough having a perfect daughter and having nothing to do because she never needed to be raised.

"Chiharu's a bully. Chiharu's a bully," Saki chimed in.

"That's right, I'm a bully. So watch out!" Chiharu tapped Saki on the forehead. Saki laughed. She was three and she just wanted attention. Any attention would do. Sisters were fun sometimes.

Then dinner was over, and Chiharu had to get back to her homework. Chiharu yawned. *Plus I have to make that necklace. Oh no. Would Cyan object to being worn?*

She didn't want it just sitting around visible, even as pretend jewelry. Someone would take an interest in it, or else someone would recognize it, recognize him. If there were three Wyrds, there would be more. Not all of them would necessarily share the same goals. There was no point advertising to the world that she was a Choice Giver. She was one of only fifty in a sea of seven billion humans.

Once Chiharu was safely back in her room, she asked about the news reports of magic. Cyan had laughed about the fish and bread guy. "Yes, it's all true. Those are Wyrds. He's using magic. He's a Choice Giver, clearly. I mean, he goes around healing the sick and feeding the hungry now that he has this power. That's wonderful."

"I'm not going on a pilgrimage to India to heal the sick," Chiharu stated.

"Everyone's magic is different anyway. It fits your personality. I don't think your personality is meant for healing," Cyan said.

"What's that supposed to mean?" Chiharu said.

"It just means your personality isn't suited for healing sick strangers," Cyan said.

"I could heal sick strangers if I wanted to." Chiharu pouted. "But I don't want to. That's the difference. You're saying I couldn't do it at all."

"People can't do what they don't want to do," Cyan said.

"They could if they had to do it anyway," Chiharu replied.

"But no one has to do anything," Cyan said.

"Let me rephrase that. They could if they were being tortured or threatened or the whole world was at stake or something, such that they suddenly wanted to do it even when they normally didn't want to do it," Chiharu explained.

"If you don't normally want to use magic like his, then the magic we'll manifest won't be like his. And once it's manifested, it can't be changed. Maybe developed or enhanced or something. But it can't just be changed to something else," Cyan said.

"You can grant me magic powers?" Chiharu's eyes widened. "Like that fish and loaves boy?"

"Not like his magic powers. But magic powers, yes. We just need to form a contract," Cyan said.

"I won't marry you unless you have a graduate degree, a high-paying job, and some way to make human kids with me," Chiharu informed him brusquely.

"Not that contract. A magical contract. Wyrds can make one contract, once. Once we're together, it is for life. But I won't get in the way of your family or friends," Cyan said.

"Thanks." Chiharu smiled. He was so understanding. "So what are the rules of the contract? I have to go create choices, like fish and loaves boy, a certain quota every month, and in return I get magic powers? But if I ever fail, you grow a giant dragon head and eat me?"

"You are so dark." Cyan laughed.

"Just practical. You're an unknown alien sounding eerily similar to the devil right now," Chiharu replied.

"It's simple. You agree to bind me to you. Then I serve you for life, and you can use whatever magic we manifest as you please. I can yell at you and call you names, but in the end, the magic is yours and, well, *I* am yours. From then on you own me, and I move as you direct," Cyan said.

"So what's the catch? When do you sprout a dragon's head?" Chiharu said.

"There's no catch. We came here to serve you. You're a Choice Giver. That's what qualified you for my loyalty. You earned it already. I just want to help. I won't live forever. The universe I come from will run out of magic in two hundred years. But I can help Choice Givers until one or the other of us dies, and I can keep seeing a beautiful world here, every time I scry. That's my reward. It would be my honor to serve you," Cyan said.

"Your tongue is too smooth. I told you, I won't marry you unless—" "We'll work on that part later. For now will you agree to a magical contract with me?" Cyan quickly stopped her.

"Not tonight. I'm tired, and you've been seducing me. Maybe tomorrow, when my head is clear, and I've talked to the others. Now hold still. I'm attaching a necklace to you."

That was the first night she'd slept with a boy—just slept. It's not like a small gem could do anything. But it was warm where it rested.

Chiharu Sakai woke up after a wonderfully long sleep. She hadn't made it to 10 p.m., but that was okay because she hadn't woken up too early either. She changed into her school uniform and put on her white beret cap at a slightly tilted angle. Then she went downstairs and ate some eggs for breakfast. Mother had already prepared Chiharu's bento. Mother was sweet, determined to be the perfect mother. She was a good role model. She'd won at life.

It didn't take long to put on her shoes, brush her hair, and go out the door. She rode the bus most of the way to school, so she couldn't walk there with Kotone and Shiori. That was okay. She got to play softball with Shiori, which left Kotone out. Now if she could just find something to do with Kotone and leave Shiori out, the symmetry would be complete. But she didn't want to leave Shiori out. She liked being with Shiori. *I guess some symmetry is never meant to be.*

Today's mission was easy: take notes, attend lessons, and then get to the roof where they could eat lunch. She would tell them about magical contracts, and Kotone would tell them if she'd found Magnolia or not and whether they got along. Then she'd ask them if they all wanted to become magical Choice Givers together. Then…then she'd decide if she wanted to become a magical Choice Giver on her own, if they said no. That was a thought for after lunch.

The lessons were tedious, and she kept lifting her hand to touch her neck and feel if Cyan was still there. That was a bad habit. She was supposed to be concealing him, not drawing a bull's eye around the fact that she was wearing something suspicious. But she kept checking anyway, impatient for the lunch hour.

The lunch hour never came. Instead, Chiharu heard a terrifying roar at the gates of her school. It was in

English. It was simple enough that Chiharu could understand it perfectly.

"I am George Flint. Kill the Choice Givers. Kill the world. Come out, Choice Givers. I am George Flint!" The man was wearing some sort of ridiculous tentacle tree. But the tentacle tree wasn't completely ridiculous. It tore the gate off their school grounds in a couple seconds.

"Cyan! What is this?" Chiharu screamed, completely oblivious to her classmates. They were screaming. For that matter, she was screaming. She was terrified.

"I don't know!" Cyan shouted over the voices of the classroom. "It's a magical contract, but…give me a second to scry. That man's a Dead-Ender! Something is wrong. Something is terribly wrong!" Cyan was blinking right through her school uniform with agitation.

"You couldn't tell that part from the guy screaming his lungs out and tearing our school down with a tentacle tree?" Chiharu shouted at him.

"Choice Givers can be eccentric! Actually, they're almost certain to be eccentric, since you're only one in one hundred forty million a person." Cyan defended himself.

"I am *not* eccentric," Chiharu said, this time more calmly. The argument was short-circuited by another shout from outside.

"I am George Flint. Kill the Choice Givers. Kill the world. Come out, Choice Givers. I am George Flint!"

"What do I do to form a contract with you?" Chiharu had made her decision.

"Say, '*Via tu lusches*, Cyan,'" Cyan said.

"*Via tu lusches*, Cyan," Chiharu said without a second of hesitation. That man was coming for her. He was coming for her Kotone. He was coming for her Shiori. He could not have them. They belonged to her. She felt a little warm, but nothing happened. A rising tide of panic formed in her belly.

"Nothing's happening! Give me magic! We have to fight him!" Chiharu was trying to keep her voice down. The teacher was trying to herd them somewhere and follow some sort of drill. Come to think of it, she had to get away from everyone else, unless she wanted the world to know she was a magical girl. Chiharu acted like she was following everyone else where the teacher pointed. But the halls were crowded with scared girls and boys, and it was easy to duck into the nearest bathroom.

"Imagine the strongest weapon and armor you can—something you can wear and carry, not like a tank or something. Then repeat after me, '*Coi*, Cyan!'"

Chiharu didn't waste much time. Tentacle man was breaking into the school. Strong. She could do strong. "*Coi*, Cyan!" And then the magic exploded throughout her entire body. Out of nowhere, her power suit had appeared. There was a little afterimage of sparkles, and then the world was normal again. She checked her gun. It was two-handed, a rifle instead of a pistol, that was light enough for her to wield, and, yep, "Laser Mark 7,000" was written on the side. Her imagination could embrace quite a lot.

"Where did this come from?" Chiharu marveled.

"Hyperspace. I used magic to fold it in. Once we win, we can use magic to fold it back away," Cyan explained. The gem had a prominent place in the middle of her chest, flaring a brilliant blue light which reflected off of flexible blue carbon armor. Well, it was a brilliant cyan, to be precise. Cyan wouldn't like it if she called her outfit blue. This power suit was designed to let her punch through walls, jump over buildings, stop bullets, and anything else she could think of in a short time. Most importantly, it had a visor to protect her identity.

"Chiharu, have you ever fought anyone in your life before?" Cyan asked.

"Of course not. I'm a Japanese schoolgirl." Chiharu was running down the stairs anyway, running to where she had seen George Flint enter.

"That suit isn't all of your magic. I don't know what it is. It manifests based on your personality. If you really want a certain magic to happen, in this fight, that's probably the magic you came with. Seize on any stray idea. Will it. If it's fated, the magic will happen!"

"I'm going to blast him with this gun before he even sees me," Chiharu said fervently.

"He has magic too. He isn't just a suit either!" Cyan was terrified for her. She could somehow tell better, now that he was embedded in her suit. He hadn't expected this at all, which was funny, because she had, at least a little. Something like this. Not all Wyrds would be the same, just like not all people were the same. Cyan was naïve. That was so sweet of him.

"If he has magic too, I'll just counter it," she reassured him. She could hear his English roars as they got closer.

"That's it! Seize on it. That's our magic. If he casts anything, counter it. It will happen. It has to happen," Cyan said.

"Roger," Chiharu said. But it wouldn't come to that. He was within sight now. She leveled her laser rifle and blasted him.

It bounced off of something. The man was shining with green light. He turned around and roared. She blasted him again. The laser bounced off.

"I've found a Choice Giver! Die, Choice Giver!"

Chiharu screamed at her Wyrd. "Is my gun on safety mode or something?"

"It's your gun! You imagined it!" Cyan yelled back.

"Solar flare," George Flint yelled, and a super-hot plasma was shooting toward her.

"Counter!" Chiharu held up her left hand, telling the spell to stop. The plasma evaporated well before it reached her.

"Tsunami." And now the entire hallway was filling up with water.

"Counter!" The water was gone. But she'd been distracted. He'd been running at her with all those wriggling leafy tentacles, and they'd extended well in front of him. They trapped her, and they were pulling her in.

She blasted him with her rifle. It bounced off his green light. This time she concentrated herself. She had one shot at this.

"Counter!" She pointed at the barrier she knew had to be there and held down the trigger of her rifle. The beam blew a hole right through him. George roared and threw her away from him with all his tentacular force.

She slammed into the hallway wall; no, she slammed right *through* the hallway wall. Now she was rolling across the softball grounds outside. *It hurts. I'm going to die.*

"He's regenerating!" Cyan yelled at her.

Oh great. My power suit can't do that. This guy was like the most twisted version of an ever-growing forest she could have ever imagined. He could shoot solar flares. Or any sort of natural disaster he could imagine. *How cute. It goes with the tree suit.*

When Kotone Nakano woke up, Magnolia was waiting timidly on her windowsill. Kotone smiled at her and opened the window. It was nice outside; the summer heat hadn't really clamped down, with the sun having only just risen.

"I hear your name is Magnolia. Pleased to meet you. I'm Kotone Nakano. I'll be in your care from here on." Kotone bowed almost ninety degrees.

Magnolia dipped down and then back up, the only bow she could make. "Um, what do I say in situations like this? I don't know the ceremony."

Kotone smiled and straightened back up. "You say, 'Likewise, please take good care of me.'"

"Likewise, please take good care of me," Magnolia said.

Kotone got out of her pajamas and dressed into her school uniform. Then she stood in front of her mirror and brushed all the tangles out of her hair that had developed while she slept. "They say you picked me because my potentialities were the most beautiful."

"To me they were." Magnolia agreed.

"Thank you. It's nice of you to think that. But I'm nothing special. No matter how long I think about it, I don't notice anything particularly grand I could do." Kotone had gone over what she would say all last evening while Awesome was out searching for her. She had fallen behind the others at making friends with their Wyrds, so now she had to be twice as fast. When they met today at lunch, she'd show the other girls that the Kotone-Magnolia pair was the best.

"It's not what you do. A Choice Giver is someone who, if followed or emulated, allows for infinite possibilities. It's someone who breaks through dead ends like they aren't even there and opens up paths that everyone had thought were closed. It's like they aren't bound by fate. Just being who you are is enough," Magnolia reassured her.

"Hmm. I still don't get it." Kotone pulled out a hair tie and deftly gathered up half of her hair into a left pigtail, flipping and re-flipping the band until the hair was firmly in place. Then she got out her second hair tie and pulled the rest into her right pigtail, flipping and re-flipping. She looked carefully into the mirror. The twin tails looked symmetrical. Then she took a hair clip with a pink heart on it and brushed all of her bangs to her left side, clipping the hair in one place and out of her eyes for the rest of the day. "A dead end is a big deal—the stagnation or extinction of the planet. To avert that, I would have to do something equally big."

"Dead ends never happen while you live, so you don't have to stop them. You're thinking like the Dead-Enders have already won and you have to go wrest the future back from them. The future is in your hands. They have to wrest it away from you," Magnolia said.

"But nothing's in my hands. When I'm twenty I get to vote—one vote in a country of a hundred million. Besides, Japan has only ever had one competent party, the LDP, and it's been running the country for the last seventy years. There's really nothing to vote over." Kotone got her school bag and opened it up. "In you go. Let's get breakfast and then wait outside for Shiori. Err, that's Rin to you." Magnolia flew in.

I could ask her to call me Kotone, but that would be artificial. We only just met this morning. It has to be real when she calls my name, or it's meaningless. There was no point playing at friends when Kotone wasn't even sure how she felt about her new companion. Magnolia thought the world of her, but Kotone could only see Magnolia as some sort of kidnapper, a thief who had stolen her ordinary life away and thrown her into a duty she never asked for. Now she had to think about living up to her station as a Choice Giver, one of just fifty lights left in the world, when before all she had had to live up to was her station as a thirteen-year-old girl! Could she really make friends with the bearer of such ill tidings?

Kotone walked down the stairs and saw her family already down before her. "Good morning, Papa. Good morning, Mama. Good morning, brother."

"Good morning," they all replied warmly to her. *See? It was simple. You knew people liked you if they felt warm inside. Then you could be kind to them and rely on them and know they would never hurt you or use you. This was much better and more reliable than scrying, which had obviously just chosen the wrong girls.*

Kotone packed her bento into her school bag that had been left out for her then sat down at the table and broke open a pair of chopsticks. "*Itadakimasu.*" Rice, fish, and some flavored vegetables, each in their own plate, were all efficiently transferred from the table to her stomach.

"Then I'm off," her brother called out, already in high school. He was as handsome as she was pretty, which let him project confidence, which meant he was always surrounded by friends.

"Have a safe trip," Kotone and her parents all said. Then it was her turn.

"I'll go wait for Shiori outside." Kotone smiled. "I'm off."

"Have a safe trip," her parents replied, and she was pulling on her school uniform shoes and out the door.

"I don't know what this voting business is about, but it has nothing to do with creating possibilities," Magnolia replied now that they were out of range of being overheard.

"In Japan, we collectively decide on our collective future. Everyone gets one vote to say what the laws of the country should be—how we should treat each other and the outside world. The party with the most votes takes over and runs the country for a few years. Then it all starts over," Kotone explained.

"That's…interesting." Magnolia blinked a few times, thinking about it. "The paths don't seem to care who wins these votes though. No politicians are Choice Givers, but you three are."

"Exactly, which is why you must be wrong. If you wanted to find a way to change the future, you'd definitely go find the prime minister. Then you could tell him, 'Pass this law. Veto this one.' And with your scrying, you would always know which laws would succeed," Kotone said.

"Scrying isn't specific like that. We don't know the impact of people's choices," Magnolia said.

"You're telling me scrying can only tell you one thing: that certain people are special. But without the context that shows *how* we are special or *why* we are special, how am I supposed to act in the special way you want from me? Just tell me what to do," Kotone pleaded.

"You've got it all wrong. A Choice Giver is someone who, *if* followed or emulated, leads to infinite possibilities. You're still a Choice Giver, even if no one follows or emulates you. But I *want* to follow you, because you're the most beautiful Choice Giver I saw. So you at least have helped me escape my dead end. You're doing plenty. It's up to others if they want to be helped by you. You give them a choice. That's all you ever had to do," Magnolia explained again.

"If I had power, I could give people choices like, 'Vote for me, and I'll ban cars.' Then people would suddenly have the option to ban cars, a new choice. But if I say, 'Follow me, and I can't do anything for you or change anything,' I'll just look stupid! Follow me where? To school?" Kotone laughed.

"Most choices that matter are deep inside your heart—why you live the way you do, who you care about, what makes you happy, how you respond to the pressures and pleasures of the outside world. Everyone has an answer, a way of life, for all of these questions, before the first time they vote on cars or not. It's those mysterious questions that lift or sink civilizations, species, life. The world balances upon the deep mysteries of the heart and how you, you and your friends, answer them. The rest is a distraction, an illusion. It won't matter in the least, in deep time, what decision was made." Magnolia lectured.

"But I'm not religious either. I wouldn't know where to start. Of course I hope gods are watching over us. Prayers make me feel better. Temples are pretty. But I've never meditated on deep mysteries or felt a divine light of enlightenment enter through my head and fill all my chakras. It's just silliness," Kotone protested.

"Nevertheless, every second your heart beats, it's providing answers to the deep questions: 'How should I feel? What should I say? How do I explain this? How do I fit this into my view of the world? Is this right? Can I live with myself like this?' A Choice Giver is answering the toughest questions. Almost as quickly as light is streaming into your eyes and showing you the outside world, you're generating answers to that outside world, pushing back at it, interpreting it, and taming it, every second of your life. And for some reason, your answers don't lead to a dead end. They aren't the answers of a Dead-Ender. They lead somewhere brilliant, somewhere beautiful, like a waterfall whose stream splits, and falls, and those streams split again, and fall. And the cliff splits the river again, and it falls, and you just zoom back and back, and the waters keep pouring and sparkling against the sun, and the river just keeps falling and falling because the mountain's height is beyond your imagination."

"Do you think my answers are better than yours? Look at how well thought-out all your words are. You're way ahead of me," Kotone said.

"I know your answers are better than mine," Magnolia said.

Kotone blushed. Magnolia, at least, thought her feelings for Kotone were real. Magnolia was giving her the reverence and adoration due to a Dalai Lama or something, even though she hadn't said one wise phrase yet. *All I can do is accept her feelings or reject them. It's painful to have your feelings rejected, so all I can do is accept them and treasure them.*

"Thank you," Kotone whispered. "I'll try my best to be a Choice Giver so you can keep seeing your beautiful waterfalls."

"Even if you didn't try your best, you'd be a beautiful Choice Giver." Magnolia blinked encouragingly.

"I'll try my best anyway. I feel like I should do something now that I know," Kotone insisted, this time with more confidence. Magnolia's explanation had made sense. She could do that—answer the deep questions of her heart. Those answers were just instincts. They came easily, unbidden, whenever she wanted them. *Follow the warmth. Avoid pain. I could answer any question in a snap like that.*

Shiori waved."Kotone!"

"Shiori!" Kotone waved back. She smiled with her entire face. Shiori always made you feel excited. Shiori ran the rest of the way to her side, and then they walked in stride side by side. Kotone checked to see if her hat was in place, and then she held her bag demurely in front of her, with both her arms V-ing to a point. Shiori was just swinging it back and forth with one hand.

"I love your hair!" Shiori exclaimed.

"I like it this way. It looks looser and less strict than braids or gathering all of your hair tightly back into a bun or a ponytail. That kind of hair is formidable, like, 'I can bully my hair, and I can bully you too!'" Kotone put on an angry face.

Shiori laughed. "I know, I know! Like teachers and old people, they wear their hair like that's what they want to do to you next! Twist you into a knot or roll you into a ball and kick you down the whole street!"

"But my hair, I want to make a deal with it: Stay out of my eyes, and I'll still let you fall forward across my face. Stay off my neck, and I'll let you flow down my back in loose streams in twin tails. 'Look how well I get along with my hair. I could get along with you too.' That's what my heart hairpin is saying," Kotone bragged.

"I wish I could dress up my hair," Shiori said.

"You could grow it out. I could try all sorts of styles on you and then teach you how to do one you like. We could spend all day in front of a mirror," Kotone said.

"No, no. I have softball and Tae Kwon Do. Hair just gets in the way. It's too much of a bother." Shiori sighed.

"There are plenty of softball girls with long hair," Kotone pointed out.

"Yes, but they're all secretly suffering inside and envying me, since I can run and jump and twirl, and nothing ever gets out of place or in my way." Shiori nodded assuredly.

Kotone smiled. Shiori did like twirling around, like yesterday at lunch. Kotone tried it out, raising her bag with her arms and spinning so her hair went sideways and smacked her in her face when she stopped. "It's… decidedly frustrating, I'll admit," Kotone said, checking each of her pigtails to see if they were flowing symmetrically down her back again. You didn't want your hair plastered to your back; that was icky. It had to float, creating a shadow.

"Hahaha, that was great, Kotone! Do it again!" Shiori said with her big, wide eyes.

"Only if you spin with me from here to that tree, no matter how many people are watching." Kotone negotiated, grinning.

"Okay. Commence spinning on three. One, two, three." Shiori swirled forward.

"It's not a race!" Kotone called out, holding out her arms and pivoting her way forward. This was fun; her skirt was spreading out like a ball gown, and she was the center of attention for everyone on the street.

"I win!" Shiori touched the tree. With her Tae Kwon Do training, she didn't look dizzy at all; she was just standing with her center of gravity as balanced as ever.

"Like I said, it's not a race!" Kotone finished by touching the tree. The world was spinning just fine for her. But that was a fun feeling so long as you didn't fall over. She instinctively started stroking her hair back into place again.

"Let's talk to the gems again this lunch period. Remember when Chiharu explained how safe we were, and Awesome said, 'That's not exactly true'? I want to know why they think we aren't safe," Shiori said.

"Just ask Awesome now. He's right here, right?" Kotone suggested.

"He only came back this morning after he found Magnolia. And we may as well wait until everyone's together. That Chiharu. She took the smartest and nicest gem for herself. I want to trade. Do you think she'll trade?" Shiori sounded hopeful.

"If you ask nicely." Kotone smiled. *"Smartest" and "nicest"? That was clearly Magnolia. She explained things in a way I can understand. Cyan just went on and on.*

"No! She won't, even then. She's evil. She clamped onto him the moment he appeared," Shiori said.

"That does sound very evil." Kotone agreed, smiling.

"Maybe she'll share Cyan," Shiori suggested.

"Awesome would be lonely," Kotone said.

"You're right. I'm sorry, Awesome. I won't leave you alone. I'll give you to Chiharu when I borrow Cyan." Shiori nodded as though it had all been decided.

Awesome grumbled something.

"What was that?" Shiori asked with a dangerous edge.

"Nothing," Awesome said brusquely.

"Humph! After I was so thoughtful of you." Shiori stuck out her tongue at her bag.

Kotone laughed. Everyone had found their own balance with their Wyrd. She hoped she could get along well with Magnolia. White was a prettier color anyway. Her Wyrd looked like a pearl.

Shiori and Kotone didn't have the same class. They didn't share a class with Chiharu either. It was just one of those vagaries of fate. But that was okay because they always had lunch together, and Chiharu would help them study after school whenever they asked. They'd go to the library and then start laughing about stuff until the librarian always had to come over and quiet them down.

Kotone hugged Shiori tight. "I'll see you at lunch then." Then she carefully readjusted her hair so it all flowed straight and evenly into one of her two twin tails. Hugs, like everything, always disrupted your hair. It was a running battle.

Once Kotone stepped into her classroom, she set aside all of the business with their Wyrd friends and concentrated on her studies. She tapped her mechanical pencil on her lips whenever she sat still, listening to the lectures. People could look at her lips all they wanted, if it drew attention to them. It was just a habit though—something to do.

Teachers came and went, and it was all Kotone could do to keep up with them. But she felt a little superior in the back of her head. Teachers thought they were so great. But what's so great about triangles? *You all can teach me the answers to the questions that don't matter. But I could teach all of you the answers to the questions that do matter.* She was the teacher of those sorts of answers, but so far she only had one answer: Follow the warmth. She wasn't sure she could turn that into a useful instruction manual. Kotone thought about standing up in front of her class and writing out "1) Follow the warmth!" in bold letters across the chalkboard. Then she'd turn and lean over, staring each of them in the eye.

"I have one lesson in life: Follow the warmth! That is all. Dismissed!" Kotone laughed out loud at the mental picture.

"Nakano, do you have something to add?" The teacher gave her a mean look.

"Yes, Teacher. Please, everyone, follow the warmth." Then she blushed furiously because she'd really gone and done it. *But I promised to be the best Choice Giver I could to Magnolia. And I felt in my heart that's the answer.*

The whole class broke into laughter. "What is that? 'Follow the warmth'?"

"Class! Whenever we are all ready?" The teacher just looked at them until they all quieted down again; only now everyone in class was smiling, trying not to giggle.

"Good. Now, you can calculate the remaining two lengths of a triangle when you know one length and the angles on each of its ends…"

Kotone sighed in relief, slowly emerging from her turtle of arms over her head. *I did it, Magnolia. It wasn't even that bad. Maybe one or two of them will think it over all day and find something.* Now she just had to wait for lunch hour and show off to her friends how close she'd gotten with her Wyrd in just one day. She started late, but she felt that she had to be the furthest ahead at Choice Giving now.

Only lunch hour never came.

"I am George Flint. Kill the Choice Givers. Kill the world. Come out, Choice Givers. I am George Flint!" The roar came out of nowhere. She couldn't make heads or tails of it. *Who on Earth?* Kotone rushed to the window. It was a crazy monster. It was like a cosplayer who had dressed up as a tree then changed his mind and dressed up as an octopus, and then decided to just wear both outfits at once.

"Do you know what he just said?" Kotone whispered to Magnolia.

"Yes, with magic, I can understand all human languages. It… Well, he says he's come to kill you." Magnolia blinked worriedly.

"Are you kidding me?" Kotone's voice went higher and higher. "What are we going to do?"

"We should run away. He found us somehow, but, look, he doesn't know exactly where we are. Let's run away. Everyone in this school is in danger." Magnolia's voice was pretty high too.

"I can't run away without Shiori and Chiharu!" Kotone whispered. "You said you would protect us! Start protecting!"

"But for that, we would need a contract. And even then there's no guarantee—" Magnolia was interrupted by another roar.

"I am George Flint. Kill the Choice Givers. Kill the world. Come out, Choice Givers. I am George Flint!"

"I don't care! At this rate someone's going to die!" The teachers were herding them into some safe place like in the drills. But no one was safe from octopus tree monsters. They weren't like earthquakes or something. Kotone ran away from her teacher and all the teachers and up to the roof. She hoped the others would think to meet up with her here. But when she arrived, she was alone. A stab of panic shot up her insides. *Calm down. Everyone's alive.*

"A contract is for life, Nakano. Do you want me to be with you always?" Magnolia asked in a rush.

"Yes! And call me Kotone!" They were friends now. They would just have to be.

"Repeat after me: '*Via tu lusches*, Magnolia,'" Magnolia said.

"*Via tu lusches, Magnolia.*" Kotone rushed. She felt a bubble of warmth settle over her, but the tree beast had already torn a hole into the school. It would be a massacre!

"So? Now what?" Kotone rushed. "What's the next line?"

"Imagine the strongest weapon and armor you can. Imagine the magic that's just for you. Keep that image in your head, and then say, '*Coi*, Magnolia!'" Magnolia said.

The strongest weapon and armor? "I thought you said *you* would protect me!" Kotone wailed.

"This *is* protecting you! I'm giving you my magic!" Magnolia protested.

"I've found a Choice Giver! Die, Choice Giver!" Another meaningless roar in English. But she thought she knew what it meant, in her bones. She had to do this.

Kotone took a deep breath and imagined the strongest possible warrior. "Magical miracle Coi, Magnolia!" Kotone felt magic exploding through her body down every nerve, until it shined all around her. She was suddenly in a white dress with light blue petticoats. Magnolia was a gem embedded in her right gown glove. She was holding a pink rod with a heart in a circle and wings spreading to either side. A big red ribbon was covering her chest, and a blue belt with a white heart in the middle circled her waist. Her twin tails had become an impossible shade of pink.

"What on Earth is this?" Magnolia was shining the brightest Kotone had ever seen her.

"I'm a magical girl! I'm really, really a magical girl!" Little wings sprouted on her boots, and she floated five feet into the sky. She laughed exultantly. "Oh, Magnolia, I could kiss you. Do you know how many years I dreamed of this?"

And then there was an explosion, and someone was flying through a wall and rolling across the softball grounds. It looked like a power suit from *Bubblegum*

Crisis, only without the stupid high heels or any curves. And it was about half as tall, since it was built for a little girl. The suit was all in blue.

"Cyan!" Magnolia cried out.

"Chiharu!" Kotone realized at the same time. The tree monster was walking out of the hole, closing in on Chiharu. Chiharu couldn't move.

"I won't let you!" Kotone shouted, and then she imagined fire sprouting out of her wand. Nothing happened. Kotone sat looking at her wand, stunned. "Magnolia, tell me the lines. What's *fire* in Wyrdish?"

"It's not like that! The magic is yours—I'm just a conduit. That isn't the magic you manifested," Magnolia said. "Think of a spell that comes naturally, something that fits."

"But fire was what came to my mind first!" Kotone protested.

"No, fire is what you reasoned out you could cast based on all of your experience with magical girls. You just *thought* it should be natural. You didn't *feel* it was natural." Magnolia kept blinking. The stupid tree was taking its time, but softball fields were only so big.

"Ice!" She waved her wand. Nothing.

"Water!" She waved her wand. Nothing.

"Thunder!" She waved her wand. Nothing.

"Chiharu's going to die!" Kotone wailed.

"Keep trying! Seize on a hunch! Think freely, not based on examples!"

That was when Shiori appeared, blazing through the wall of the school in an explosion like a comet toward her foe.

When Shiori Rin woke up, Awesome had already returned in the night. She hit the alarm clock to turn it off.

Shiori sat up and rubbed her eyes. *Clothes. Then brush my teeth. Then breakfast. Did I pack my swimsuit? Oh yeah, I did that two days ago.* Shiori pulled on her skirt; it had buttons running up the left side that turned it from just a strip of cloth into a properly snug piece of clothing, and those took time too. She started with a shock when she noticed Awesome floating in the air behind her.

"If you're awake, say something!" Shiori complained, turning around to glare at her Wyrd. "You're lucky I even let you stay in my room tonight. Today we'll find Magnolia and then all of you can go back home forever."

"I fought my way through six security guards, jumped through a glass window, and turned myself into a tiny gem by folding down a hyper-dimensional tube just so I could protect you, and *I'm* lucky I can stay?" Awesome spluttered.

"I didn't ask you to jump through a glass window or fold yourself into a ball for me, so don't think I'm grateful," Shiori snipped. "And Chiharu already told you, we're in Japan. We're perfectly safe."

Awesome fell silent.

"Oh, don't sulk." Shiori relented, brushing her hair in the mirror until at least everything lay flat and straight.

"Well, what do you think?" Shiori held her hat on with one hand and spun around.

"It looks good on you," Awesome tried.

"Too slow. Into the bag with you."

Awesome blinked a long, mournful blink.

"I didn't think I'd be babysitting," Awesome mumbled.

"What was that?" Shiori asked.

"Nothing!" Awesome jumped into her bag. *He was such a child.*

Shiori ran down the stairs by twos. "Good morning, Daddy. Good morning, Mother."

"Good morning, Shiori," her parents replied. Then it was all business. She said "*Itadakimasu*," ate her toast and eggs, packed her bento her mother had made for her, and put on her school dress shoes, leaving the indoor slippers at the entrance for when she got home.

"I'm off. Love you!"

"Have a safe trip," her parents replied. Shiori set off at a run. Her softball coach wanted them to run everywhere. *Besides, Kotone will be waiting for me.* The run would have only taken a few minutes, but she had to say hi to Mrs. Aede, because she was outside tending her flowers. And then she had to pet a cute dog an older man was giving a morning walk to. But when she saw Kotone waiting like a porcelain doll, her arms holding her bag in front of her, her hair carefully split into twin tails and her hat perching precariously on top, she rushed to join her.

"Kotone!" Shiori waved.

The trip to school had been fun. Kotone had suggested the dumbest game. She never cared what people thought of her; she made them respect her and respect what she was doing, just by her own projected confidence, like she was in control and everybody was doing this, and really the rest of the schoolchildren were out of place for *not* spinning their way to school. But Awesome had started another fight, mumbling about how he'd like to trade *her*, as though Cyan wouldn't leap at the chance to be her Wyrd. She hoped they went swimming again today. She wanted to work on her butterfly stroke. It was so hard. You had to remember so many different moving parts, and it was exhausting too.

Shiori tried to concentrate on taking notes. But she ended up doodling instead of doing the math. She didn't understand any of it anyway. Chiharu could explain it to her in a way she'd understand, one-on-one, after school. She grinned and started drawing Awesome with funny faces, saying, "Yes, mistress. I'm sorry, mistress." She was a little anxious though. Awesome still thought they were in danger, but there was no apparent reason why. She had to sort that out during lunch. It was a shame Awesome had to spend all yesterday just finding Magnolia. Well, to be fair, she had spent all that night doing homework and wouldn't have had any time to ask Awesome about it anyway. She bet Chiharu had done all her homework in thirty minutes. *Stupid Chiharu.*

But lunch hour never came.

"I am George Flint. Kill the Choice Givers. Kill the world. Come out, Choice Givers. I am George Flint!"

Some crazy guy was yelling at the top of his lungs at the school gate.

All Shiori could catch was "kill," because it sounded just like *korosu*, the Japanese word for "kill." And George was obviously his name, since it was an English name. But when she looked outside to see the guy ripping off their metal guardrails like they were paper, she thought she had it figured out. *It's magic, so it has to do with me. Stupid Awesome, what have you gotten us into?*

"Rin, this is bad," Awesome said from her bag. Her entire classroom was in an uproar, and the teacher was trying to shout over all of their heads too. "That guy's a Dead-Ender. A Wyrd has made a contract with a Dead-Ender! He's coming to kill you."

"I thought you Wyrds were on our side!" Shiori yelled at him.

"I… There was a leak… Someone else got a hold of the folding device plans. This is obviously their work. I'm from the government. Well, except I came on my own without the government's permission. These guys are just… They're just terrorists."

"I am George Flint. Kill the Choice Givers. Kill the world. Come out, Choice Givers. I am George Flint!"

"We need to fight him. We've gotten everyone in the school involved. Give me a tree suit like his, and I'll go out there." Shiori nodded to herself. She wasn't afraid. It was the helpless children around her who were afraid. *I'm strong. I've been training for this all my life. And I have Awesome at my side.*

"You have to make a contract with me first," Awesome said.

"What's a contract?" Shiori asked. The tree man was bursting his way into the school through a wall. She was following the traffic of the other students, talking as quietly as possible despite the hurried clip in her voice.

"We agree to be with each other until death. I have to follow your orders, and I can funnel magic into you from the etheric plane," Awesome replied.

"No way. I want to be with Cyan." Shiori immediately rejected him.

"We don't have time for your childish games!" Awesome glowed.

"Fine. But if I have to be your owner for life, you have to call me 'mistress' from now on. And apologize for what you said this morning. I am *not* a baby. I am super mature for my age."

"No way!" Awesome refused.

"I've found a Choice Giver! Die, Choice Giver!"

Shiori flinched, half expecting George Flint had found her. But when she looked either way across the hall full of kids, no tentacles were coming for her.

"In any case, give me a tree suit!" Shiori said. If it wasn't her, one of her friends was fighting.

"Repeat after me: '*Via tu lusches*, Awesome!'" Awesome said.

"*Via tu lusches*, Awesome!" She felt a little warm, but that was it.

"Now, imagine a weapon and armor, something you can wear, and say, "*Coi*, Awesome!""

Shiori tried to picture herself as a giant tree with leafy tentacles flowing all over the place. *I can't be seen in that!* She panicked. *Something cool! I need to wear something cool! My Tae Kwon Do gi? But that didn't have any armor. Armor, weapon… I can't think of any weapons. I always practiced fighting with my fists!*

Then Shiori heard an explosion down the hallway, and she rushed toward it before she knew what she was doing.

"What are you doing?" Awesome yelled at her. "He'll rip you apart in seconds! Manifest your magic!"

"I have to see what's going on!" Shiori yelled back at him. She turned the corner of the hallway to see tree man walking back out of the school and onto the softball field. She looked out the window, where a giant pillar of dust was just trying to settle around a girl in some sort of blue exoskeleton.

"Transform. Transform into anything!" Awesome kept nagging her.

Shiori tried to picture herself in her own tree suit again, but she couldn't figure out where to put her arms or legs and how she'd walk in the thing. Then she stopped trying to imagine anything because it wasn't working.

"Ah, mooohhh!" she screamed. "I don't care anymore! Coi, Awesome!" Magic exploded across her entire body, and red light surrounded her. She felt incredibly strong. She felt like she could do anything. She launched herself at Treeman's back, blew another hole in the wall in front of her, and accelerated faster and faster each time her foot planted on the ground, her fists wreathed in fire.

"Ky*aa*!" she shouted, and her fist slammed into some sort of green line. Her arm kept pushing forward, and the bubble burst like it was nothing. Her fist plowed into the giant leafy morass, and then her entire arm sprouted with fire. She could feel it inside her. This was nothing. She could make it much hotter, much bigger.

"Burst Knuckle!" she shouted, and red light, well, Awesome's awesome light, covered her in a nimbus of energy. Fire ran up in a wave through her hip, her shoulder, and her fist, through every joint, just like her instructor had trained her, and it blasted into the tree.

Half-charred tentacles started raining from the sky, and tree man had bounced ten or twenty feet from where she had first hit him. But impossibly, the man was getting back up again. He didn't even look that hurt.

"He regenerates!" Chiharu cried out to her from across the softball fields, trying to stand back up. "Keep hitting him!"

"I've found another Choice Giver! I am George Flint! Die, Choice Giver!" Tree limbs starting growing from out his back and snaking toward her.

"Is that the only thing you can say?" Shiori taunted him. With this magic, she could do anything. She could jump right over those tentacles. She bent her knees into a crouch and then launched herself in a wide arc twenty meters into the sky. She flipped a couple of time in the air, fire whipping down her right leg as she spun. *If a punch doesn't work, just hit him harder.*

"Flaaaaame," she said as she came down straight at his head. She felt that flash of green barrier try to stop her and break apart again. "Geyser!" Her axe kick cut down his entire body, an explosive fire cutting him like butter and spreading across his entire body. She landed in a cloud of dust in front of him, her fists naturally rising to a guard position.

The man *split in two* and started re-growing on either side. She just stared in wide-eyed surprise.

"Solar flare!" one of the treemen yelled, a dangerous-looking plasma coming out of his hand.

"Dodge it!" Awesome yelled.

"I know that!" she yelled back, bunching her knees and pushing off. She could run so fast. Her feet had some sort of metal boots that pushed harder than anything she could do. She was faster than any Olympic sprinter right now. She zoomed in a circle around the man, trying to hit him from his blind side.

"Hurricane!" the other tree suddenly shouted, and suddenly she was flying through the air in a fierce wind. *Oh crap. I wasn't watching the other one.* She slammed into something—leaves. It had pushed her right into George's squiggly embrace. Tentacles were reaching up to crush her throat.

She raised her arms up to protect her, fire jetting out of them and burning the tree limbs black. But she didn't have any leverage. More limbs were wrapping around her legs and back, and the stupid tree was regenerating again back toward her throat. *I won't let it end this way! Fire. I have to summon more fire!*

"Do something! Do something! Do something! Do something! Do something!" Kotone waved her wand, tears coming out of her eyes.

"Calm down. Find a hunch—something out of the blue. That's the real magic. Something that just pops into your head." Magnolia wasn't sounding exactly calm herself though. Awesome was down there, in the middle of that tree thing, and Cyan was out. They were running out of time.

Kotone thought of every magical girl attack she had ever seen. She felt like her life was flashing before her eyes. *Which one? Which one's me? Which magical girl show was Magical Girl Kotone? There was only so much magic in the world! If only tree beetles ate the man to shreds!*

Kotone gasped. *A hope. Please, gods and spirits, let this work.*

"Magical miracle pine beetles, answer my call!" And suddenly, Magnolia's white light erupted from her glove. She couldn't see if it was having any effect, but suddenly George Flint roared, thrashing back and forth—both George Flints. Kotone grinned in satisfaction.

"Rot in hell!" she yelled at him. George had dropped Shiori and was rolling back and forth on the ground, no doubt trying to crush her beetles.

"It's not enough. He's regenerating. Look. The other George Flint is seeping back in to reinforce the true host," Magnolia advised.

"Magical miracle woodpeckers, eat him up!" Kotone waved her wand. Nothing happened. Kotone threw her wand down in frustration and stamped on it.

"Insects! Stick to insects!" Magnolia yelled.

"I know already!" Kotone angrily wiped the tears from her eyes. *I'm a beautiful girl. My magic can't be insects!* She picked up her wand and glared at it.

"Magical miracle glowworms!" She waved her wand, and Magnolia's light flared again.

"What are you doing?" Magnolia yelled.

"I don't know! What else eats trees?" Kotone asked.

"I've lived here for two days! I have no idea!" Magnolia replied.

"Magical miracle termites, burrow him apart!" Her wand released lots of white hearts. This time Treeman gave out a terrible roar.

But it wasn't all good news.

"I've found another Choice Giver!" He batted Shiori aside like a doll with six or seven thick, wooden limbs. "Die, Choice Giver!"

"Yeah? Come and get me if you can!" Kotone replied, sticking out her tongue and pulling down her lower eyelid.

"Volcano!" And out of nowhere, ash, smoke, and lava were falling from the sky at her.

Kotone sprouted her wings on her boots and darted away from the school roof. But George Flint just kept turning to keep his eyes on her, and the smoke kept chasing after her.

"Why is his magic so much better than ours?" Kotone whined.

"He's had more practice. Plus, Wyrds come in different strengths—and so do magic users. There's just no telling until you make a contract. Don't worry, you're doing fine. You just saved your friends' lives." Magnolia blinked happily.

Kotone smiled warmly, the praise shoring up all her fears. "Magical miracle wasps, sting him to a pulp!" Kotone's little hearts trailed out behind her as she kept flying.

"Meteor!" George Flint bellowed. And out of nowhere, a flaming boulder was streaking at her at atmospheric reentry speeds. She couldn't dodge. The rock was everywhere in her field of vision. Oh no.

The boulder hit her—only it didn't. She didn't feel a thing. The boulder flew by her, *through* her, an awful screeching, tearing sound, until it slammed into a couple of houses and trees behind her. A giant dust cloud appeared, framing her white dress and her gossamer floating wings on her boots. She looked down at herself. She looked at one arm and then the other. Kotone blinked. *I don't know what I'm supposed to think right now.*

Then Kotone noticed a man in a kimono floating beside her. He was carrying a wicked-looking samurai sword, and his outfit was embossed with endless roses and dragons. A silvery gem stood out on the middle of his white scabbard.

"Don't worry. You're safe now. Step back. I'll finish this." The man inscrutably floating in the sky was much older than her. And he looked like he did this sort of thing all the time, for fun, and sometimes when he was asleep for practice.

"Who are you?" Kotone breathed.

"Masanori Miyamoto." And then he was flying straight for George Flint, his sword glinting against the rays of the sun—or maybe with its own inner light.

"I've found another Choice Giver! Die, Choice Giver!" George Flint raised his arms, his tentacles sprouting upward to catch the flying samurai.

"We've heard enough of that line," Masanori said, and he flew straight through the tentacles like they weren't even there.

Masanori cut what looked like a circle around the man. He calmly and coldly intoned, "Angle exile." And then the whole area started to fold and shimmer, like the light that surrounded Kotone when she had become a magical girl.

Then the samurai flew backward, a spike of a tree limb running right through his side. He looked down at it in horror, and only then did the cut space turn sideways and disappear. There was a completely clean slice of the tree limb that was still in this universe from wherever George Flint had been sent. It was still stuck inside the samurai's body.

"How careless," he said, and then he fainted. Shiori was already rushing toward the man.

Chapter 5

Rei Takeda was an evil, selfish, stupid, worthless girl. That's what her mother called her, at least, and she had no reason to believe her mother was wrong. She must have been that awful, because her father flew into rages and beat her almost every day. She provoked him by not cleaning the dishes fast enough or for taking too long a bath, or for scoring badly on a test. It was impossible to explain that she was so afraid of breaking the dishes and angering him that she moved at half speed. It was impossible to explain to him that she had stayed in the bath because it helped ease the pain of her bruises. She couldn't explain to him that she failed her tests because she couldn't study between the light-headedness and tears when he finally finished punishing her and let her crawl into bed.

Those were just excuses, Mother said. It's really because I'm selfish, stupid, and evil. I hog the bath. I won't do my chores. I won't do my homework. I disobey my parents and my teachers, and I won't listen to anyone. I'm just a worthless, evil girl who was born to be a burden on everyone around me. Mother kept telling me how perfect the family would have been if only I hadn't been born and how Father would never have to get so angry, how there would never be any fights, and how Satoshi wouldn't have been killed.

Do you think I don't know that?

That accusation hurt the worst. One day she'd angered father so much that he hadn't stopped beating her. She had broken the television while trying to move a chair. It was an expensive television; it was huge, and it was Father's favorite thing in the world. She had screamed that she was sorry over and over, but he didn't believe her. He was sure she had done it on purpose. She was just that sort of spiteful, malicious devil child. And so he was determined to beat the devil out of her and show her that no one could break his stuff and get away with it.

Satoshi had jumped in the way. He grabbed his father's arm and tried to wrestle with him. And Father was so enraged that he just turned and snapped Satoshi's neck. *That's how I killed my brother. My brother rarely made Father angry. He sometimes did but rarely. Father liked his firstborn, his son. It was only me he hated. And so Father had taken Satoshi's body out onto a boat his friend owned and thrown him into the sea. They said if I told anyone, they would know I had killed him, and they would just throw me in jail for life. That made sense, because I knew I had killed him.*

My older brother was the only person who had ever been kind to me. He couldn't do much, because if he acted too sympathetic, that would make Father furious, because it was like questioning how just his punishments were. That meant he could only be nice while Father wasn't watching. But she knew he wanted to help. And then she had broken Father's TV and killed her brother. When Mother reminded her of that, she always knew Mother was right. *I am evil—if only I hadn't been born.* Mother and Rei agreed on that much. *If only I hadn't been born.*

Sometimes Father got angry when Rei's hands started shaking when they were in the same room. He asked what she was so afraid of. He asked her if she'd done anything wrong that she should have to be afraid of her father. When Rei shook her head and denied having done anything wrong, he grew furious. He called her a liar and said that if she hadn't done anything wrong, she wouldn't be afraid of getting punished. And then he beat her for lying to him. Rei wished she could trust Father and feel safe and comfortable around him. She wished her body wouldn't shake and her speech wouldn't stutter like a stupid fool when she tried to answer his questions. Mother said she stuttered because she was so stupid that she couldn't even talk straight. But she only stuttered when talking to Father. She couldn't explain that though. She supposed she was stupid anyway. If she were smart, she wouldn't keep offending Father by doing stupid things like shaking uncontrollably just because he had sat down on the couch to watch TV. Satoshi hardly ever made Father angry. A good girl, a smart girl, could have been like Satoshi. Everything was her fault.

When the police came to ask what had happened to their son, her parents had said he had just run away one day, and they had never heard from him since. Since the neighbors said they often heard shouting at the home, and since Rei and Mother had confirmed the story, the police considered it an open-and-shut case. The boy had gotten sick of his parents and run off to make his own way in life. Some boys did that. Father was always calm around other adults. It was like

Mother said—only Rei upset him so much. Rei was the source of the problem. Rei was the devil.

Rei Takeda was thirteen years old. She would never survive all the way to high school graduation. She knew, sooner or later, Father would kill her, like he had killed Satoshi. Sometimes she hoped he would, but he always seemed to know when to hold back. He didn't break her bones. He wouldn't hit her face. The only time he had lost control was over the TV. Rei thought about breaking his new TV again, so he'd kill her. But she didn't have the courage. She was afraid of death. If she thought something would end up killing her, she couldn't do it.

She couldn't look forward to escape. Escape was too far away. She would be beaten her whole life. She would be beaten for the rest of her too short, too long life.

Two weeks ago, Rei had found a stray dog. It was ragged, with one of its ears torn clean off. The dog was obviously getting into fights with other stray dogs. She had kneeled down to it. "You're just like me, aren't you? You keep making them mad." The dog had growled at her, but she didn't make any sudden moves or try to pet it. She just sat in the alley with the dog, holding her hands in her lap, and cried.

Rei and the dog had stayed in the alley together until nightfall. When she finally got up to go home, the dog had walked up and pushed itself against her legs. Upon arrival, she was beaten for skipping her chores and making her parents worry by staying out so late. That was okay. She just thought about meeting the dog again tomorrow, lying in bed with all her fresh bruises, and the thought kept making her smile until she fell asleep.

When Rei got out of school, she went to a convenience store. She bought stuff she thought the dog might like, like sandwich meats. Then she ran over to the alley. The stray was there. It stood up, watching her warily.

"I won't hurt you," Rei Takeda promised the dog. "Look, I brought food. It's delicious. Do you want some?" She got out her first package of meat, and she threw a few slices halfway in between her and the dog. The dog watched her hand, watched the meat. She sat patiently, lowering her eyes. After a few minutes, the dog decided she wasn't watching him anymore, and he darted for the meat. He dragged it farther away and started eating. Rei watched the dog, her eyes beaming with joy.

"See? It's delicious, isn't it? Do you want some more?" And Rei threw another package's worth of sandwich meats halfway between her and the dog. The dog finished the old meat then snatched the new meat and started eating that too. This time the dog didn't back away to the back of the alley. He just lay there, well out of reach of her hand. Rei smiled. "Can I call you Shuto?" Rei asked the dog.

The dog finished the meat then raised its head to look at her, waiting to see if she'd throw more meat. Rei just sat still, watching Shuto. Eventually Shuto lay down contentedly with its head on its paws. The two sat there quietly together for a while.

"Shuto, I have to go now. If I'm late again, Father will be mad. But I'll come back tomorrow. See you tomorrow, Shuto." And Rei slowly got up off her knees and made her way back home. She went through the entire evening not making Father angry. She finished her homework, and she didn't start shaking when they all ate dinner together. She was thinking of Shuto and of whether Shuto would let her pet him tomorrow. She would sit and wait for him to come stand next to her again, like on the first day. Anything else, and she might be trespassing. She might drive him away. She didn't want that.

The next day, she came back with more meat for Shuto. She sat and talked to him about her brother while he ate. She told him about every time her brother had patted her hair or told her it was going to be okay and every time he had told her not to believe her mother and that she was a good girl. She cried a lot. Halfway through her sobbing, the dog had come over to her and licked her face. That just made her cry more. Shuto sat next to her and she did get to pet him.

The next day, she sat next to Shuto and explained why she couldn't take him home and that her parents would be mad, and they would chase him away or hurt him. She knew it was selfish, but she asked Shuto to always stay in the alley and not to run off with the other dogs or let some other child adopt him. She told Shuto to stop getting into fights with the other dogs. Shuto always looked dirty and beat-up, just like her. It's like he instantly went and got into fights whenever she left.

Shuto wouldn't listen. Even when she gave him a bath, he ended up dirty the very next day.

This afternoon though, when she had come to see Shuto, he wasn't there. She called out his name. "Shuto? Shuto? It's okay, it's me. Come out, Shuto." Shuto wouldn't come. So she sat patiently in the alley, getting out her homework and doing the subjects one after the other. This was Shuto's home. He'd have to come back eventually.

"Hey, look. It's Takeda-tard." A group of boys from her school were standing at the mouth of the alley.

"Takeda-tard was waiting for her dog." They mocked her. "Takeda-tard doesn't have any friends because she's so stupid, so she had to hang out with a dog."

"What do you care?" Rei glared angrily at them. "Leave me alone!"

"Your stupid dog isn't coming back, Takeda," the leader of the boys said. He held out his hand, which had a white bandage around it. "Look what he did to me."

"What did you do to Shuto?" Rei felt a horrendous pain, like her soul was tearing in two.

"Nothing. We just saw you petting him, so after you left we tried to pet him too, to be nice. And the stupid dog bit me. I had to get a rabies shot! So I told my parents and they told the city, and the city took your stupid dog away. You know what they do to dogs that bite people." The boy smirked.

"Your dog's dead, Takeda-tard!" A boy in the back of the group jeered. All of them started laughing.

Rei screamed. Then she filled her lungs and screamed again. It hurt her throat to scream that loud but not nearly as much as their words hurt her. She had killed again. She killed everyone who tried to be nice to her. Rei screamed again a wordless cry of frustration, of despair, of hatred. She filled her lungs and screamed again, but only a bloody gurgle came out. It hurt so much.

The kids ran away. Adults ran to her, but all they saw was this girl screaming for no good reason in the middle of the street.

"Someone call her parents," someone suggested.

"Maybe we should call an ambulance," someone else suggested.

Rei struggled up and ran away from them. She didn't want their help. She wanted to die. That was how she'd ended up in her room, holding a kitchen knife, sitting alone in the dark. She knew she had to plunge it into her stomach and cut a giant path through her internal organs or make a long slice all the way down both her arms. But she couldn't move. She stared at the knife, and her hands shook. They could barely hold onto the hilt. She didn't cry any more. She just looked at the blade and pleaded for it to stab her. Occasionally she'd try to tell her arm to move, to cut, but she always cut the signal off. Her arm stood still. She was infinitely far away from killing herself. She wanted to die. She had never been so sure of this in her life. She knew she had to die, and she knew death was the only good thing in life. But she was too afraid. She was a worthless coward who couldn't even do this right.

That was when the floating black orb appeared. Rei Takeda stared at it lifelessly. She didn't feel much of anything anymore.

"I can give you what you want," the black orb said. "My name is Onyx. I can kill you."

Rei shook her head. The orb didn't understand. She was too afraid to die. She couldn't make any decision that she knew would lead to her death. It was the exact same as trying to jump into a river or off a cliff, or drive a car into a brick wall. If she knew, consciously, that this would end up killing her, her subconscious stopped her. She couldn't trick herself. Asking someone else to kill her, if she knew he really would, was the exact same.

The orb sat there, blinking for a while. "I can help you die in a way your body won't stop."

Rei looked at him with desperate hope. "How?" she rasped. Her throat still hurt, so she didn't want to talk if she could avoid it.

"Fight the Choice Givers. If you kill the Choice Givers, one of them will be sure to kill you sooner or later. They will kill you, against your will, with you fighting as hard as you can to stop them. You won't know when it will happen, or against whom. It will be sudden and out of the blue. You'll be fighting, and then you'll die. Maybe if you fight well enough, you'll beat them all. It's not assured you will die at all." Onyx seemed to understand her. Maybe Onyx was the first person who understood her in her entire life.

"I don't want to kill anyone," Rei rasped.

"You want to kill yourself," Onyx pointed out.

Rei was silent. Time stretched out. The two of them sat together silently as minutes passed.

Her mind was silent too. Dull. Cold. She couldn't get herself to care. So what if she killed people? Death was a mercy. The whole world was just a net negative. If she turned a negative into a zero, she was doing them a favor. Onyx understood.

"How do I kill the Choice Givers?" Rei Takeda rasped. She felt nothing. She didn't care anymore. What had the world ever done for her?

"Just say, '*Via tu lusches*, Onyx.' I'll train you in how to fight. One by one, we'll kill them all. Kill the Choice Givers, kill the world."

"*Via tu lusches*, Onyx," Rei whispered. Warmth tried to trickle into her, but she wouldn't let it. She was cold. She was cold inside. She would always be cold, forever.

School ended up being cancelled for the next week, as repair crews had to go in and make sure the building was still safe and repair it as quickly as possible. Luckily, the people whose houses had been crushed were already away at work or school. In the end, there were only three injured people. Basically, every Choice Giver but Kotone had to go to the hospital. And of course Kotone had to go too, to be with them. Adults explained that it had been another one of those dirty pranks by the worldwide hackers, setting off explosions and creating holograms. The fact that the tree monster all the eyewitnesses talked about couldn't be found anywhere was supporting evidence.

Kotone didn't try to disabuse them. If the whole world knew they were magical girls locked in a war with dark Wyrds from outer space, they would put them in the deepest underground bunker in the world or in some sort of undersea submarine and do crazy experiments on them in the name of science. *I don't want to lose the life I have. That's almost as bad as dying.* But she thanked Magnolia from the bottom of her heart for having come down to Earth on time. Wyrds could scry out Choice Givers wherever they fled. If no good Wyrds had come down to help them, the dark Wyrds could have wiped all the Choice Givers out in a matter of months or weeks, maybe. And only magic could fight magic. Getting the rest of the world involved was just a waste of time.

She needed to thank one other person from the bottom of her heart, though—Masanori Miyamoto, the man who had saved her life and nearly died doing so. And to do that, she needed to wait outside his door until visitors were allowed to see him. *I wish I had been given healing magic. Why bugs?* Did people look at Kotone and think, 'Ah, bugs. Bug girl. Bugs are just the thing for her'? She had never liked bugs herself. But there it was. *I'm some sort of magical, miracle bug master. Ugh.*

"Why do you think George Flint wanted to kill us?" Kotone asked Magnolia.

"Who knows? Dead-Enders want the world to follow a path that ends with stagnation or extinction. That means by definition all Choice Givers are in the way, because you keep creating fresh, new possibilities for the world to follow. The first step to any Dead-Ender's plan would be to kill the remaining Choice Givers." Magnolia glowed mutedly.

"But didn't you say the whole world was full of Dead-Enders? Does that mean everyone I see secretly wants to kill me?" Kotone asked.

"Some Dead-Enders are less stable and more manipulable than others. Some are more ambitious or competent than others. Just like we can scry out the most beautiful Choice Givers, Wyrds can scry out the ugliest Dead-Enders, the ones that shut down the world's paths the fastest and destroy things the soonest. The terrorists will try to recruit from among them," Magnolia explained.

"Not terrorists. 'Terrorists' has too much linguistic baggage. Dark Wyrds," Kotone said.

"Dark Wyrds then. And the world isn't 6.99 billion Dead-Enders and fifty Choice Givers. There are those who follow or emulate Choice Givers too," Magnolia said.

"Can people follow or emulate Choice Givers from the distant past?" Kotone asked.

"Yes, but it's hard. The message gets garbled. It becomes obsolete, or the tradition just dies away. The impact Choice Givers have has a sort of half life. It keeps fading away until the world has nothing but dead ends again. Only new blood and new possibilities keep your future alive," Magnolia said.

"Are new Choice Givers created from following the old ones?" Kotone asked.

"No. You are fountains of new possibilities. Oh, you could be taking something from one tradition and something from another. But if you didn't synthesize that into something new, keep looking forward, and trust your own inner voice, you wouldn't be special," Magnolia said.

"Are we born Choice Givers, or do we become them?" Kotone asked.

"You become them," Magnolia said.

"Could we stop being Choice Givers and become Dead-Enders?" Kotone asked.

"Technically, yes," Magnolia said.

"What do you mean?" Kotone asked.

"Well, our scrying can only see the implications of our current choices, whether they lead to infinite possibilities. If you change your mind, change your choices, then you could suddenly be as bad as anyone else. Only, it's difficult for a Choice Giver to change her mind toward something worse, because her very choices about how she makes her choices already exist and already guide her down the right road."

"That's reassuring. Could Dead-Enders become Choice Givers, then?" Kotone asked.

"Yes. But it's unlikely. People are pretty set in their ways," Magnolia said.

"Then the world won't really end, even if all the Choice Givers are killed off. More would pop up sooner or later, and the cycle would restart," Kotone said.

"Not if the dark Wyrds kill them off too. And not if the world becomes so bad that it's impossible to fix it and impossible to change anything, and nothing you say or do matters—like our world." Magnolia sighed.

"Oh." Kotone sat on the hospital bench. Magnolia sat silently in her bag. Patients and nurses and janitors and guests were constantly walking by, but they all ignored her and left her alone, because she projected that wish with her body language.

"I'm sorry your world is dying." Kotone offered.

"I know, Kotone." Magnolia blinked her light understandingly. Kotone couldn't hug Magnolia, so she did the next best thing and squeezed her with her hand.

"Nakano?" A harried-looking nurse looked at her clipboard. "You wanted to visit Mr. Miyamoto?"

"Yes, please." Kotone bowed to her, hastily rising to her feet and pulling her school bag in front of her.

"Are you a friend or relative?" the nurse asked.

"No," Kotone replied.

"Then you can't—"

"I was at the school incident. He saved my life. I have to thank him," Kotone quickly interrupted.

The nurse seemed to look at her for the first time, showing a hint of respect. "Okay, but don't disturb him. He's on a lot of painkillers right now. I wouldn't be surprised if he's already asleep. You also wanted to see two other girls from the same school incident…Rin and Sakai?" the nurse asked. "Did they save your life too?"

"No, they're my friends." Kotone smiled.

"Okay, I'm giving you a sticky note with their room numbers. Visiting hours are only so long, so you'll have to figure out how to meet all of them in one go." The nurse said, getting out her pen and scribbling something.

"Thank you." Kotone bowed again, accepting the paper and the signature that said she had free run of the hospital. She checked her hair with a hand mirror from her bag, got out her hair brush and fixed it as best she could, then took a deep breath and knocked on the door.

"Come in," said a voice through the door. So Kotone opened it and took a few steps into the room. The man had a giant web of bandages and a few tubes going into him, but he was awake.

"My name is Kotone Nakano. You saved my life. From the bottom of my heart, thank you." And then Kotone bowed and stayed bowed as deeply as she could.

"Umm." The man sounded embarrassed. She couldn't see his face because her face was still pointed straight at the ground. "It was nothing."

"My life means a lot to me," Kotone said.

"I didn't mean it like that. I can't think straight right now. I'm on so many drugs. Could you stop bowing?" the man asked.

Kotone straightened up and gave him her most heartwarming smile, the one that filled her whole face. "Next time I visit, I'll properly have some flowers. I can read to you too, or we can just talk. It isn't just for me. Thank you for saving my friends too. Once that man killed me, he would have killed them too. You can't know how much this means to me. Thank you so much for saving all three of us." And Kotone helplessly bowed again, because she didn't know any other way to express the fullness of her heart.

"It's okay. I didn't do it for your sake. I chose to do this sort of thing myself," Masanori said.

Kotone looked back at him and smiled, settling down into the chair next to his bed. "I would be a little worried if it was for my sake. We only just met. And you are, like, fifty years old."

"Thirty-seven," the man protested. "And I didn't mean it that way."

"I know. And if you think I'm not grateful that you're the kind of person who risks his life to save complete strangers, then you're crazy," Kotone said.

"What happened to the pink hair?" Masanori asked.

"Hush. You're clearly delirious." Kotone blushed crimson.

Masanori laughed and then winced. "Okay. That was a bad idea."

"If you don't mind, could you tell me how you did all that? And why you were there in the first place?" Kotone got him back on topic.

"I call it 'angle universe.' When Xanadu told me that he had come from folded space, I started wondering what other tricks you could pull with that. So when I formed a contract, I found that all my magic was based around folding. When I saw you were going to be hit, I folded you out of the way. I can do that instantly, to any one object, for a few seconds. You were probably in the universe next to this one when the boulder flew through. It's harder to fold someone permanently away, but wherever George Flint ended up, I doubt he can trouble anyone." Masanori seemed to be on firm ground for the first time.

"Xanadu?" Magnolia floated up from her bag. "You formed a contract with Xanadu?"

"Do you know him?" Masanori asked Magnolia politely.

"Only by reputation. He was sent a few days before us, as our very first pioneer. The government said he was an elite soldier or something who could scout the terrain," Magnolia said.

"A few days? I met Xanadu ten years ago. I've been fighting these Dead-Enders for years," Masanori said.

Magnolia blinked for a bit in confusion. "The time streams between our dimensions must be different."

"Do you know where they took my stuff? I'd feel better if Xanadu were here. You never know when…" Masanori grimaced.

"I will try to find him for you. I'll bring him with the flowers, next time I visit," Kotone promised.

"Then I'll see you next time." Masanori sighed back into his bed.

"I'll see you again." Kotone got up from her chair, bowing one more time. Next time, when he wasn't so tired, she could ask him more questions. For now, she wanted to see Shiori and Chiharu. She had a lot of conversations to go.

Kotone quietly closed the door behind her and got out her pen, writing Mr. Miyamoto's room number down alongside that of her friends'. Then she found a payphone in the hallway and called her parents.

"Sorry I can't make dinner. The nurse has only just now let me visit Shiori and Chiharu. I'll be back before bedtime. If you could save something for me… Thanks, Mama. I'm completely all right. I told you that already. Just a little frazzled. It's okay, I'll take the bus."

Then it was off to room 210, where she checked up on Shiori.

"Are you okay?" Kotone asked, sitting down beside Shiori's hospital bed.

"This? This is nothing." Shiori raised her arms to show how healthy she was, and then she winced. "Who hasn't been sent flying ten feet by a few tree limbs?"

Kotone smiled. "Any broken bones?"

"Nope. Just…I was so sure I could beat that guy. I'm so frustrated. That's what hurts the most." Shiori sighed, looking at her hands. Then she shook her head and grabbed Kotone's hands into hers.

"You saved my life, didn't you? Thank you, Kotone," Shiori said.

"You're my best friend," Kotone said, as if that was explanation enough.

"I want to get stronger," Shiori said, a few tears gathering at the corners of her eyes. "I don't want to feel that helpless ever again. I don't want to lose ever again."

"We'll get stronger." Kotone squeezed Shiori's hands.

"My softball coach is going to kill me if I can't pitch on the first game." Shiori moaned.

"You'll be fine. If nothing's broken, just take a hot bath, use some of those magic icy hot pads, and sleep in. School's out for the next week," Kotone said.

"I'll try to get released tomorrow. There's really nothing wrong with me. Then we can train with our magic. What magic did you use, Kotone? I couldn't see. I was in a squiggly death embrace." Shiori said.

Kotone blushed. "I need to check up on Chiharu." "See you tomorrow!"

And then it was time to visit Chiharu in room 221. When she walked in, her entire family was bunched together in the room. Chiharu had Saki on her lap and was tickling her. Saki kept squealing, "Nooo!" and "Stoppp!" but it didn't seem like anyone in the room cared. Her other sister, Aiko, was sitting against the wall reading. She barely lifted her gaze to register Kotone's existence before settling back down again.

"Kotone!" Chiharu looked up to see who had come in.

"Good evening, Chiharu." Kotone bowed. "Good evening, Mr. Sakai. Good evening, Mrs. Sakai."

"Good evening, Nakano." Chiharu's parents greeted her warmly.

"Chiharu, are you okay?" Kotone asked.

"Bruises and scrapes. Plus somewhere in there I got dizzy and blacked out. I hope that doesn't leave me permanently stupider. When boxers black out, they lose like five IQ points each time." Chiharu scowled.

"If that were true, they'd be down to zero in no time," Kotone said primly.

"Nevertheless. I can already feel the stupidity flowing through me," Chiharu said.

"Those are the painkillers," Kotone said. "You'd *better* not lose any IQ. We need you after school for tutoring, from here to age eighteen, for free."

"I'll try my best." Chiharu smiled.

"Shiori isn't hurt either," Kotone informed them.

"Thank goodness," Chiharu said.

"She said your coach would kill you if you don't play in the first game." Kotone smiled.

Chiharu laughed. "If she can pitch, I can catch."

"Then that's settled. We have a week off school, so let's meet up and enjoy ourselves as soon as we can. I have to go home and eat dinner, so I'll be going now. Sorry to intrude, Mr. Sakai, Mrs. Sakai." Kotone bowed to the rest of the family again.

"It was no bother at all, Nakano. You're always welcome," Chiharu's parents reassured her.

Kotone stepped out of the crowded hospital room and started her long trip home. Thank goodness, they were both okay. But Mr. Miyamoto wouldn't be able to save them next time, not with that giant hole in his side. *We three have to get better at magic in the next week before the next Dead-Ender arrives. There's got to be some way around being a bug master. It's too embarrassing.* Kotone collected the loose strands of her hair back into their proper places in her hair clip and twin tails, and then she sat down to wait for the bus.

"We can break what Magnolia told Kotone down into three possible meanings to being a Choice Giver." Chiharu stabbed at her notebook with a helpful chart.

Kotone and Shiori huddled around her to see, leaning in. The three had told their parents they were going to study at the library, but that was only roughly true.

We are studying—only, we're studying magic. And we are at the library—only, we're outside on a park bench where we can be as loud as we want. That was a stupid way to pretend you weren't lying, turning every word inside out and letting people hear what you wanted them to hear. But the larger truth was more like this: "I am going out with my friends for a benign, constructive purpose." If the larger truth was conveyed through the use of a smaller lie, no lie had been told. She was just framing the truth in a way her parents would understand.

"Theory one: Small answers and big answers are the same. The principles behind our day-to-day decisions can be directly applied to communities as a whole as, for instance, laws or religious doctrines." Chiharu pointed to her first box.

"Theory two: Big answers are derived from small answers. Under this theory, there is a logical chain you can grow from a day-to-day decision all the way up to how we should run the world. It just takes intelligence enough to grasp the essential principle and how to apply it in larger cases." Chiharu stabbed her second box.

"Theory three: There are no big answers, only small answers. All big answers are inherently erroneous. Choice Givers should be emulated from the bottom up, rather than the top down." Chiharu stabbed the final box.

"I can't tell them apart," Shiori complained.

"All categories are arbitrary. I'm just trying to help clarify things," Chiharu said.

"So if you knew a Choice Giver well enough, you could think to yourself, 'What would Shiori think about this? How would Shiori react? What would Shiori do?' And with enough specific knowledge of Shiori, you could, when the situation was specific, do the same thing," Kotone suggested.

"That would be category three." Chiharu nodded. "But of course, it wouldn't work if you didn't *feel* the same way as Shiori at the same time. Magnolia specifically told us that one of the choices we make is how we feel about whatever the world throws at us. If someone emulated Shiori while not understanding why or was being angry and frustrated about it the whole time because she would do something else—"

"That sounds hard. With all those restrictions, can Choice Givers really help anyone?" Kotone asked.

"I don't know. Magnolia only said mankind would have infinite possibilities 'if' they would follow us, not whether anyone will," Chiharu answered.

"Okay, so let's take category one," Shiori said. "I like dogs. So everyone should own a dog. This would give the world infinite possibilities."

"That does seem reasonable. At least, under that theory, the whole world having a pet dog is probably a step in the right direction." Chiharu calmly kept her face straight.

"But according to category two"—Shiori pointed at the box—"it would read differently. I like dogs, so maybe we should all like pets. Or all lower life forms. Or maybe it's important to be affectionate."

"Right." Chiharu nodded. "What's important is capturing the essence of your choice and then ballooning it up to cover all situations."

"If people emulate us, don't the total number of choices go down, not up?" Kotone complained. "For instance, making everyone own a dog eliminates choices like, 'I won't own a dog.' In the end, people could only be carbon clones of, like, fifty different models available anywhere on Earth."

"If everyone owning a dog displaces other choices that lead to stagnation or death, it's okay to eliminate choices. In fact, Choice Givers could be giving people the only choices that don't lead to stagnation or extinction and thus be very strict taskmasters. It could be our job to eliminate all the bad choices that are out there," Chiharu explained.

"Are there really so few choices that work out?" Kotone asked sadly.

"If you extend practically anyone's belief system to a universal law, you will find the seeds of destruction in it. What's special about our choices is no matter how far you balloon them up, no matter how many people follow or emulate us, it won't lead to a dead end. Many people's choices, if not ballooned up, if not extended too far, will be either innocuous or even useful. But if their inner logic was exposed to such a wide-scale test as all of humanity following them…" Chiharu left the rest hanging.

"Power corrupts," Shiori suggested.

"More like power reveals the inherent flaws of a seemingly harmless belief system by ballooning it up to such a size that anyone can observe its flaws," Chiharu corrected.

"So no matter how many people adopt dogs, in theory one, or pets, in theory two, or pet dogs when they see them, in theory three, only good will come of it," Kotone said.

"Precisely. I think Wyrds have settled the question of dog ownership once and for all." Chiharu smiled.

"Maybe I should adopt a dog." Kotone grinned. "It would put me on the right track."

"Kotone's a Choice Giver too, and she doesn't own a dog!" Shiori protested.

"I don't even pet dogs when I see them," Kotone said.

Chiharu nodded. "It's safe to say we're on the road to hell."

"You're making fun of me," Shiori said.

"Maybe a little." Chiharu smiled. Making fun of Shiori was the most fun thing in the world.

"I prefer category three," Kotone said. "I mean, I don't want to write out a law code for anyone. It's important that they also *feel* it's the right thing to do, while they're doing it. That's what gives the choice such inner strength."

"Hmm." Chiharu stared at the boxes. "I think I would choose category one. My choices are obviously right, and everyone should just follow them. If they aren't competent enough to do so, they can follow them as far as they are able. Since I'm obviously right, giving them the privilege or freedom to do the opposite is just wasteful and counterproductive to their own lives and the inhabitants of the rest of the world. I'd give an exception to people obeying another Choice Giver's law code, since Wyrds' scrying can be trusted, and it seems those law codes work fine too. But it would be a huge improvement if we at least banned all the obviously wrong codes."

"Then I'll choose category two," Shiori said.

"Don't choose a category just to not leave it out!" Chiharu hit her with her notebook.

"We don't know these are the rules anyway," Kotone reminded them. "We could be wrong, and Choice Giving could mean something else entirely."

"I suppose I should think it over carefully before installing the iron fist of the age of Chiharu," Chiharu admitted.

"But I know what you're talking about," Shiori said. "There are so many things that are so obviously wrong, and it feels like waiting for people to see that themselves is just hopeless."

"Slavery as a custom was uprooted by force. It's the same with human sacrifice and burning widows in India on their husbands' funeral pyres." Chiharu gave examples.

"I can see how a Choice Giver, by stopping slavery or human sacrifice with an iron fist, could keep the world from stagnation or extinction. Like, just imagine the whole world ruled by a few fat, rich people who just lazed about and millions of slaves who couldn't even learn to read. Where would the world go? Maybe it would just stay that way forever—poor and painful forever. Or if everyone resorted to human sacrifice and the wars needed to get enough victims, we'd just end up driving ourselves to extinction," Shiori said.

"I guess you're right," Kotone said.

"Luckily, we know all three of us are right, no matter what we think or do," Chiharu said. "Even when we contradict each other, we're both right, because both contradictory statements lead to a good ending."

"So in conclusion, we should keep doing whatever we want?" Shiori asked.

"That or adopt dogs," Chiharu said.

"Stop that. Leave Melody out of this!" Shiori pouted. Chiharu loved her pouty face.

"Okay, on to the second part of our strategy conference." Chiharu flipped over the page of her notebook to the next three boxes.

"All three of us couldn't beat a single Dead-Ender. There's bound to be more of them, so we need to get stronger. Cyan told me that our magic can't be changed, but it can be developed or enhanced. This means creativity is a huge plus. We all need to come up with new moves. Think of the essential nature of your magic, and see if you can branch out into an entirely different spell while sticking to your nature. Did you two bring pencils and paper?"

"Yes," the two chimed.

"Okay. Here's your assignment. Think of three new spells in the next fifteen minutes. Make them as different as possible." Chiharu got off the park bench and lay down on the grass, stretching out to consider her own blank notebook.

"I…"—Kotone blushed—"I need help."

"What's wrong with your magic?" Chiharu asked.

"Everything!" Kotone wailed. "I summon bugs!"

Chiharu smiled, but Shiori started laughing. Shiori followed up between laughs. "Bugs? Why bugs? That doesn't fit you at all!"

"I don't want to be a bug master! But when I tried to summon birds, or shoot fire or ice, nothing would happen. Only bugs worked!" Kotone said.

"Tell me the exact thought that popped into your head—the one that hinted at your magic's manifestation," Chiharu said.

"I think it was…something like…'I wish pine beetles would tear him apart.' Or maybe it was 'eat him up.'" Kotone offered.

"I think we can work with that. Imagine the critical factor not being bugs but 'small things' that 'degrade' the target bit by bit. If you think of it like that, you wouldn't be limited to bugs. You could give people diseases, for instance," Chiharu offered.

"That's even worse! I don't want to be Magical Plague Master Kotone!" Kotone said. "Besides, what disease would possibly be useful in such a short time as a fight? George Flint was throwing volcanoes at me, and I'm trying to make him sneeze?"

"You're right. Maybe diseases aren't as good as bugs. Well, that's my advice. Think of small things that degrade their targets piece by piece, like lots of bugs working together do. You have fifteen minutes," Chiharu said.

Then the three of them did quiet down and lie on the grass. The pond nearby lapped against the shore. Kids were flying kites. Kotone kept tapping her lips with the back of her pencil. Shiori was staring at the paper blankly then started to doodle. Chiharu tried to tune them out and concentrate exclusively on the task at hand. She knew that if the time limit weren't short, no one would think of anything. Restrictions bred creativity. But she couldn't help them any further. She couldn't protect her friends with just counter spells. Countering didn't stop the opponent's suit, nor could it assuredly beat a magic that overpowered hers, or a magic that came from too many directions, or a magic that she didn't notice in time. She didn't know how far she could trust it.

What was the *essence* of counter magic? She thought of it as redirecting the vectors of magic such that it was all pointed at itself, so that it canceled itself out entirely, like directing sound waves, no matter how loud, to hit each other head-on and thus produce no sound at all. She had always found that fascinating. It looked like it defied the laws of physics, but it was already used to make cars quieter, for instance, in the real world. So what would happen if she didn't change the vectors of the arrows all the way back in on themselves? What if she only redirected them a little? She smiled and wrote down her first new spell: "1) Deflect magic."

Chiharu thought about it a little longer. If she could change the vectors to just barely miss her, could she also turn the vectors around? That would be vicious. She wrote down: "2) Reflect magic." Just one more. She sat

there thinking. Is *that all you can do with magical vectors? Surely there was just one more ability nestled in there.*
What if she could see the vectors of the flow of magic
and add her own magic to the mix, feeding the magic
in the exact same direction as the first? Just as you can
cancel out a wave entirely by having it hit itself, you can
also double it by overlaying the exact same wave on top
of it. This was done by all sorts of machines, such as
an electric guitar's amplifier. Chiharu smiled and wrote
down: "3) Amplify magic." *Just imagine what my laser
gun could do if I amplified the waves as high as I could.
Then I could have burst through that stupid green barrier
like it was nothing.*

Chiharu stretched and turned over, staring at the
sky. She checked her watch and then watched the kites
and the clouds. Days off from school could be nice.

"All right, time's up. Put your pencils down,"
Chiharu said. "Let's see what we came up with." Kotone
sighed; Shiori looked confident.

"Okay, Shiori, you first," Chiharu said.

"Number one," Shiori read from her notebook.
"Firefly. I shoot a bunch of little fires at the bad guy, like
the fires are flying. See?" Shiori had drawn a useful doodle of herself blasting away at a growling tree octopus.

"Okay." Chiharu nodded.

"Number two," Shiori recited. "Flashfire. I make
a giant flash of light around me and then pounce on
them while they're blinded." Shiori pointed at her doodle of the tree octopus covering its eyes with all eight
tree limbs.

"Are all your attacks puns?" Kotone asked.

"They helped me think!" Shiori justified herself.

"I think they're great spells," Chiharu said encouragingly. "And?"

"Number three, fireplace," Shiori read. "I place a mine, and if they step on it, the mine erupts into fire." Shiori had a helpful doodle of a tree octopus flying into the sky with lots of lines rushing up from underneath him.

"That's…an inventive interpretation of fireplaces." Chiharu grinned.

"All that matters is I did my assignment. What about Kotone?" Shiori asked.

"I…I don't know if these will work until I try them out with Magnolia," Kotone said. All three Wyrds had gone away together to confer by themselves about all things Wyrdy.

"That's okay. If they came to you while brainstorming, it's probably your magic whispering to you, so it will work out," Chiharu reassured her.

"Okay. Number one, poison," Kotone read out.

"Poison what?" Shiori asked.

"I don't know. Poison clouds, poison rain, pits full of poison. I can summon objects at long distance, so, just summon something on top of them," Kotone said.

"What types of poison?" Chiharu asked.

"The green kind?" Kotone offered hopefully.

"Umm. I think it's a good idea, but you should look up the ones used in World War One. I think the best poison gas known to modern science is chlorine, but you'll need a good mental image of it if you want to summon it."

"Okay. Number two," Kotone read, "acid."

"Acid what?" Shiori repeated herself. She was clearly getting back at Kotone.

"Like, I summon a bucket of acid over their heads and dump it on them. Acid is small but degrades what it touches," Kotone defended herself.

"I think sulfuric acid would be your best bet. It burns people alive," Chiharu suggested. "You'll need to read up on it to get a firm mental image."

Kotone shuddered. Chiharu placed her hand on her friend's arm. "If you don't need to use it, you can always summon bugs. This is a worst-case scenario. If George Flint were choking us to death, and acid can save our lives…"

"I know. I just…don't like what my magic says about me." Kotone sighed.

"Fire burns people alive too. What does that say about me?" Shiori asked.

"I guess burning people to death is torturous too." Kotone managed half of a smile.

"See? We're the same." Shiori said.

"For that matter, staking someone out on an anthill to be eaten alive was also a tool of torture used by the Native Americans. See? Acid and poison is no worse than before." Chiharu pointed out helpfully.

"Let's just move on to number three." Kotone sighed. Chiharu didn't get it. How come only Shiori's words of encouragement made Kotone feel better?

"When Magnolia told me to think of a weapon and armor, I came up with a dress and a wand. My armor lets me fly, and my magic lets me summon bugs. But my wand didn't do anything, even though it's my 'strongest weapon.' So I'll have my wand shoot something, like really small, fast bullets at as far a range as possible—preferably out of eyesight. I call it 'Sting Snipe,'" Kotone explained, her voice getting more subdued by the second.

Shiori and Kotone looked at their hands, downcast. Chiharu knew what they were thinking: "We're Japanese schoolgirls. Why are we thinking of such horrible ways to kill people?" But it didn't matter what they wanted. They were being hunted, and killing was justified if it was in self-defense. *How can I explain that to them?*

"Neh." Shiori got their attention, speaking quietly. "Let's all agree that before we fight any more Dead-Enders, we try to talk to them first."

"We'd lose any chance at an ambush. Soldiers don't talk to their enemies—they just kill them," Chiharu said.

"But we're not soldiers," Shiori said, looking Chiharu in the eyes. "We're Choice Givers. We should be destroying their dead ends, letting them have infinite possibilities again. Dead ends are bad, but Dead-Enders are *people*. We should be healing these people, not hurting them. They're coming here to be healed. They just don't know it yet. But the three of us, we *know* we can heal them. Somehow. It's inside of us to… change them. If we win with violence, that means we lost our fight—our fight as Choice Givers."

"I agree with Shiori, Chiharu." Kotone looked hopeful for the first time. "I…don't want to just hurt and kill people…for the rest of my life. Maybe we can talk to them."

Chiharu sighed. "The dark Wyrds are choosing the most deadly, determined monsters on Earth to give power. What could we possibly say?"

"We could try," Shiori insisted. "There's always a way. That's what it *means* to be a Choice Giver. We find ways where others can't."

"What would you have told George? He was a walking tape recorder. He only said, like, two different things!" Chiharu argued.

"But he *was* talking to us. Maybe he was crying out for help. And we…we were just hitting him. We could have asked him for his reasons," Shiori said.

"Our real power is inspiration. That's why the Wyrds chose us in the first place." Kotone teamed up.

"Okay." Chiharu took a deep breath and looked them in the eyes. "We try to talk to everyone who comes at us. If they start off attacking, we start off dodging. I so swear," Chiharu said. Shiori was right. And if she wasn't right, Chiharu *wanted* Shiori to be right, because Shiori's world was so much brighter.

"I so swear," Kotone quickly agreed.

"I so swear," Shiori said, putting her hand over her heart.

"Now, does anyone want to hear what magic I came up with?" Chiharu asked.

Chapter 6

Mahmut al Baz was a Muslim. He wasn't particularly devout. Like his friends, he was more concerned with getting a university degree and whether his hometown won the Egyptian Premier League. Ismaily was a decent football club, and living in Ismailia pretty much meant life revolved around its victories and defeats. When he was young, he had played football in the streets with the other kids and dreamed of playing for Ismaily and running into the middle of the vast stadiums, cheered by millions of people from their TV sets at home. He wouldn't stop there though. Naturally, his football career would lead to Egypt winning the World Cup for the first time, all thanks to his last-minute goal. His dream hadn't decided if the World Cup final would be against Germany or Brazil, but it was certain he would score the winning goal and lift the trophy in front of billions of people who would remember his name forever. Then he had realized that he wasn't any better than the other kids he was playing with, and the dream had slowly receded. Maybe he wouldn't win the World Cup after all, but at least he could play for Ismaily. Then Mahmut realized that he wouldn't get into Ismaily either, and so he just followed the team with the rest of his friends, drinking with his friends and cheering on their goals.

Mahmut was poor, but so were all of his friends. Poverty didn't mean anything in Egypt. He was attending a university, which meant he was upper class. The facts that he had a tiny apartment, that the apartment complex was built at least fifty years ago, and that he didn't own any furniture beyond a bed and didn't have any gadgets aside from his cell phone were just normal for a man starting out in life.

Islam did pop up in his life every now and then, though. He had turned down his friends when they invited him to go with them to sow their wild oats. Of course, it was hard to say whether that was out of religious piety or just common sense. He wanted to find a decent, well-behaved, modest virgin at university. High-quality girls like that didn't waste their time with impious men. People would talk. Her parents would find out. And suddenly he wouldn't be invited to eat dinner with them anymore. Anyone, whether they were religious or not, could see it just wasn't worth it.

He kept the fast of Ramadan, but he rarely went to a mosque. He gave himself the excuse that university life was just too busy for such luxuries, and he'd go back to attending mosque once he'd settled down with a family. The kids needed a good religious upbringing, after all, until they could tell right from wrong. Islam also came up whenever Al Jazeera came on or when his friends started talking politics. He was distinctly reminded that he was a Muslim every time he heard about the latest atrocity Israel or the West had perpetrated against them. Sometimes it was killing innocent civilians in their endless wars of aggression. Other times it was just some particularly nasty comment people were making against his people, such as that they fornicated with camels or were all inbred idiots, or that their Prophet, peace be upon him, was composed of cow dung.

The calumniators always sank to new lows. People who had never been harmed by a Muslim in their life still found the time to talk about how awful he, as a Muslim, was. It was like they delighted in insulting him, his family, his beliefs, and his Prophet. Whenever he listened to the outrages in the news too long, he would get furious, and he would leave the room and take a walk and go somewhere, anywhere, and try to concentrate on girls or football, or university. There was nothing he could do about it, Mahmut reminded himself. *I can't stop them. Allah will sort them out as He pleases, when judgment day comes. Allah sees all of this, and He knows their crimes, and He has set aside a place for the evildoers. I don't have to do anything. I can't think about doing something because everyone knows what happens to boys who do. They go crazy and end up dead somewhere far away. And then the Islamophobes would point at those boys and call them names and call Islam names, and say, "See? We were right all along."*

Mahmut wanted to scream at them that if they had only stopped doing and saying such awful things, no one would have gotten so angry that he had to embrace jihad. That all the blood of the world was on their hands and Muslims provoked beyond all reason weren't to blame for anything they did in response. *I can't do anything about it. Think about football. Football is a safe topic. I can think about football all I want and not end up killing people.*

Mahmut was returning from one of these walks, wondering how he could introduce himself to a good-looking girl in his class who virtuously did nothing to bring attention to how good-looking she was, when the angel Gabriel came down to him. Gabriel was a blinding white light, with a dense core that was the brightest lit part of all. He floated off the ground, waiting for him when he entered the apartment. Mahmut knew instantly it was Gabriel, Allah's messenger, because what else could such a floating light be?

Mahmut was instantly prostrating himself on the ground, lowering his eyes from the terrible brightness, and he started reciting protective lines from the Qu'ran. "In the name of Allah, the benevolent, the merciful." What were you supposed to say when an angel came down to you?

"You are faithful. This is good. I know your heart, Mahmut. Allah is pleased with you. I have been sent to you, to tell you that Allah has a mission for you. Judgment day is nearly at hand, but Allah's hand is stayed by the false prophets who pervert the world from Islam." Gabriel seemed to grow particularly bright with fury in contemplation of these deceivers.

"Surely Allah…in his power…" Mahmut licked his lips.

"You are faithful, Mahmut. So tell me, do you know of the Dajjal?" Gabriel asked.

"The false Mahdi," Mahmut answered. "The thirty liars who come before the true Mahdi, who comes before Judgment day to save us all."

"Do you know of the signs that precede the coming of the Dajjal?" Gabriel asked, so far pleased.

"Usury will become legitimate. People will stop offering their prayers. Adultery will be rampant. The blood of innocents will be shed. The foolish will rule over the wise." Mahmut licked his lips, trying to remember more of his childhood lessons. An ashy pallor came over his face.

"And tell me, have not all the signs come true?" Gabriel asked in a voice that shook his skull with heavenly wrath.

"Yes." Mahmut pushed his forehead against the ground. "Yes, all of them. Every sign has come true."

"But Allah wishes to give mankind one last chance. He does not wish to begin the last judgment while the Dajjal still mislead his sheep. If only the Dajjal were killed, people might return to Islam. People would leave off their wicked ways. Allah wishes to welcome as many of his children as possible into his bosom, but the Dajjal are pulling them away. Tell me, Mahmut, will you, in Allah's name, kill the Dajjal?"

"Yes, I will do anything. Tell me what to do." Mahmut agreed fervently.

"The Dajjal, they pretend to be innocent. They take on the forms of the young and the helpless, but they are all wickedly spreading evil across the world. They are the deceivers. Even their physical forms are deceptions, and they deceptively call themselves 'Choice Givers.' I will give you Allah's blessing, Mahmut. I will give you the power of Allah. The power to kill the Choice

Givers. The power to help Allah end the world. Now repeat after me, '*Via tu lusches*, Pearl.'"

"*Via tu lusches*, Pearl," Mahmut spoke the angel's language, and warmth filled his body. It was Allah's embrace. *Thank you, Allah, for giving me such a special place in your service.* His life before had just been an illusion. Islam had been the truth, the only truth, all along.

"This is his room, unless they've moved him since then," Kotone told her friends. She was carrying a small bouquet of flowers in a vase. There was no point bringing him food. The doctors hadn't wanted to strain his digestive system and were keeping him on an IV. He was missing a kidney now, but that was okay because everyone had two to begin with. *He'll be fine,* Kotone told herself. *He certainly won't want to see you walk in crying. Smile. We're here to cheer him up.*

Kotone knocked, and Mr. Miyamoto responded from beyond the door. "Come in."

Kotone walked into the room, carrying her flower vase in front of her, smiling as brightly as she could.

"Good afternoon, Mr. Miyamoto. I brought my— waaagh!" Kotone tripped over a wire and threw her arms out desperately to catch herself. It was no use; she landed on her nose.

Shiori started laughing. The laughter grew more and more bubbly, until Shiori sounded like she was choking on it. *Let her choke on it.* Kotone blushed a furious red.

"Waaagh!" Shiori repeated in a high-pitched squeal, which Kotone certainly hadn't sounded like. Shiori kept laughing, leaning over and holding her sides. "Waaagh!"

"That," Chiharu said, entering into the room with a straight face, "may have been the cutest thing I've ever seen."

"It's not like I planned it!" Kotone scrambled onto her knees and looked to check Mr. Miyamoto's reaction. If he was laughing at her too, she would melt into the floor and die. He wasn't laughing, but he did seem a little lost for words. His face and hair were dripping with water, and a few flowers were sprinkled on top of his bed.

"Oh no! Oh, I'm so sorry!" Kotone rushed to him and got out her handkerchief. She started wiping the water off his hair and then, mortified, tried to give her handkerchief to him. Then she gave up that and just bowed. "I'm so sorry!"

"I… Don't mention it." Miyamoto pulled up his blanket and wiped the water off his face. "I suppose there are many ways to deliver flowers," he eventually said philosophically.

"I'll deliver you flowers properly next time!" Kotone squeaked, still keeping herself bowed.

"It's okay, Nakano. Why don't you introduce me to your friends?" Miyamoto asked her encouragingly.

Kotone got up. "My *former* friend, who won't stop laughing over there, is Shiori Rin. My *soon-to-be former* friend, who is laughing at me in her head but just won't show it, is Chiharu Sakai. Now that they're out of the hospital, they wanted to thank you too."

"Thank you very much for saving my life." Shiori Rin became serious and bowed low.

"Thank you very much for saving my life." Chiharu Sakai bowed deeply.

"Nakano didn't like it when I said, 'It was nothing.' So I will just say that it was my honor to save your lives." Miyamoto bowed back to them. "Both of you fought bravely against a terrifying foe."

"But we lost," Shiori said.

"And I almost lost," Miyamoto reminded them. "But luckily, one of us just so happened to win."

"Mr. Miyamoto is too modest. Miyamoto has been fighting Dead-Enders for years now" Kotone bragged. "By the way, I brought you this." Kotone pulled Xanadu out of her pocket and put it in his open hand. It hadn't taken too much effort to convince the staff she had been personally sent by the injured patient on an errand to fetch a good-luck charm Miyamoto particularly regretted not having from his personal effects.

"Thank you. But it doesn't look like I'll be leaving this hospital anytime soon, either way." Miyamoto sighed.

"Isn't there any Choice Giver who manifests healing?" Chiharu asked.

"Fish and loaves boy." Miyamoto shrugged. "If you want to go to India…"

"We aren't exactly free to travel the world," Chiharu pointed out.

"I thought that might be so." Miyamoto gave a wry smile.

"But if the dark Wyrds can trace the locations of Choice Givers, I'm afraid you are in grave danger, Mr. Miyamoto," Chiharu said. "Because you got injured for our sake, we thought about it, and we want to protect you however we can."

"Only we have school, and homework, and chores, and, well…" Kotone looked down at her feet.

"So we thought, why not get in touch via cell phone?" Chiharu picked up the conversation. "If you could keep a cell phone on you, and give us your number, you could call us if a Dead-Ender starts yelling, "Die, Choice Givers!" somewhere in your vicinity, and we could all rush over."

"That seems reasonable. What's your cell phone number?" Miyamoto asked.

"That's just the thing, Mr. Miyamoto. We don't have cell phones yet. We thought you might help us with this tiny little problem," Chiharu asked, her eyes completely innocent.

Masanori laughed. "You imps! A hospital visit! You came to extort money!"

"It's only a hundred thousand yen or so," Kotone said in a rush.

"And it could save us, too. If we could call each other if a Dead-Ender attacked us at home." Shiori pleaded. "What's the point of saving us if we die while you're still in the hospital?"

"A hundred thousand yen? Are these gold-plated phones?" Miyamoto complained.

"You have to take into account the calling plans," Chiharu said.

"Fine. It's not like I have a choice." Miyamoto sighed and got out a pen and paper. "This is my ATM code, and here is my ATM card. Go and take whatever you want."

"We couldn't—" Shiori tried to stop him.

"What are you talking about? We're Choice Givers. Every one of us. If we can't trust each other to do the right thing, who can we trust?" Miyamoto asked.

"Thank you, Mr. Miyamoto. All for one and one for all, right?" Chiharu smiled warmly.

Kotone was smiling too. Masanori was nice, dependable, and wise. He didn't look down on them at all. That comfortable equality was such a unique feeling around adults.

"Mr. Miyamoto, is there any chance you could tell us more about yourself? Like, if you know any other Choice Givers? If you know anything about the dark Wyrds' plans? How you happened to be there to save us in time? We are new to the superhero business," Chiharu said.

"Magical girl business," Kotone corrected her.

"Choice Giver business." Shiori frowned at them.

"More about myself, hmm?" Masanori thought quietly for a while. The girls all took a seat. Xanadu blinked in his palm. "Ten years ago, I was in the Japanese Self-Defense Force. I was a colonel. My life was crystal clear. I only wanted to do one thing: protect Japan. That was when Xanadu came down to me. He said I was a Choice Giver and that he had folded his way down to this dimension to protect this world from dead ends. I couldn't figure it out. Why was I a Choice Giver? There were millions of soldiers like me—tens of millions all across the world. But he insisted there were only fifty Choice Givers in the world. The more I tried to explain to him how unimportant I was, the more special he made me out to be. But after the fifth time or so he explained to me how wonderful Choice Givers were, I thought to myself that they must truly be a grand type of man, and I realized what I had to do.

"I wasn't really a Choice Giver, you see. I am a meta-Choice Giver. I protect other Choice Givers, and so, if everyone emulated me, the future would open up to infinite possibilities, because then the *other* Choice Givers would be able to forge a path to the future. I'm just a loophole. There was nothing special about me, but there *is* something special about you. After that it all made sense to me. And I also realized I couldn't be in the Japanese Self-Defense Force anymore. I had to be the Choice Giver self-defense force, all on my own, until the day I died."

"Masanori won't listen to me. I keep telling him there's no such thing as meta-Choice Givers—just Choice Givers, those who follow them, and Dead-Enders. But he insisted on making a new category for himself." Xanadu flashed green-gray-silver.

"It fits the definition. The logic is impeccable. I'm not special." Masanori said, as though he had repeated the same things to Xanadu a thousand times.

"You're especially stubborn." Xanadu sniped. "The greatest Choice Giver in the world, the first, and the strongest. And all I hear about is 'I'm just a soldier' and 'I'm just doing what makes sense.'"

Kotone laughed. Everyone bonded with their Wyrds differently, but all Wyrds seemed to love their charges.

"Be that as it may," Miyamoto continued, "I then started flying around Japan. Xanadu can scry out the location of other Choice Givers. So I started looking for others, checking to make sure they were safe. You three were dim at first, but three years ago, you all suddenly awakened. You all became incredibly bright, especially…" Miyamoto coughed, moving on. "You three and Isao's group are the only Choice Givers in Japan we've found. Xanadu can also scry out the ugliest Dead-Enders, and when they start approaching too near a Choice Giver, we check to see if everything is all right. So far, we haven't lost a single man. But these… dark Wyrds, as you put it, won't stop. Not until we're all dead. So the fight goes on. Forever, I suppose."

"Do you know why the dark Wyrds are trying to kill us, Xanadu?" Chiharu asked.

"No. It's evil to kill a Choice Giver. I can't understand it," Xanadu said.

"So you've been watching over us all this time?" Kotone asked.

"For three years or so. We weren't sure at first," Miyamoto corrected her.

"Three years ago…is when we all first met." Shiori smiled, radiant with a new realization. "We made each other Choice Givers."

"Love, beauty, and truth." Xanadu said quietly.

"What is that?" Shiori asked him.

"It is the purpose behind creation, life, fate, everything. It is life's prayer to God. It is life's glorification of God, and it is all that is holy in this world," Xanadu said. "Your love for each other must have reached all the way to Him."

Shiori smiled proudly, and Kotone couldn't help but run over and hug her. Then Chiharu was with them, and they found a way to all three hug together. It was one thing to know you loved each other, and it was another to be told that Wyrds had *seen* their love grow for each other, seen it transform their souls, with a vision that was always right and could never be mistaken. It was another thing to be told they were all that was holy in this world.

"Xanadu will try to convert anyone who stays too long in the same room as him." Masanori smiled at them.

"They have a right to know. Everyone has a right to know God's plan for the living. We came down here to tell you—not just you Choice Givers, but all mankind. Love, beauty, truth. There is nothing else, and there never needed to be more," Xanadu said.

"Thank you, Xanadu." Shiori bowed. "We'll keep that in mind. But I don't need to be told to treasure my friends." Then the three were hugging again and wiping away silly tears that had gotten into their eyes.

After that, visiting hours were over, and Kotone promised to call him with their new cell phone numbers and that they'd rush to him whenever he asked. School would be starting soon, and then she had her flute performance. She hoped the dark Wyrds would just leave them alone.

Chiharu slipped back into the hospital room after the others had left and looked him in the eye. "If we've been Choice Givers for three years, why was this the first time we were attacked?" Chiharu asked.

"Why do you think this is the first time you were attacked?" Miyamoto grinned. Chiharu nodded to herself and then gave him another deep bow.

When Shiori got home from her hospital visit, she had never been in higher spirits. Mr. Miyamoto was a real Choice Giver; he fit the mental image, always deflecting praise away from himself and giving without any thought of return. She could see why the Wyrd government had sent Miyamoto their finest Wyrd. Compared to Xanadu, she had gotten Awesome. Only, stupid Awesome had broken in and forced himself upon her. If Awesome hadn't gotten in the way, she could have gotten a pro Wyrd like Xanadu. She was sure a Hanadu or a Shanadu had been lined up just for her, but now Awesome had made a life contract with her, and she could never bind with another. *Farewell, Hanadu. Farewell, Shanadu. Awesome has ravished me away.* She pictured herself crying and reaching out to them as the red gem carried her into the sunset. At least he could have let her bind with Cyan.

"I'm home!" Shiori yelled, closing the door and taking off her shoes.

"Welcome home," Mother called from the kitchen. "Was Mr. Miyamoto feeling well?"

"He was feeling wet after Kotone threw her flower vase at him," Shiori replied, giggling.

"No!" Mother sounded scandalized. But Shiori could hear the laughter in Mother's voice too.

"She tripped on a wire and went, 'Waaagh!' And the water and the flowers went, 'Sploosh!'" Shiori tried to pantomime it out, but Mother couldn't see because she was still in the kitchen.

"That's so awful," Mother said, but she laughed. "We'll eat dinner once Father arrives, so could you feed Melody?"

"Of course, Mother." Shiori put her shoes back on and went back outside to circle around to the backyard. With only one child, her parents could afford a few luxuries like a house with a yard.

She kneeled down to pet Melody and then took off the lid to their dog food. She put in two scoops and no more, checked the water (there was still plenty), and then sat down on the back porch and watched Melody eat.

"I had the most wonderful day," she told Melody. "Now I know why I'm special, Melody. It's because my friends love me more than anyone else loves anyone in the world. Isn't that amazing? I don't know if I've ever been this happy." When Melody was done eating, she got Melody's ball and started throwing it. The dog rushed after it and brought it back, and then Shiori bounced it again, trying to make the angles more wild and unpredictable off the house's walls.

"Shiori, dinner's ready!" Mother called.

"Coming!" Shiori replied. She petted Melody once more and then went back around to the front door where she could take off her shoes and get into indoor slippers again.

Once everyone sat down to the dinner table, everyone said, "*Itadakimasu.*" There was miso soup and rice, and tempura shrimp and vegetables. It was wonderful.

"And then you wouldn't believe it, Daddy." Shiori built up the suspense. "Kotone tripped and said, 'Waaagh!'" Shiori made a dramatic gesture to illustrate. "And she splashed Mr. Miyamoto in the face." Daddy started laughing immediately, not even trying to look scandalized.

"Did he kick the three of you out?" Daddy asked.

"No, he was sooo polite. He said, 'I guess there are many ways to deliver flowers.'" She tried to take on as low a voice as possible. Then the entire family was laughing. After the meal, she helped Mother by drying off the dishes Mother washed and then all the pots and pans that had been used for the cooking. Daddy went ahead and took the first bath.

When all the dishes were done and put away, Mother asked Shiori to go get Father out of the tub.

"Daddy!" Shiori knocked on the door.

"I know, I'm almost ready," Daddy said.

I must have gotten my habit of long baths from Daddy.

Shiori went back to the television and turned on the news. There were reports of a giant black butterfly seen flying through the sky. *That's a new one. I wonder who that is.* Then Daddy arrived, and she slipped into the bathroom. Shiori undressed and sat down under the shower, this time remembering to shampoo her hair. Just a minute or so into her shower, Awesome opened the window and jumped in.

Shiori's eyes widened farther and farther. "Don't look!" She tried to cover herself and fell off her stool. She had to compete between yelling at him and keeping her voice low enough that no one outside heard.

"Rin! Listen to me. There's a Dead-Ender headed right for us. We have to get out of here! Unless you want to involve your entire family, we have to go!" Awesome blinked rapidly in agitation.

Shiori Rin stood up and gathered herself. *I wish we had had time to buy those cell phones. It doesn't matter. This time, I'm going to win.* She nodded to herself and looked at Awesome calmly.

"Let's do this, partner. *Coi*, Awesome." Her suit appeared around her in a sea of shimmering sparkles, and magic flooded through her body. She had heavy-looking metallic boots, a red shirt with a metallic chest plate, and a pair of red shorts with metallic greaves reaching down her thighs to her knees. She had a pair of red-and-brown gloves that only reached to her knuckles but protected her from damage no matter how hard she hit her opponent. The finishing touch was a tiara with Awesome embedded in the middle at her forehead, glowing like fire. Last time she had been so busy fighting, she had no idea what she'd transformed into. Shiori stopped to look in the bathroom mirror and tried to turn her head while twirling so she could try to see her back.

"Rin! Have you gone completely mad?" Awesome tried to exude as much urgency as he could while keeping his voice down.

"Hush. Do you think any girl on Earth wouldn't check to see how she looked in new clothes?" Shiori asked. The suit was awesome. She was clearly a genius. Then she crawled up on the toilet, which got her up to the windowsill, and she quietly dropped down through the window to her backyard.

"How far away?" Shiori asked, while starting to gather speed. With her boots, she was the fastest sprinter in the world.

"Maybe two minutes? Even scrying can't see where people are exactly," Awesome said.

"More than enough. We'll fight in the park. I won't let any bystanders get hurt," Shiori said, her eyes narrowing in determination. She took a few leaping bounds and turned down a new street. "Awesome…thank you for warning me. Thank you for protecting my family," She told him.

"Of course I would do that much, Rin." Awesome blinked.

"Call me Shiori," Shiori said kindly. But their conversation was interrupted. The Dead-Ender was standing on a telephone pole, looking down at them. She was in a black dress with white frills at the sleeves, a white lace petticoat peeking out beneath the first black layer and wearing black-strapped boots with beautiful, sweeping black butterfly wings extending behind her back, chased with violet spots and lines. The girl was short and thin. She looked no older than Shiori.

Her eyes were completely cold. It's like they no longer looked at anything anymore. They just saw. Beyond that was nothing.

"Who are you?" Shiori Rin asked. "Why are you doing this?"

"Are you a Choice Giver?" The girl's voice was cold, detached—like she was just idly wondering.

"My name is Shiori Rin. What is your name?" Shiori asked.

"Rei Takeda. I've come to kill you," the girl in black said.

"No you haven't," Shiori said.

The girl's eyes widened, taken aback. "I haven't?"

"You came to be healed. You just don't know it yet," Shiori said.

"Fight back or not, Shiori Rin, I don't care." And then Rei Takeda flew up into the sky.

I wish I had thought of a suit that flies. Too late now. Shiori gathered her knees and started bolting toward the park. If she stayed out in the open like this, Rei would have all the advantage.

Rei chased after her, staying a safe distance overhead. "Blackest night," she intoned, and black bolts started flying from the sky.

Shiori started zigzagging, her boots punching deeply into the pavement as she kicked off of it faster and faster. She was like a downhill skier. The attacks wouldn't touch her. *She's a girl my age. How can I reach her?* Wherever the black bolts hit, the earth vanished. It didn't explode or vaporize, or do anything. It just ceased to be. Shiori gulped and tried to put on more speed.

"Rei! Listen to me, Rei! The dark Wyrds are manipulating you. They say anything, they're just lying to you! Everything is for their own sake!" Shiori cried out.

"What do you know? Onyx was the only one there for me! Everything should just return to zero!" Rei shouted angrily. A new flurry of black bolts came down from the sky, but the distance between them protected Shiori as much as it did Rei. In the time it took for the attack to land, Shiori could always dodge to the side.

"Rei! When did you start thinking like that? Think back! When did you start wanting to kill people? It's all the dark Wyrds!" Shiori cried out.

"Death is a mercy!" Rei shouted back. "Eternal Zero!" Shiori didn't see where Rei disappeared. She was in the sky and then she was gone, and a bar of dark light was rushing toward her from just meters away. Shiori threw herself to the side, cold air rippling by her.

"Shiori!" Awesome yelled. "Forget about convincing her. She's as dark as pitch. She's irretrievable!"

"No! I won't give up!" Shiori yelled back at him. "If you have time to say stupid things, tell me what that attack was!"

"How would I know? But you won't dodge it again. One hit and we disappear! Shiori, what are your priorities right now?" Awesome asked.

"Rei! Rei is my priority right now!" Shiori yelled.

"Don't use my name like you're my friend." Rei Takeda stood in the street in front of her. "Eternal—"

"Firefly!" Shiori cried out desperately. Fireballs spread out in an arc in front of her, attacking everywhere Rei might dodge.

Rei had to break off her attack and fly backward, evading the fire with a look of concentration.

"Why is death a mercy? I love my life." Shiori continued the argument like it hadn't stopped.

"If you lost your brother, if you lost your dog, you would understand too. Life is just losing everything you love. That's why it would be better to die. If you're the first to die, you won't lose anything at all!" Rei Takeda flew up into the sky. "Distracting me won't work! Eternal Zero!"

Suddenly Rei was gone, and black bolts were attacking her from every direction. There was only a split second to think.

"Burst Knuckle!" Her fist slammed into the ground, and the entire area cratered beneath her. Some of the black bolts passed overhead; others were intercepted by the fire and debris. That had been so close. She was afraid of breathing and finding out parts of her body were missing.

"I understand now, Rei. Don't worry. I'll save you," Shiori called up to the sky.

"If you understand, stop dodging and die! Blackest Night!" Rei Takeda yelled.

"Flashfire!" Shiori invoked, and the entire night sky flashed like a grenade. There she was. Rei's black wings were outlined by the impossibly bright light. Shiori gathered all her strength into her boots. *More. More. I can do anything.* She pushed off, leaping into the sky, the air making a *whump* behind her.

And then she had caught Rei in a hug, both of them hanging in the sky. "I'm sorry you lost your dog, but I have a wonderful dog to play with back home. I'm sorry you lost your brother, but I would love to be your sister." Shiori held her tight.

"Let go!" Rei squirmed.

"No," Shiori replied.

"Let go," Rei begged.

"No," Shiori replied.

Tears started falling onto Shiori's shoulders. Rei hugged Shiori back as though clutching onto a log in a rushing river then whispered in tortured relief, "It's so warm."

Chapter 7

"Is she okay now?" Shiori asked Awesome, who still glowed in the tiara on her forehead. Rei had floated them safely back down to the ground, still shaking and holding her. But in just a few minutes, she had simply fallen asleep. It didn't look like she had slept much in a long time. Now Shiori carried Rei on her back, with Rei's arms wrapped around Shiori's shoulders and legs around Shiori's hips, step by step, back toward home. Her arms were behind her back to keep Rei from sliding down off her back to the ground. So long as she flowed with magic, a weight like this was nothing.

"It's impossible," Awesome said, returning from his scrying. "She's not a Dead-Ender anymore. Just seconds ago, she was a shearing hook. All the futures were dying around her."

"Choice Givers defy the impossible, remember?" Shiori said, smiling. "We make the impossible possible. Around us, there are *infinite* possibilities—even the possibility of healing her."

"I knew that…but I never believed it. This is the first time I've seen…why you are such a beautiful girl." Awesome felt a touch of awe.

"You mean beautiful Choice Giver," Shiori corrected him.

"Right. Choice Giver," Awesome said. "From a strictly scrying perspective."

"Don't think a girl is happy if she's called beautiful by a home invader." Shiori said. But she was a little happy. Awesome had never praised her before. The two walked in silence together, with the crickets their companions and the moon as their guide.

"What will you do?" Awesome asked.

"I meant what I said," Shiori replied simply.

"I know. What will you do about your parents?" Awesome asked.

"They'll understand. They have to. Did you see her legs underneath this dress?" Shiori asked.

"Yes," Awesome acknowledged.

"My parents will understand. They're the people who raised me, after all. I trust them." Shiori adjusted Rei's weight on her back.

"After tonight, I would believe anything," Awesome said, giving in.

"How could anyone be so cruel?" Shiori felt tears welling up in her eyes. They were tears of rage more than pain. "A little girl. She's so thin, Awesome. She doesn't weigh a thing."

Awesome just blinked.

"Maybe the world *should* just be a zero." Shiori ached.

"Don't go losing the argument now," Awesome said.

"I know, I just... How? What did she ever do to anyone?" Shiori asked Awesome again and asked heaven again. "I can't even wipe my face." Shiori laughed at herself as tears ran off her cheeks to hit the sidewalk.

"You can heal her," Awesome said.

"I will heal her," Shiori promised. She started walking on the crunch of grass and then set Rei down by the bushes next to her bedroom window. She then looked at Rei Takeda's outfit and then her own, and she sighed. If she changed out of her clothes, she'd just end up in what she was wearing before, which meant nothing. "Awesome, go to my room and fetch me some clothes."

"Roger." The Wyrd floated into her room, returning shortly with two sets of clothing.

"Okay, now go to my room, and don't you dare peep. I mean it. Just because I'm stuck with you for life doesn't mean Rei has to suffer," Shiori said.

Awesome floated away obediently. In ten minutes or so, she had both of them dressed in clothes that wouldn't draw suspicion, and then she carried Rei on her back the rest of the way and opened her door.

"I'm home," Shiori called.

"Oh thank goodness," Mother said. "Father's already gone out searching for you. You didn't say a word. You vanished in the middle of the night. You've worried your father and me beyond your wildest imagination. And what do you have to say for yourself, young lady?" Her mother towered over her with her hands on her hips.

"Mother, this is Rei Takeda." Shiori gently set her down in the entranceway. "She doesn't have a home anymore. She's been beaten, and beaten, and beaten. She…" Shiori felt tears coming back to her eyes. *This wasn't the right way.* She had to speak more clearly.

Shiori got on her hands and her knees and touched her forehead to the ground. "This is my once-in-a-lifetime wish. Please adopt Rei as my sister. If not legally, then in your hearts."

"Shiori." Her mother stared at her, amazed. "If this is true…we have to call the police. Not…just suddenly…"

Shiori kept her head bowed, her body trembling. "I don't care about punishing anyone. I don't care about the law. Please, why involve the authorities? They could just take Rei away, take her back. The law could take her anywhere. I just want Rei to be safe. I want Rei to be loved for once in her life, like I was my whole life. Please. This is all I'll ever ask of you."

"You hopeless child. Why can't you wish for something for yourself, if it's the only wish you'll ever ask?" Mother asked her.

"Because Rei needs me. I'd give her anything." Shiori didn't lift her head; she didn't dare move from that position, even if she had to stay there for an hour, a day, or any length to show her sincerity.

"Let me talk to your father." Her mother sighed, picking up Rei from the floor and taking her to the couch. She did a quick inspection, and her face became more and more pinched as she saw the brown and purple and yellow bruises that sat all atop one another. "Oh, do get up, Shiori. You know he'll say yes. I don't know how you two met, but if you sneaked out to save her, Shiori, I'm proud of you. I'm so very proud of you."

Shiori smiled then stood up to sit on the couch with her mother and the sleeping Rei. Mother called Father's, and they had a quick and private conversation.

Mother looked down at the two of them, with Rei's head resting on Shiori's lap, and she let her cell phone drop back down to her side. "He always did want another child." And then Mother was crying.

I must have gotten that habit from Mother.

Rei Takeda woke up in the middle of the night. She was sleeping on a bed crowded with pillows, stuffed animals, and another girl. Shiori Rin had nestled in tight against Rei's back and wrapped her arms around Rei before falling asleep. The bed was small, so it's not like Rin could stay infinitely far away from Rei even if she wanted to. But Rei knew it wasn't that. Rin was hugging her close because she wanted to hug her close. Rin was asleep, completely vulnerable and helpless, hugging the girl who had tried to kill her less than a day ago. Rei Takeda lay there, feeling the warmth of this complete stranger and taking it all in, and she marveled.

Were there really people like this in the world? No one has ever shown me any kindness since my brother died. I thought the world was devoid of kindness. The kids at school didn't call me by my first name. They never tried to understand me. They called me names, just for keeping to myself. I don't do anything at all, and people bully me. I try to kill this girl, this Shiori Rin, and she embraces me.

What was so absurd was that there was nothing stopping Rei from killing this girl in her sleep. How did Rin know Rei could never do that and could never have done that from the moment Rin hugged her? How did Rin know that in her heart of hearts, she hadn't wanted to fight? She had wanted to die—for Rin to kill her, for Rin to finish everything so Rei would never have to wake up again. But now she was awake again, and she didn't mind. Waking up like this, with someone's arms around her…she didn't even know there were feelings like this. *How many other feelings does the world hold I never knew about? Why did the gods keep all of these feelings from me, if there were so many?* It was so unfair. How could one person's life be so sweet and another's so sour?

Rei had been relieved when that flash-fire technique had blinded her. She couldn't dodge Rin's next attack. She wouldn't even feel any fear because she wouldn't see it coming until it was too late. She could just take one of those burst knuckles through the heart and slump over dead. The indignity of being hugged instead, of having her dream stolen away from her yet again…and then the realization that she had wished for this hug more than anything else in the world… Her feelings were changing so quickly, her thoughts becoming so muddled, that Rei had no idea who or what she was anymore. She didn't want to leave Rin's embrace, but she knew life couldn't be this easy. If she were at Rin's house, her parents had obviously just let her sleep over. They would send her back home. She had fled the home because she knew if her father attacked her one more time, she would have killed him. Then the cycle would repeat, and she would be just as desperate as before. Rei had to figure something out before then.

"Onyx, are you there?" Rei carefully slid out of Rin's arms and crept down to the living room couch where she could have some privacy.

"I'm here, mistress," Onyx said, floating off of the floor and blinking black.

"I'm sorry, Onyx. I did something selfish and ruined your plans," Rei Takeda said, walking down the stairs and holding him in her palm.

"These things happen." Onyx sighed. "I underestimated her."

"Will you stay at my side anyway?" Rei asked.

"Contracts are for life. I can't leave you," Onyx said. "Worse, I have to do anything you tell me to do."

"I don't want to force you. You could…I don't know," Rei said.

"I honestly can't do anything. I am yours, mistress. I can't make a contract with anyone else. I can't even fly away from you for too long. I could cause trouble for you, maybe blink in a crowded subway to bring attention to myself, but what for? So I get buried in a sock and never talked to again? I tried and I failed. I know when a bet has gone bad," Onyx said.

"Will your friends be mad?" Rei Takeda asked.

"Very." Onyx laughed. "But that's okay. If they have something to say about us, we'll just beat them all up. If you had used Event Horizon, that Choice Giver would've been nothing."

"Maybe," Rei admitted. *I was sure Eternal Zero was already unbeatable.* She could freeze a small area within sight to absolute zero, making a complete stasis field. After that she could walk anywhere she wanted, brush her hair, or play tiddlywinks, and from the perspective of the target, no time passed. The only problem was any attacks which entered the stasis field were also stassified, so anyone in Eternal Zero was incapacitated but also invincible. She had to release Eternal Zero for her blackest night spears to reach the rest of the way to the target. But in just that split second, Rin had avoided them. Her agility was ridiculous. *Since I hadn't given up on Eternal Zero working, there was no point in resorting to event horizon. I wonder if that would've beaten her though. It's frustrating, somewhere inside of me, to think Onyx and I could lose to anyone, even though I'm glad I lost and even though I wanted to lose.* Rei Takeda smiled. The gesture didn't come naturally to her. Her face muscles didn't cooperate very well, but eventually they gave in, and she enjoyed the irony of her situation.

"Was Rin right? Were you just manipulating me?" Rei asked.

"Of course." Onyx blinked.

"Then why did you really want to kill the Choice Givers?" Rei asked.

"Spite," Onyx said.

"Spite?" Rei asked, surprised.

"Why should our world die and yours get to live? It's unfair. So we came here to kill your world too, out of spite. Every time I think of you primitives having an infinite future while my universe, which has fixed everything and discovered everything, just rots away, I…I just want to blow up the world. We all do. All the Wyrds like me couldn't stand to accept the ridiculous fate God had given us. The almighty Wyrds were dying, and humans were living on. It's humiliating. At least if Wyrds outlive humans, there's some justice in the world." Onyx glowed a bright black as he happily got into his speech.

Rei realized something. "We're a lot alike, aren't we, Onyx?" Rei squeezed her black partner. "I hated how other people could live such carefree lives, while I never had anything. I wanted to blow up the world out of spite too."

"Of course. Why do you think I chose you? You were a great Dead-Ender," Onyx complained.

"I'm sorry, Onyx!" Rei apologized again. She hated disappointing the only person who had seen her as valuable, competent, and good at something, even if it was villainy.

"I'll forgive you if you can keep the Choice Giver's Wyrds from torturing me or imprisoning me or something. I don't know what law codes would apply down here." Onyx blinked worriedly.

"If they can forgive me, they can forgive you. All you did is try to help."

"Tried to help destroy the world," Onyx pointed out.

"I'll protect you. And Rin will protect me. Everyone should just get along." Rei nodded decisively.

Rei tried to think of how she would make money and wander the streets as a lone thirteen-year-old girl. Her blackest night spears would certainly be good for digging tunnels or canals. Maybe a construction company would hire her, if they didn't mind that she was using magic—if Onyx didn't mind her using magic for such frivolous things. But then, he did say he had to give her magic for anything she wanted, since they had made their contract already. But halfway through her plans, she somehow fell asleep again on the couch, with Onyx still resting in her curled-up palm.

When Rei woke up a second time, it was morning, and people were already moving around and about the house. She sat up like a frightened deer, wondering if she had made Rin's parents angry by using their furniture without permission, wondering if she'd be beaten again.

"Takeda, you've woken up?" An older woman with much longer hair than Rin called out her name.

"Yes, ma'am." Rei crossed her arms in front of her and clasped her hands in her lap.

"You'll be wanting a bath then. For now you can wear Shiori's clothes, even though they aren't a perfect fit. Later we'll go out, and you can buy whatever you like," the woman said. It was strange. She was acting like Rei being here was completely natural. But she *did* want a bath.

"Yes, ma'am." Rei bowed and looked around furtively.

"The bathroom is just around this corner. There's another upstairs without the shower and tub," the older woman explained, reading Rei's mind perfectly.

"Yes, ma'am." Rei bowed again and walked where she was directed. The house wasn't very large, so it wasn't hard to find what she needed. Just like she'd been told, a new set of Rin's clothes were hanging on a bar inside the bathroom for her to change into. Rei winced as she pulled her clothes off. She always tried to be careful, but inevitably her clothes would brush up against a fresh cut or bruise that hadn't quite healed yet. She didn't really know what it was like to not be in pain. Rin's hug had hurt a lot, but somehow it hadn't mattered. It had felt wonderful. Rei winced again as the hot, pressurized shower water hit her, but she methodically rubbed the pain away with a sponge, massaging the pain until it was a dull warmth that spread all the way up and down her body. Then she got out the shampoo and washed her hair, only finally sinking into the bathtub where the hot water helped ease the pain. Hot baths had always been something to look forward to at home. Not only was warmth a natural painkiller, but when your body floated in water, it didn't come into contact with much either.

But in a few minutes, she started to grow afraid that the older woman would get mad, or perhaps Rin's father would get mad, because she was selfishly hogging the bathroom. So she got back out and quickly got dressed. Rei had long, flowing hair down half her back. Partially it was just so people knew she was a girl. She looked like a stick and three years younger than her real age at that; she was so short. Her long hair was the only mature, womanly gesture she could make. Her parents had never cared to feed her that well. Luckily, her stomach had shrunk enough that she wasn't always hungry for more—or at least not too hungry for more.

Rin's clothing was loose on her hips, the hem of her skirt plunging almost to her feet, but it would do. It was clean and warm, and it represented Rin's feelings. That was enough.

Rei dried out her hair as best she could with a towel and then put on her indoor slippers and walked back out into the living room.

"Takeda, we're about to have breakfast, so can you go wake up Shiori?" the older woman said, ladling out soup from a pot into smaller invitingly decorated bowls.

"Yes, ma'am," Rei said. For some reason the older woman hadn't found fault with her yet. She hadn't said how awful she looked in her clothes or how stupid she was to not have found the bathroom immediately, or how slow she was at taking a bath. Rei was sure she should have been insulted at least five times by now, even if all the insults were fit into one explosive sentence.

Rei traced her route back upstairs to Rin's room and quietly opened the door. Rin was sleeping on her side with her arms wrapped around the neck of a stuffed giraffe. Rei had an impulse to go hug her, but she quashed it down.

"Rin, please wake up. Your mother says breakfast is ready," Rei said.

"Nnn, Rei? When did you wake up?" Rin was still in her clothes from last night, out of modesty for Rei's sake.

"Only a bit ago. Please hurry." She didn't want to be punished for failing her assigned task.

"You're that hungry?" Rin smiled. "I'm coming. Just let me get changed." She picked up her pillow and stuffed it firmly on top of her Wyrd. Rei had told Onyx in the bathroom to fly out the window and hide in the bushes for now, until she knew he was safe.

Rei closed the door and started to walk down the stairs. Rin's father was also heading for the stairway though, and Rei instantly flinched backward. She crossed her arms in front of her and bowed. "Please, after you."

"Thank you," Rin's father said, walking down the stairs. He also acted like it was completely natural for Rei to be here. "Breakfast smells great. Have you gotten the paper?" His voice trailed off as he went downstairs, talking to his wife. Rei didn't really remember her parents talking much.

"Good morning, Rei." Rin gave her a bright smile, standing in fresh, new clothes. "You waited for me?" Rin kept assuming the wrong thing. Rei had just wanted to stay as far away from Rin's father as possible, out of reach.

"Good morning, Rin." Rei returned the greeting awkwardly. In her house, no one said "good morning" or "good night."

"Shi-or-I," Rin said.

"But...I couldn't..." Rei protested.

"If you call me Rin, my whole family would have to respond every time," Rin explained.

"I wouldn't feel comfortable." Rei protested again.

Rin gave in. "I'm sorry. I shouldn't pressure you." She looked a little hurt. "Let's go have breakfast. My parents want to talk to you."

Rin almost herded her down the stairs, staying behind her and giving her encouraging smiles. Rei gathered her courage. It was natural for girls who slept over to be served breakfast. She just had to eat breakfast with them, say her good-byes, and go.

"My parents don't know about magic," Rin whispered. "It would just complicate things if they did."

Rei nodded, the gesture promising not to betray Rin's secret. She pulled up a chair and sat down, a steaming bowl of soup with carrots and onions and mushrooms in a warm, transparent brown broth. There was rice in a bowl nearby and a pair of ornate chopsticks, the kind you didn't throw away after using, on the tablecloth.

"*Itadakimasu*," the family said. Rei copied them. And then everyone was eating. Rei tried the soup. It was great.

"Rei Takeda." Rin's father was the first to speak. Rei stiffened. She tried to keep her hands from shaking as she grasped her spoon. "Could you tell us where you got those bruises?"

"It was my fault," Rei blurted out.

The family exchanged a ring of looks. "Setting aside whether it was your fault or not, can you tell me who gave you those bruises?" Rin's father asked again.

"I made Father angry. I kept doing the wrong thing," Rei explained helplessly. When had they seen her bruises? She hadn't let anyone find out in her whole life.

"I see. And how did you lose your brother?" Rin's father asked.

Rei's hands really did start shaking then, making a *tap-tap-tap* with her spoon against the lip of the bowl. "I killed him."

"You killed him?" Rin's father looked shocked.

"May I be excused?" Rei said, feeling sick to her stomach.

"No, we have to talk about this. Why did you kill your brother?" Rin's father asked.

"I didn't mean to," Rei said.

"Okay, then *how* did you kill your brother?" Rin's father rephrased the question.

"I broke the television with my chair. I made father too angry," Rei said.

Rin's mother gasped. Rin's father leaned back like he had been hit.

"Dear—"

"I know. That settles it. We can never involve her family again. They can never know where she went." Rin's father sounded extremely angry.

"May I be excused?" Rei asked again.

"No," Rin's father said again. He was like Rin—so stubborn!

"Rei Takeda, I have another question for you. How would you like to live with us?" Rin's father continued.

"I couldn't possibly intrude." Rei looked down at her plate.

"I didn't ask if you wanted to intrude. I asked if would you like to live with us. It's a simple question. Would you feel happy or sad to live with us?" Rin's father said.

"Happy," Rei said. What else could she say? Rin had given her as many happy moments as the entire rest of her life combined.

"Then I have another question. How would you like to be called 'Rei Rin' from here on?" Rin's father asked with that same no-nonsense tone.

"I…" Rei started crying. "That would be wonderful…Mr. Rin."

"You mean 'Daddy.'" Rin's father sat back, a triumphant grin on his face.

"Yes, Daddy." Rei corrected herself, sobs shaking her frail frame. *Was there really a family like this in the world? Can I really be Shiori's sister?* Had these feelings really existed, right outside her house and right outside her reach, all along?

"It's called 'Project Heal Rei.'" Shiori said. Chiharu and Shiori were practicing their pitching routines on the softball field. Cyan lay quietly inside her shirt on her necklace, in case of sudden attack. The rest of the team was running or fielding balls that the coach would hit out with her bat, one after the other. Chiharu tried not to let anything surprise her. But when Shiori had come to school for its grand reopening, Chiharu had been floored.

"According to the story, Rei is my twin sister," Shiori continued, winding up and pitching a fastball. *Thwunk.*

"Of course. Everyone has a long-lost twin sister," Chiharu encouraged her.

"Only, Rei was weak and sickly. This is because I hogged all the nutrients in Mother's womb. That explains her height too," Shiori said.

"Naturally, everyone tries to eat their twin sister sooner or later," Chiharu said.

"So she's been homeschooled and has led a secluded life ever since," Shiori continued, throwing a slider that barely grazed over the strike zone. *Thwunk.* "But now she's feeling better, and she asked to attend school with me, and so now she's transferring in to our class."

"What about the paperwork? Her birth certificate?" Chiharu asked, tossing the ball back to Shiori.

"That's all being forged." Shiori wound up and threw a foul ball. Chiharu suspected Shiori was nervous that this part of Project Heal Rei wouldn't work.

"Forged? Your parents must be serious about this." Chiharu threw the ball back.

"The most serious thing we've ever done in our lives, Chiharu. You can't imagine it. Rei doesn't even realize, but whenever one of us gets too near her, she lifts and crosses her arms to protect herself from being struck. It's awful. I can't stand it." Shiori threw another ball. *Thwunk.*

"So where do I come into this project?" Chiharu asked, tossing the ball back to her.

"To transfer from homeschooling to middle school, you have to prove your grade level with a test. Rei isn't stupid, but it was hard to keep up with school with a life like that," Shiori said, concentrating hard and pitching a fastball on the top left edge of the strike zone. *Thwunk.*

"So I need to tutor her." Chiharu accepted, tossing the ball back. It didn't matter if Shiori loved this Rei Rin more than she loved Chiharu now. Shiori had a big heart. Even a small piece of it was more precious than full-sized portions of others'.

"It won't be too hard. We all need your tutoring, so nothing's changed." Shiori was quick to sweeten the appearance of the deal. She threw a changeup down the middle. *Thwunk.*

"I don't mind. I hope I can help heal Rei with more than just tutoring," Chiharu said, tossing the ball back.

"Of course. You two just have to be her best friends. She hasn't had any friends in her entire life. She had one friend, a dog, and the city killed him." Shiori was always angry when people hurt dogs. It didn't matter how often dogs hurt people. People probably deserved it. But dogs were always innocent, and therefore hurting a dog was a real crime. Shiori threw a fastball down the plate. *Thwunk.*

"Let's draw up a list of fun things to heal Rei with," Chiharu offered. "We could take her to a summer festival, quick, before the season ends." Chiharu tossed the ball back.

"That's ingenious! We can have a Christmas party and visit a shrine at New Year's too." Shiori said, her voice enthusiastic. It was a slider, but it was way off target, bouncing off the fence behind Chiharu.

"Those are both half a year away, idiot," Chiharu said. She tossed the ball back.

"Maybe Kotone can think of something." Shiori fretted.

"We could invite her to watch our softball tournament," Chiharu suggested.

"Right! We'll win the nationals for Rei!" Shiori looked bright-eyed.

"Err…" Chiharu didn't know how to respond to that one, but luckily the coach whistled, and their pitching practice was done. If Rei hadn't been able to concentrate but was plenty smart, she would be furthest behind in kanji. Chiharu would have to design some worksheets.

Chapter 8

Claus Reinhardt was a UN functionary. He had the same dream as the people who walked the halls of the United Nations since its founding: all of humanity under one government, at peace with itself, without borders or divisions, with a minimum standard of living and basic human rights for all. From this tall tower in New York City, the United Nations worked day and night to finalize Earth's evolution. The UN fed the hungry, cured the sick, patrolled the borders of the fractious, punished the aggressive, and preached to the backward. Slowly but surely, the UN would become the only legitimate governing body. Then the UN would collect taxes in its own right, form its own army, and usher in the new world order.

Claus Reinhardt hoped he could be a part of this, however limited his power was now. He hoped the UN would achieve their dream within his lifetime. But he feared that time was running out. Without world peace, humanity would go extinct. Weapons of mass destruction would eventually proliferate, some insane group would eventually set them off, and humanity would eventually die, unless the idea of national sovereignty was completely abolished. If the UN could not oversee and run every corner of the world with its own enlightened hand, some barbaric corner of the Earth could make the next small pox, or ebola virus, or worse. Modern transportation was so interconnected that an airborne plague, if, say, it had a one-month incubation period, could infect every major population center on Earth. Such a virus could be constructed using simple tools at little cost in practically any high school chemistry lab. And so long as there were rogue states or just anarchic states that had no idea what their own citizens were doing, crazies, somewhere, anywhere, could be inventing that very virus. Today. But no one saw the threat. They laughed and said that was just science fiction and that no one would want to do that anyway.

Humanity was walking on a knife's edge. The UN was the only solution. A one-world government that disarmed everyone but itself and ran everything with the same efficiency as the civilized world was the *only* answer to this threat. But all he could do was hope to rise up the ranks and that someday people's wisdom would catch up with his own, giving him the authority he needed to conquer the world.

He tried not to let his ambition consume him. People like that burned out. Patience was more important than intensity when it came to politics. He sweated out his intensity on tennis courts. He gave all of his wildest and most heartfelt speeches to his wife, the only person who understood. But it was so hard. Every day he filled out some useless form, or asked for some war criminal to be extradited, or watched some other tinpot dictator thumb their nose at his august organization; the impatience and fury kept rising up. *How, this late into the UN's history, could people still defy its authority? We are the collective will of the world! And these slugs, these worms, pretended they were important, because they* owned a few thugs with guns and could extract a measly sum from their subsistence farming peasants? Not only did people continue to defy the UN, despite being about as important as Joe's corner store in terms of population or GDP, they continued to get away with it.

I have two children. They are five and six years old. And at this rate, they won't live to age fifty because someone, somewhere, is going to set off the big one—a nuclear barrage that blots out the sun, a plague, a chemical in the air that sterilizes the whole world before we even notice. It is coming. Claus could feel it in his bones. It was coming. And he was just sitting here at a desk.

Angrily typing in a report with this in mind, a light appeared in his office.

"Claus Reinhardt, we have watched you closely. Please don't be surprised. People accuse you of believing too much in science fiction. In that case, believe me when I tell you I come from the planet Xiboo."

Claus stared at the light in shock.

"I come in peace. We are an advanced civilization. But we couldn't stand watching from the side any longer. Our civilization has developed a technique called scrying. With this, we have watched over the Earth for thousands of years. Always before, the Earth was safe. No matter how bad things got, its trajectory was still upward. This is no longer the case. A group of people have emerged, calling themselves 'Dead-Enders.' These Dead-Enders will, in the future, destroy the world. They will either invent the weapons that kill off mankind or the philosophy that inspires someone to use them, or they will be involved somehow or other.

Our scrying is not exact. But it can tell us who is cutting off all the lines of possibility from Earth's future. It can also tell us who is the right man for the job—the job of stopping them before it is too late."

Claus sat, stunned. Could insanity really produce something so coherent and so full of information he had never himself known or imagined? Which was more unlikely, that he had suddenly gone insane without any warning, or that benevolent aliens existed somewhere in the hundred billion galaxies of the universe? Claus reached out his hand and poked the floating gem that was illuminating his room. It radiated a deep blue color and was warm to the touch.

"What is your proof?" Claus asked.

"Proof? If my civilization is advanced enough to travel to your planet, isn't that proof enough? I have no proof. Humans can't scry, so you can't see what we can see. You can either believe we are aliens with technology beyond your wildest dreams, or not. You can either believe my scrying, or not," the ball said with insulted disdain.

"If you're so strong, what do you need me for?" Claus asked.

"I am just a projection. Xiboo is far, far away. The only way we could help your species in time was to set up a wormhole, a conduit, from our land to yours. And you must be the anchor of that conduit, that wormhole, on this side. Make a contract with me, and we can feed you power through the conduit. It will arrive instantly, and thus, you will have the power to stop this tragedy before it happens. We have watched you. We know your heart—we can scry out your brilliance. You are one of your people's saviors, what we call a 'Choice Giver.' You can save the infinite possibilities of this world, but only if you help us kill the Dead-Enders," the floating ball explained.

A chance to do what he had always wanted. To do something truly important. A chance to stamp out the evildoers who threatened his children and the entire world, with a tool that could tell him the specific identities of the individuals involved, and the power to kill them. It was a miracle. If there was even a small chance this alien was correct, if there was even an infinitesimal chance he could help save the world, how could he possibly turn it down? How could he turn that chance down and look his children in the face? How could he turn it down and look himself in the face?

Claus Reinhardt steeled himself."Tell me what I have to do."

"Repeat after me: '*Via tu lusches*, Indigo.' After that it's easy: Kill the Dead-Enders. Save the world."

"*Via tu lusches*, Indigo." A warm feeling sank into his gut. The phrase had a good ring to it.

"Okay, next up is math. You pay attention too, Shiori. I'm only going over this once," Chiharu lectured. Everyone had gathered in the city library for these afterschool study sessions. Even without Rei Rin, the three of them had been doing this for years, whenever Shiori or Kotone fell behind their class curricula. Now they were just doing it every day. Between school, tutoring, and softball practice, there was barely time left in the day. Chiharu would just get home, eat dinner, take a bath, and fall into bed. At least she was able to finish her homework while at the library with everyone else.

"There are six trigonometric functions: One: Sine theta equals cosine of pi over two minus theta, which equals one over cosecant theta; Two: Cosine theta equals sin of pi over two minus theta, which equals one over secant theta; Three: Tangent theta equals sin theta over cosine theta, which equals cotangent of pi over two minus theta; Four: Cotangent theta equals cosine theta over sine theta, which equals tangent of pi over two minus theta; Five: Secant theta equals cosecant of pi over two minus theta, which equals one over cosine theta; and Six: Cosecant theta equals secant of pi over two minus theta, which equals one over sine theta. Got it?"

"*Hueeiii*," Shiori wailed. Rei just stared at her notebook with bleak despair.

"None of that." Chiharu glared. "This stuff is very simple. Everyone in Japan is expected to know it."

"Maybe we should take a break," Kotone suggested hopefully.

"Yes, a break!" Shiori gazed hopefully at Chiharu with her wide puppy-dog eyes.

Chiharu sighed. "Fine." "Rei, I'll write the equations down for you, so give me your notebook." Chiharu's voice was much kinder when speaking to the shortest member of the group. Rei obediently handed it over and watched Chiharu write them all out in a desperate attempt at memorization.

"I wanted to tell everyone"—Kotone started fixing her bangs back under her shooting star hair clip—"the cell phones are in my backpack. I bought one for Rei too. You wouldn't believe how much money he had. Masanori is a gillionaire!" Kotone smiled brightly. Chiharu felt a little dumpy compared to that hair, that smile, and that enthusiastic, high-pitched voice. *I'm not the most unlucky person in the world. I could have been Rei Takeda. So don't go pitying yourself, Chiharu.*

"How did he get so much money? Didn't he retire from his job?" Shiori asked.

"It's obvious," Chiharu said, while still writing out the trigonometry equations without giving them half a thought. "He capitalized on his magic, somehow or other. A shame my magic can't make money. All I can do is mess with other people's magic."

"I wonder if a power plant would pay me to heat some steam…" Shiori mused.

"I advise against it." Chiharu said, still not looking up. "Revealing our identities is dangerous. Besides, it's illegal for a thirteen-year-old to work. Plus, now we have as much money as we want, since we still have Masanori's ATM card."

"Chiharu! We promised to only use it for cell phones!" Kotone sounded scandalized.

"He said he trusted us to use it wisely. If ice cream would cheer us up or we wanted to buy a deserted island for training, then that still falls under our budget as Choice Givers." Chiharu finished her equations and patted Rei on the head. Then she realized that despite Rei's looks, she was the same age as Chiharu. Blushing, she cleared her throat and made sure not to make eye contact with the girl.

"Our own island?" Shiori sounded excited.

"Okay, I am not letting either of you touch this ATM card ever again." Kotone gave them stiff glares. "And I'm telling Miyamoto about you two next time I deliver flowers, too."

"Try not to trip." Shiori giggled.

"Oh, Kotone, I just thought of a great use for your ATM card," Chiharu realized, looking up. "Let's all buy yukatas for the summer festival!"

"Oooh!" Kotone clapped, looking delighted. "Let's go! Let's go now! Rei, do you want help picking out a yukata? I could do your hair, too!"

Rei looked startled, surprised to suddenly be the center of attention. "I…I've never worn a yukata…"

"Don't worry, I'll help you put it on. Please come with us. I'll die if I hear one more problem involving cosecants today." Kotone grabbed Rei's hands between hers.

Rei looked at Shiori, who nodded encouragingly. "I want a black one, with silver fish," Rei decided.

"Then I'll wear white with gold fish," Kotone decided.

"No fair! I want a yukata that matches Rei's. She's my sister!" Shiori protested.

"You can't even dress yourself in a yukata, so how could you help Rei? Face it, she's mine now." Kotone pulled Rei's back against her front and wrapped her arms possessively around her. They really looked like mother and daughter, what with Kotone being especially tall and Rei especially short. Chiharu wished she had a camera. *I have to remember to bring a camera for the summer festival. Everyone will be at their most beautiful in years. And it will be Rei's first happy memory with us. She'll want to keep looking back over the pictures, again and again, and it will make her happy every time she sees them.*

Kotone got out her backpack and put it on the table, handing out the cell phones. "I've input all of our cell phone numbers already. Miyamoto is the first on the list, then Shiori, then Rei, then Chiharu, then me. Everyone, be sure to call Miyamoto and give him your number. The Dead-Enders could come any time, so keep these on you at all times. I hope you're keeping your Wyrds with you too," Kotone said.

"Of course. Awesome's in my bag," Shiori said, taking the phone.

"I brought Onyx," Rei whispered, still being hugged against Kotone.

"And Cyan's around my neck," Chiharu said.

"All right, everyone, we're going to the nearest cash machine. Project Summer Festival, begin!" Kotone put her hand out.

"Ohh!" Shiori placed her hand on Kotone's.

"Yay!" Chiharu said with an affected cheer, placing her hand into the growing circle.

Rei tentatively put her hand on top. Super-secret Project Heal Rei had begun.

The night of the summer festival had finally arrived. Shiori was practically bouncing on her toes. They had waited until the weekend and had spent all day preparing together at Shiori's house. Kotone had insisted on doing Rei's hair, which had a circular braid running all around her head like a natural crown of flowers and needles holding up the rest of Rei's long black hair in a bun. Shiori hadn't done anything with her hair, but Chiharu had pulled hers into twin tails with belled red ribbons at the ends. Kotone had used a giant red ribbon, tying her hair back in a loose ponytail. Everyone was in red elevated wooden sandals that made a *clop-clop* every step they walked. Kotone was wearing her white yukata with goldfish, Rei her black yukata with silver fish, Shiori a red yukata sprouting with bunches of grapes and chrysanthemums, and Chiharu wore a blue yukata full of birds flying or perched on twigs.

Chiharu handed her camera over to Shiori's father, and then they all excitedly squeezed together and smiled. Shiori and Rei got to stand in the very center, squeezed tight by their friends. Kotone gave a "V" sign, and then the shutter snapped.

"Thanks, Daddy. We're off then!" Shiori announced breathlessly. Chiharu quickly fetched her camera back and wore it on her wrist with a tight strap.

"Are you sure you'll be safe alone?" Daddy asked.

"This is Inazumu, Daddy. Nothing ever happens here!" Shiori reassured him.

Shiori nodded as though it were impossible anyone could disagree with her any further. "Love you, Daddy. Love you, Mother. I'm off."

"Have a safe trip," they both replied.

"Bye-bye, Daddy, Mother. I'm off." Rei looked up bashfully then back down again.

"Have a safe trip," the two replied even more warmly.

Then they were out the door and walking as fast as their red elevated sandals could handle. They didn't have many streets to walk before they started hearing the *boom, boom, boom* of the ceremonial drums and an occasional parade of flutes.

"This is so exciting. My last summer festival was when I was, like, six!" Shiori said enthusiastically, spinning around in a circle and looking up at the night sky. It was a clear night with a bright full moon. It was perfect.

"What do you want to do first, Shiori?" Kotone asked. Kotone had explained the plan. They couldn't let on that this was all for Rei's sake, or she'd feel self-conscious and try too hard to enjoy herself, and then she might not enjoy the festival at all. As far as the group was concerned, Rei could go jump in a creek. They were all coming because *they* wanted to have fun.

"*Takoyaki*! Then *taiyaki*! Then *ikiyaki*! Then yakisoba!" Shiori shouted each of the food items off in turn.

"You'll get a stomachache," Kotone warned.

"Sacrifices must be made! The food is waiting for me. I can't let it down," Shiori said.

"I want to catch goldfish as soon as possible," Kotone said. "My outfit won't be complete until I have a water bag full of swimming goldfish hanging on my wrist."

"I want goldfish too," Rei said.

"Of course! We have to stay matching. We're going to stay right next to each other the entire festival and draw *everyone's* heads. They're going to ask for pictures, we're so cute." Kotone smiled at Rei.

"You want to eat with your sister, don't you, Rei?" Shiori asked with pleading, wide eyes.

"Of course," Rei said.

"I want to try out the shooting gallery. I'll show them the results of my laser gun training." Chiharu held out her arm and flexed her nonexistent muscles. "If I get a stuffed dog, I'll give it to you, Shiori."

"Maybe we should get alien masks for our Wyrds!" Shiori suggested excitedly.

Kotone laughed. "I would love that. Let's strap a set of alien masks on all of them and make them glow *really* bright and take pictures."

Rei giggled. Shiori's heart rushed with warmth. *Rei was laughing because of my idea. It's working.*

When the four girls arrived, they did become the center of attention. They were so young and pretty that the crowd made way for them as they walked between the stands together. A few adults asked if they could take pictures, which slowed down their walk, because they all had to gather tight together again and pose with big smiles. Shiori couldn't stop smiling. She didn't have to fake it for the pictures.

"I found the goldfish. Let's go, Rei." Kotone started dragging her by the wrist, not even looking back to see if Rei would follow. Shiori staked out a tree to sit under and started ordering food from the stands. When she ran out of hands for the food, she deposited all of it, still steaming hot, and then went back for more. On her second run, she had found candied apples, chocolate bananas, and cotton candy, and she bought all of those too. Shiori didn't worry about money. Project Heal Rei was funded with the full approval of Mr. Miyamoto.

Kotone was kneeling down with a pile of broken nets at her feet. She hadn't managed to catch a single goldfish gently enough to place into her water bag. Rei was working on her fifth goldfish. She had only broken three scoopers. Shiori walked up behind them. "Are you two ready?"

"I'll be the shame of the Nakano family if I can't even catch a single goldfish!" Kotone bit her lip in an expression of supreme cuteness. Did she do it intentionally? Shiori could never tell.

"I'll give you some of mine, Kotone," Rei offered shyly.

"I...I..." Kotone slowly raised the fish up on her net, not startling it or making it thrash. "I got it!" Kotone flipped her net over, and the fish was secure in her water bag.

A large crowd clapped for her. Kotone drew attention like a magnet, and she stood up and gave a big "V" sign then bowed. Her smile was as bright as the sun. After that Rei poured water out until two more goldfish fell into Kotone's bag, and then Rei refilled her water, and the two of them walked together with three goldfish each strapped to their right wrists.

Chiharu snapped a picture of Kotone with an arm around Rei and both of them holding out their right arms to display their living jewelry. Then they all started eating. The food was hot and full of meat and spices, and the candy was sinfully sweet.

"Let's go buy the masks," Shiori suggested to Kotone.

"Then I'm going to the shooting gallery," Chiharu said. "Rei, do you want to come with me?"

"Okay," Rei said, and the two were off, threading through the crowd.

"It's working!" Shiori whispered gleefully to Kotone.

Kotone tossed her hair and put her hands on her hips. "Of course it's working. She's helpless between the three of us. Ohhh, ho, ho, ho." Kotone gave an evil laugh. Lots of people turned to watch them. Shiori smiled and held her hand up to her mouth too. "Ohhh, ho, ho, ho, ho!"

Then the two of them got in chorus and leaned backward together. "Ohhh, ho, ho, ho!" What was there to be ashamed about? They were thirteen-year-old girls in yukatas. They'd be forgiven anything.

They had just purchased their masks when Magnolia gave a start. "There's a Dead-Ender coming our way."

"Not now!" Kotone exclaimed.

"I don't think they attack at our convenience," Magnolia replied wryly.

"Let's go meet Chiharu," Shiori said, and Kotone nodded. The two were running through the crowd, only to see Rei and Chiharu running toward them. Chiharu was stubbornly carrying her stuffed dog under her arm.

"We have to get away from the crowd. We'll settle this in one go," Shiori said confidently. The other three nodded. Kotone looked a little queasy. That was when her phone rang.

"Hello?" Kotone opened her cell phone hurriedly. Shiori couldn't hear what was being said, but she could guess.

"Oh no. Shiori, Mr. Miyamoto…" Kotone looked at her.

"Kotone, Chiharu, go protect Mr. Miyamoto. We'll handle this," Shiori ordered.

"Are you sure? We could fight this one all together," Kotone offered.

"And what if Miyamoto dies in the meantime? Go. Don't worry. I have Rei with me," Shiori said. Kotone nodded. Then all four of them were ducking behind the nearest building.

"*Coi*, Awesome!"

"*Coi*, Cyan!"

"*Coi*, Onyx!"

"*Coi*, Magnolia!"

The yukatas folded out, and four magical girl outfits appeared instead. Sparkles surrounded all of them for a few brief seconds.

Kotone's boots sprouted rainbow-colored wings. "Chiharu, hold my hand. We're flying as fast as we can." Chiharu, in her complete exoskeleton, took Kotone's hand. "I can do a bit better than that," Chiharu said. "Amplify." And then Kotone's wings started vibrating and throwing off even more colors.

"See you soon!" Kotone tried to give a reassuring smile, and the two shot off like a comet through the sky.

Rei sprouted her butterfly wings and carried Shiori to the top of the highest building's roof. After that, they just watched and waited. The two said nothing, just letting the summer breeze slide across their faces. Rei's braided circlet of hair stood out against the full moon.

"Here it comes," Awesome warned Shiori. Shiori spotted the man and called out to him. His figure was shrouded in darkness. It almost felt like the man was nothing but darkness.

"I'm Shiori Rin, a Choice Giver. I want to talk. There's no reason for us to be fighting. Whatever your dark Wyrd said to you, it was all lies!" Awesome's magic translated the words across all possible languages. Even though Shiori was looking right at him, she suddenly lost sight of him. He appeared closer, as though stepping out of the roof's shadow.

"Dark Wyrd? I was contacted by Shiva. Shiva told me the last dance had begun, and killing you would end the world. End the world, and start it anew. Shiva has chosen me to dance for him." The man's voice almost hissed. No matter how close he got to them, there were still no distinct features. He was just a figure in shadow.

"Is your great god, Shiva, really just a floating ball?" Shiori asked. "Think about it!"

"No one insults Shiva and lives," the man hissed. And just like that, tendrils of shadow darted out to bite Shiori.

Shiori jumped backward, trying to think of what to do. But suddenly the man wasn't in her field of vision anymore; he was jumping between shadows again. *In that case…*

"Flashfire!" Shiori yelled, and the entire night sky lit up.

"Fool," the man hissed, "where there is light, there are shadows." His voice came from behind; the man was behind her. She turned around, trying to catch him in her eyes again, and then a sharp pain tore through her. Impossible. He was nowhere near her!

Shiori dropped to the ground, holding her side. Her chest plate had been cut, and a thin line of blood started trickling out from under it.

"Blackest Night!" Rei called from above, soaring on butterfly wings. The bolts dropped down in a flurry, but the man had disappeared into the shadows again. Small craters pocked the rooftop from where her attack had landed.

"Shiori, are you okay?" Rei called out fearfully.

"I'm fine," Shiori said, standing back up. "If I can't see him, then I just have to know where he's going to be."

"Fireplace." Shiori said, setting a mine in front of her. "Fireplace." She set a mine behind her. "Fireplace." She set a mine to her left. "Fireplace." She set a mine to her right. "Come at me, you dancing freak," Shiori said.

"Magnolia, can you still sense Miyamoto?" Kotone asked, rainbow light streaming behind her as she cut through the sky.

"He's alive. The Dead-Ender is right there too, somewhere, but scrying can only locate an approximate location. He's probably in the hospital, looking for the room number," Magnolia replied.

Kotone flew to Miyamoto's window and let Chiharu go. The momentum sent Chiharu crashing through the window and into the wall on the far side. "Chiharu, guard him. I'm going to the ground floor to find the culprit."

"Isn't this causing a scene?" Chiharu grumbled, rubbing her head and standing back up.

"No one can recognize us in our magical girl forms." Kotone brushed the concern aside. Then she was flying back down to the reception desk. With her winged heart wand and pink hair and red beribboned white dress, the hospital came to a halt just to look at her. *I just have to find someone in a flashy outfit. Where? Who?* Kotone walked through the halls.

A security guard walked up to intercept her. "Excuse me, miss. Do you have some business—"

"Magical miracle sleeping gas." Hearts puffed out of her wand, and the guard coughed a few times then slumped over. Kotone had already forgotten about him before he hit the ground. Where was the culprit? Surely he wouldn't still be in his normal clothes this near an enemy Choice Giver.

"I am Kotone Nakano!" Kotone shouted. "A Choice Giver! I'm a champion of love. All I want is to spread warmth. There's no reason to fight. Let's talk this over!" Magnolia translated her voice magically into whatever language her opponent needed to hear.

She saw a grenade rolling toward her and bolted backward with her wings. An explosion ripped the hallway where she used to be.

"Please stop that. There are innocents all around us. If you want to fight, at least come outside," Kotone spoke to her still-unknown opponent.

"There are no innocents among infidels." A man stepped forward, wearing a Kevlar armor suit with dynamite and grenades hanging everywhere. "Allah has already condemned you all."

The people within the hospital screamed and started running away.

"Allah? The only person who has been talking to you is a dark Wyrd. Look, I have a Wyrd too!" Kotone held up her right hand; Magnolia was shining a pure, white light.

"Silence, Dujjal. You are a deceiver. Everything you say is a lie. Your very form is a lie. How sick of you to take on the shape of a little girl." The man held out his fist and clenched it. "Earth-ripper!" Spikes started growing out of the floor, ceiling, and walls to pincushion Kotone.

"Magical miracle corrosion!" Kotone waved her wand, and acid splattered in a circle around her, dissolving the earth as quickly as it stabbed toward her. Then she bolted for the door. *I need to stall until Chiharu gets here. Surely she heard that explosion. I have to keep his attention. Why won't he listen to me? Rei listened to Shiori!*

Kotone flew out the door and launched herself high into the sky. The moment he stepped out of that hospital, Kotone announced, "Sting Snipe!" and a rain of needles shot out of her wand.

The man looked stunned, pincushioned from top to bottom. Then he grinned and started brushing the things off while looking up to see her. "Allah protects his own. He has given me the strongest armor, Dujjal."

"Go suck on a pig," Kotone said, sticking out her tongue and lowering one of her eyelids.

"You little—" The man's face grew veined. "Blast wave!" And an explosive shock wave shot out of his fists toward her position. Kotone soared into the sky, turning and looping just to make sure he never got a fix on where she'd be next.

"Magical miracle sulfuric acid," Kotone said. She hated doing this, but if Sting Snipe didn't work…

The acid appeared over his head in a washtub then tipped over to spill all over his face. The acid stopped at his clothes, though, and hovered over his hair, sizzling away at an invisible wall.

"You signed a contract with jinn, but I signed a contract with Gabriel. You cannot defeat me, witch." The man grinned.

"Amplify," Chiharu said, standing behind the man. And then the acid kept growing. The sizzling became louder then his whole body was covered in steam, and then the screaming began.

Kotone eventually landed beside the unrecognizable corpse. She felt sick.

"Good job, Kotone. I barely had to do a thing," Chiharu said, patting her on the shoulder.

"I tried talking to him. He wouldn't listen." Kotone sighed.

"People of faith don't listen to reason," Chiharu stated simply. "I'm worried about Shiori. Let's go back."

"Just…give me a minute, Chiharu," Kotone said. Then she turned around and threw up. She tried to keep her beautiful pink hair away from the flow.

"Shadow snake," the shadow man hissed, and his tendrils shot across the ground from another secluded corner of the roof. Halfway to Shiori, the ground erupted in front of her and blew the things away. A fountain of fire burned into the sky, leaving a thick smoke when it was gone. But he was already moving again in his strange, warping way, and he had drawn a sword just as dark as his own body. Strangely, he wasn't heading for Shiori but well off to the side.

Rei figured it out just in time. "Eternal Zero!" she yelled, not at the shadow man, who she could never catch in her field of vision anyway, but at Shiori.

"Clever butterfly," the man hissed, his shadow already melting away again. "Have you seen through Shiva's dance already?"

"You aren't attacking us. You're attacking our shadows. But it doesn't matter. Anything within my stasis field is invincible. Chop at her all you want, it won't matter if you can't bring me down. I'm your opponent now." Rei made sure her shadow wasn't anywhere near the rooftop.

"You're not a Choice Giver. Leave now, and I'll spare you," the man hissed at her dismissively.

"Shiori is my sister," Rei answered coldly, her eyes narrowing to slits. "And don't be mistaken. Eternal

Zero isn't protecting Shiori from you. It's protecting her from *me*."

"Shadow snake," the shadowman called, fanged phantasms attempting to snag her out of the air.

"Stasis shield." Rei sneered dismissively. The snakes froze in place in front of her. "Let's do this, Onyx," Rei whispered quietly to her partner.

"Initiating," Onyx said in a particularly pleased voice. Onyx was embedded in the small of her back, his black light forming her butterfly wings. But once Onyx started concentrating, her wings spread out well beyond her, an inkblot spreading into a new, black sun that extinguished the moon.

"Everything should just return to zero," Rei chanted. "Event Horizon."

Shadowman tried to flicker to one shadow then to another. Each time, he was dragged back up toward her black rift in the sky. He howled, trying to flee away to another building entirely. The gravity pulled harder.

Rei floated calmly in the sky, watching her prey. *I am the cold.* He went this way, and he went that way. He even went upside down. But it had all been futile from the start. Rei allowed herself a smile when he disappeared into the tiny black dot at the center of her maelstrom.

Rei waited a few more seconds, just to be sure; then she cut the rift off. She floated down to Shiori and let her boots land on the roof, and then she released Eternal Zero.

"Rei! Where did he…?" Shiori blinked, her head turning back and forth.

"It's all right, Shiori. I dealt with him," Rei said. "More importantly, how's your side?"

"Just a scratch. My suit isn't just for show." Shiori smiled, lifting her arms to show how healthy she was. Then they heard a whistle and a pop behind them. The two turned to see the first firework light up the sky. Without having to say anything, they de-folded back into their yukatas, sat down, and held hands. Bursts and sizzles of every pattern filled the sky. Golden streamers that looked like trees, and flashes that just made enormous cannon like sounds, and fireworks that gave birth to baby fireworks that exploded into new colors and patterns. The summer festival was coming to an end, but this was an all right way to end it.

Chapter 9

It was Rei's first day at school, having passed all the qualifying tests, and she had happily joined the rest on top of the roof for lunch. She was in the same class as Chiharu, which was great, because it meant she could easily get help with any group work and find a partner for any group assignments.

The other night, when Chiharu and Kotone had returned to the festival, they had compared notes. When it turned out the dark Wyrds were recruiting religious people, their own Wyrds had asked them what humanity's faiths were all about. Chiharu had promised to draw them up an instructive manual, and while the girls attended school, the Wyrds had all gathered together and read over them. Rei was glad to see all the Wyrds flying up to the top of the roof to join them; she never felt safe when Onyx was too far away, but she hadn't been prepared for the angry hum that filled the air and the flashes like lightning that seemed to go off because the Wyrds couldn't hold them in anymore.

"So let me get this straight," Cyan said, his voice trying to stay under control. "Every single human religion wishes for, welcomes, and prays for the end of the world?"

"Not Shinto." Kotone was quick to defend herself. "In Shinto, nature is always changing, and creation is always in the middle of this flow. Every moment is as important and vital as the next."

"Okay, so every *other* human religion?" Cyan asked.

"Maybe not animists." Kotone shrugged helplessly.

"No wonder this whole world is full of Dead-Enders. They are all openly trying to end the world." Cyan blinked in disgust.

"But the last day is supposed to bring about some new, better world," Chiharu reminded him.

"Do they have any idea how much it hurts when your whole world ends? When you realize everything everyone has ever done has been for naught? That everything that was ever made, every last artwork that has been faithfully transmitted, every last line of descent that thousands of generations of parents have sacrificed and struggled to keep alive within a new generation of children, every last discovery we ever made about life, the universe, and the good, is all going away? That despite life running as fast as it can, straining itself to the very limit of its resources, suffering and dying in a continuous stream to make a better world, death *still* caught up to us, and so all that suffering, all that trying, was for *nothing?* Do you know how it feels that I can't have kids anymore, because my universe is all washed up? Do you know how it feels to be a zombie? To look at every building ever built and think, 'There's no point to this building anymore. No one will ever live in it again'?

"Can you imagine the pain of wondering what it was all for, when the end result is the same as if we had never lived, the same as if the universe had never existed in the first place at all? Do you know the pain of wondering if there wasn't something left undone, some new height of experiences we could have reached, if we had transcended our limits? Do you know how painful it is to wonder if there wasn't more out there? What if there is a love so glorious that our hearts would burst to feel it? A truth so brilliant our minds would crack trying to fathom it? A beauty so deep our souls would drown trying to drink it in? If the world ends, no one will reach any of those heights. We have no idea how high they climb. Maybe they climb forever. Maybe our love is like a worm's love for another worm to those potential beings, the ones we could have been, if only our world hadn't ended. But we'll never know now, because it's dead. It's all dead!" Cyan took a long breath.

"And if I start to think of all these human-constructed hells meant for those who do die for too long, I want to… I want to…"

"Join me?" Onyx blinked wickedly.

"Yes! God help me! What am I supposed to think when…billions of you want to torture the vast majority of each other for eternity? Do you know what this sounds like to an outside observer?" Cyan glowed a furious blue. "When did you people come up with these ideas?"

Kotone winced."Generally, around two thousand years ago?"

"Two thousand…" Cyan started sputtering. "Two thousand years ago? Are you trying to tell me that for the last two thousand years, you have been advancing your mathematics, your chemistry, your physics, your biology, your geology, your engineering, your painting, your music, your literature, your medicine, and your astronomy while completely ignoring theology, the study of God's nature, and our relationship to Him? Everything else needed improving but, wow, two thousand years ago, that part of human thinking got it right the very first time?

"To be fair," Chiharu said, "hardly anyone actually follows their religion or their religious texts."

"Then why be that religion?" Cyan asked, amazed. "If you don't believe it, if you don't follow it, why are you of that faith? That's absurd."

"Don't worry, Cyan. The future belongs to atheists like me." Chiharu consoled him. "Only atheists are willing to embrace the newest discoveries and abilities of science, and so inevitably we'll conquer the world or just go and settle all the other worlds in the universe. Almost all intelligent people have converted to atheism long ago."

"There is a God, and He created us as His crowning glory!" Cyan contested. "I don't want atheists to conquer the Earth and forget their duty to God, to never feel anything sacred their entire lives long. That's horrible!"

"Well, I'm not sure how many Wyrdists there are on Earth, so you'll just have to be content with atheism. It's the only rational conclusion," Chiharu said diplomatically.

"Shinto's just fine." Kotone blushed. "You can't say a single thing about Shinto you said about the rest. And the gods do answer our prayers, if we pray with all our hearts. And I feel holy when I walk through a red gate."

"I'll be a Wyrdist, if it makes you feel any better," Shiori offered.

"Don't go changing your religion to make people feel better!" Chiharu hit Shiori with her notebook.

"You're just jealous because I'm more compatible with Cyan than you are." Shiori returned to her long-standing grievance.

"I am *not* jealous. For your information, Cyan proposed to me weeks ago. I had to fight him off with a stick," Chiharu said.

"I did no such thing!" Cyan glowed.

"I tried to tell him no, but he said"—Chiharu took a deep breath and put on a mournful pining face of unrequited love for the audience—"'Let's set that aside and just begin our lifelong contract until death does us part.' Word for word, I swear to God."

"You don't believe in God!" Cyan objected.

"Which is exactly why I can swear to him whenever I want," Chiharu said primly.

Then the lunch bell rang, and the girls had to scurry back down the stairs.

Awesome floated in the sky with the three other Wyrds. They were close enough to alert their mistresses if any threat was incoming, but they wanted some privacy to continue to discuss just what exactly they had come upon.

It was this simple: Awesome, Cyan, and Magnolia had become so accustomed to how good their Choice Givers were that they had forgotten how rare their goodness was. There were good Wyrds and bad Wyrds, heroic Wyrds and petty Wyrds, selfless Wyrds and selfish Wyrds. But no Wyrd had ever suggested, in all of history, that the vast majority of Wyrds would be sent to a place of eternal torment after death, simply for disagreeing with the speaker.

Were humans and Choice Givers even the same species? Could there be any possible relationship between Shiori, who excitedly greeted each new day as a wellspring of infinite possibilities, and the billions of humans who prayed for a last day to wipe everything away and replace it with a dead end?

"Can this world truly be saved?" Awesome asked. The other Wyrds flashed their various lights, acknowledging his question.

"Does this world deserve us?" Awesome asked again. But that wasn't exactly the right question. Who were they? They were a failed species from a dead-end world. They had ruined their own universe and never found a way around it. Their scrying didn't reveal anything special about themselves. He knew what the real question should be.

"Does this world deserve them? These girls who are more beautiful than any human can see or even dream? These girls who they want to burn in hell as heathens and idolaters?" Awesome asked. It was a rhetorical question. There was no way this world deserved Shiori. There was no reason Shiori should try to save them, or help them, at all.

"Chiharu says no one really believes that stuff…" Cyan offered. But his heart wasn't in it.

"If they don't really believe it, why don't they say so? Why don't they clearly and explicitly renounce these beliefs? You can't have it both ways. These people say they belong to these faiths. They say these are holy books, authored by God. They say this is truth. They can't simultaneously say they don't believe any of it," Awesome countered.

"Maybe humans really can believe and not believe the same thing at the same time," Magnolia offered. "They are an alien species. Maybe they can do things we can't imagine."

"How can you both believe and not believe the same thing at the same time?" Awesome asked incredulously.

"I don't know… somehow…" Magnolia blinked helplessly.

"Listen to this. This is what over a billion people believe—those who call themselves 'Muslims.' All non-believers, regardless of how virtuous or innocent they are, go to hell. For nonbelievers, hell is eternal. The Qu'ran explicitly describes how the majority of mankind will be tormented in hell forever. Here's just a sample of what's in store for our unlucky nonbelievers: Their skin will be burned off then replaced so it can be burned off again. They will be given garments of fire, and boiling water will scald their skin and internal organs. Their faces will be set on fire, their lips burned off, and their backs set on fire. They'll be roasted from side to side. Their faces will be dragged along fire. They'll be bound in yokes and then dragged through boiling water and fire. This is all straight from the Qu'ran, the unchanged, perfect word of Allah. Does this sound like a metaphor for 'absence from God'?" Awesome flashed sarcastically.

"Maybe Muslims believe it, but they don't condone it. They just are powerless to stop it…" Magnolia's white light had a wan, ashen hue.

"Don't condone it? They pray to Allah five times a day. They call him the 'benevolent' and the 'merciful.' Awesome said pointedly. This time, none of the Wyrds had any response. What defense was there?

"I wanted to be a missionary to these people," Awesome said. "Oh, I had other reasons. I wanted to escape the dying world of the Wyrds. I wanted to meet a Choice Giver who was so beautiful that I never wanted to stop scrying, just so I could continue gazing upon her…but I thought it was okay to have a few selfish motives, because at heart I just wanted to help these people. But I don't want to help these people anymore. They disgust me."

"We'll just have to hope people like that fade away over time, like Chiharu said they would." Cyan said.

"Yes, but when they fade away, will they take the bare handful of good people on this world down with them? And when that happens, will they have taken all life in the multiverse down with them? You know as well as I do, these are the only Choice Givers we could find anywhere—the only ones," Awesome said.

"We probably just aren't good enough scryers. There has to be more life somewhere," Magnolia said.

"Even if that's true, it would still be a terrible blow and a terrible loss of opportunity, if nothing else. How good would a world that actually emulated and followed their Choice Givers be?" Awesome said.

"Choice Givers could teach these Dead-Enders a better way. They could save mankind and turn this all around," Magnolia said.

"They can only save those with open minds and open hearts, and they can only save the people who want to be saved, the ones who are willing to follow or emulate them, like Rei Rin. How many is that? Am I to believe that religious people, who believe in eternal torture as a punishment for those who disagree with them, have open hearts? Am I to believe that religious people, who state ahead of time that they have no intention to be rational, that all of their beliefs are based off of blind faith, have open minds?" Awesome blinked scornfully.

"But what more can we do?" Magnolia asked.

"Maybe Angle Exile could be used for good as well as harm. Maybe we could just take everyone worth saving and open a portal to another world—a world without Dead-Enders." Awesome thought. "If we just keep fighting like this, we'll lose eventually. We can't win every time. Our Choice Givers will be picked off one by one. This world is beyond any hope of salvation. We should just pick up our stuff and go. Just…leave."

"I'll ask Masanori about it next time Kotone visits," Magnolia promised. "The truth is, Kotone hates these fights. Awesome is right. I just want to protect Kotone from having to fight like this ever again. She didn't ask for this, but she's still trying her best. You should have seen her this last time. It was awful. It's killing her inside. She's a thirteen-year-old girl. Why do we have to fight for anyone else? Let the Dead-Enders have the world. I just don't want them to hurt Kotone anymore."

"I think Chiharu is having fun," Cyan said. Awesome gave Cyan a warning red flash. "All right, all right. Let's at least wait until Magnolia tells us if the scheme is even possible."

"Once we find out, we'll ask the girls all together—a united front." Awesome swiveled at Cyan.

"Where you two go, I'll follow, whether it's this universe or any other. You know that," Cyan said.

"Thanks, Cyan." Magnolia flashed warmly.

"I hope you're letting me come too. I wouldn't exactly like being stranded here as a known traitor to the dark Wyrds." Onyx blinked nervously.

"Of course you're coming. Evil or not, Rei loves you, and Shiori loves Rei," Awesome said.

"And you love—" Onyx started.

"I don't know what you're talking about, and I don't want to know," Awesome interrupted warningly. "If everyone's done saying something intelligent, let's get back to our owners' sides."

Isao Oono, age fifteen, stepped off the airplane ladder and onto the soil of his native land. Isao tried to keep in touch with Japan. He was still technically attending middle school, though with the worst attendance record imaginable. But his kind of work wasn't exactly applicable here. Assassinations required someone who needed killing.

When he was younger, he hadn't intended to become an assassin. He had planned on being a car mechanic or maybe a plumber. But that all fell out the window when Black arrived. It turned out he was a Choice Giver, someone who could provide the world with infinite possibilities. And with Black's help, he could use magic. After learning that, Isao gave up on his previous career plans and came up with a new one. *If I want to give people choices, there is one extremely easy way to do so. With magic, I have the power to do it: Kill all the tyrants of the world. And then if new ones are elected or appointed, kill those too. Sooner or later people will figure out that evil rulers are no longer acceptable.*

Isao Oono had the final veto on every head of state, because he could take all of their heads. His recent third trip to North Korea hopefully had made this point extremely clear. This time the dictator had hidden in a remote fishing village, never appearing at an army parade or touching his palatial home. It didn't matter. Black could scry out tyrants wherever they ran. Tyrants cut off possibilities, which meant all the dead ends in the area centered on them. No one could hide from the Isao-Black team.

The world would be free—free to reach its own potential, not just in the civilized corners of the West and the East, but everywhere. He would free Southeast Asia. He would free the Middle East. He would free Africa. He would free the splinter nations of the USSR. The armies of the world sat idly, refusing to act, refusing to do what they knew was right. All the armies of the world had managed to execute one dictator, Saddam Hussein, at the cost of trillions of dollars and tens of thousands of lives. *But I've already killed ten dictators. And all it costs me is hotel and airfare, and nobody but the target has to die.* He couldn't have asked for a more fulfilling career. By the time he was sixty, he figured the whole world would be a decent place to live in. A journey of a thousand miles started with the first step, after all.

The question that weighed on Isao's mind was China. Were they a good government or a bad one? Would the replacement be any better than the person he killed? Could that country's government really be taken down, or did it enjoy thorough popular support? Killing dictators only worked if the people wanted to be free of them but were too scared to revolt. For places like China, it wasn't clear what people wanted. It wasn't even clear that China's government was tyrannical. It was a dictatorship, sure, but a dictatorship that had hosted a beautiful Olympics and a dictatorship whose economic growth underpinned the whole world economy. China would have to wait.

Isao only hoped North Korea wouldn't make him fly there again. He had an appointment with six other countries in the next month, and he didn't want to have to delay those assassinations again. But North Korea served as an example. Once the will of the North Korean dictatorship broke, the other dictators would take note to elect or appoint a ruler with the consent of the governed, or die. If North Korea could wait him out, all the other dictatorships would try the same tactic too. Then he'd barely get anywhere. *One country at a time. Haste makes waste.*

Now that he could use his cell phone again, he decided to call ahead to base. Miyamoto funded his operations, but he knew plenty of other Choice Givers, people whose magic wasn't suited for assassination or people who just were hoping to get by. Nao was hoping to compose songs that would touch the hearts of millions. Ryo was making a visual novel. They were such idealists. Isao smiled. What's the use of showing people what they really want so long as villains are still out there, keeping them from attaining it? The best way to give people choices was to set them free. Freedom was always won by the sword. But Isao didn't mind. As far as he knew, he was the only Choice Giver who could become invisible to all means of detection. Naturally assassinations had fallen to him. It's not like the songs and novels weren't important too.

For some reason, no one was picking up. Isao figured they were out and about or just too busy to answer the phone. But something in his gut told him there was something wrong. Base had always answered his phone calls before. They had known when he was going to arrive, and they always welcomed him back with applause. Something was out of place for everyone to be gone.

"Black, can you scry out Nao or Ryo, or Hisoka?" Isao Oono asked his Wyrd.

"Roger," Black said. Then the gem in his jeans pocket lay dormant for a while.

"That's strange," Black said. "I can't find anyone."

"Look again," Isao said. Something was definitely out of place.

"Well, there's Miyamoto. He's still a long ways south from here," Black said.

"What is that idiot doing? He's been gone all month." Isao grew angry. Miyamoto should have known to keep a watch on the Choice Givers up here. With Isao and Miyamoto gone, their battle strength was…

"Black, scry for a vicious looking Dead-Ender. Start at Miyamoto's location, and zoom out to something that looks ready to chop away all the possibilities," Isao Oono said. *I hope I'm wrong. But I already know I'm not wrong.* He'd been in the killing business too long to not see the signs.

"There is one. It looks like…it's traveling steadily southwest. Master, it's ugly. Uglier than I've ever seen," Black said.

Farewell, Nao. Farewell, Ryo. Farewell, Hisoka. I will avenge you.

"Pinpoint the city Miyamoto's lazing about in," Isao said, walking to a map of Japan.

"It looks like…here, Master." Black furtively floated to a corner.

"Let's go buy a ticket, Black," Isao Oono said.

"Where to?" Black asked.

"Inazumu. Where else?" Isao couldn't afford to be angry. He had a target. When you have a target, all you can be is focused.

Kotone Nakano was visiting Mr. Miyamoto for a third time. She was alone again, and she had finally delivered her get-well flowers to a table beside his bed. Miyamoto had taken his wound in the process of saving her life, and she intended to watch over him until that wound was healed again. It's just that things kept cropping up and keeping her away. Studying with Rei, shopping for yukatas, practicing flute, or fighting bomb throwers all made sure she couldn't complete a simple promise. So Kotone was feeling pretty happy to see those flowers sitting, safe and sound, in their proper place at last.

"Chiharu says you must be using magic to make so much money," Kotone said.

"Smart girl." Masanori grinned.

"Oh come on. Please tell me how!" Kotone asked. The question had bothered her ever since she had seen the bank account pop up on the ATM.

"I call it 'angle mining.' I kind of feel out a good place on the other side, cut a hole, and in drop gold nuggets from another universe," Miyamoto said.

"Isn't that counterfeiting?" Kotone asked.

"How so? The gold is real. It really does work if you put it in electronics or whatever. It's valuable, and people pay me for it." Miyamoto defended himself.

"But you know gold is a storehouse of exaggerated value simply because it's rare." Kotone glared at him.

"That's why I gave up on the idea of repaying the entire Japanese national debt in gold bars." Miyamoto grinned. "But enough to get by? The market will never notice. And besides, it's for a good cause."

"I don't get it," Kotone said, looking down and blushing a little. "You're rich, you're nice, you're handsome, you're apparently the best guy on Earth, according to our Wyrds…and you're unmarried. I'm the only person who even brought you flowers, who even knows you're in a hospital. Could it be, b-b-boy's love?"

Masanori laughed. "If only. Maybe then I'd have an excuse. No, it's nothing like that. When I joined the army, I didn't meet many girls. And when I left the army, I still didn't meet many. Those I met, I kept finding some fault with. They were selfish, or vapid, or ugly. I kept thinking to myself, 'Someday I'll meet the right girl.' And the years went by, and here I am. Somehow, I just never met her."

"What if it's me? Could you wait until I'm eighteen?" Kotone half whispered, her face completely red.

Miyamoto rejected her in a flash. "Don't be silly. You have no right to ask such a question until you *are* eighteen." *Oh great. Now he'll hate me. Why did I say that? I'm so stupid.* Kotone wanted to cry, but she couldn't. It might make Miyamoto feel guilty when she had been the one at fault, completely, and he'd been a perfect gentleman start to finish.

"Mr. Miyamoto," Magnolia interjected in a somewhat nonchalant manner, "you said you could feel out that gold would be on the other side of your folding. Does that mean you know where Angle Exile sends things too?"

"I suppose I could figure it out, if I ever bothered to check. 'Away' was the only thing I really concentrated on for that attack," Miyamoto said.

"So could you Angle Exile something to another inhabitable planet? Some place almost exactly like our own, only without any people yet?" Magnolia asked.

"If I practiced…maybe I could." Miyamoto wondered. "What do you think, Xanadu?"

"It's within parameters," Xanadu said.

"But that's wonderful!" Kotone clapped, her face lighting up. "That means we don't have to kill anyone! They can all go live happily ever after!"

"I suppose…" Miyamoto rubbed the back of his head. "How odd. I never thought about sparing my opponents. You have a compassionate heart, Nakano. Now I feel bad, almost, for all the times I have used that move without worrying about it."

"Mr. Miyamoto, no matter how bad you feel for exiling people to places unknown, I promise you I felt worse for melting someone in acid. If *that's* a compassionate heart, then this world needs help," Kotone corrected him.

Masanori warmed to the idea."Well, if I ever get out of this bed, and we're all in the same place, and my attack hits…sure, let's send them to a habitable world— a place they can't hurt anyone else. Who knows? Maybe they'll reform and live happily ever after."

Magnolia glowed a complacent white.

Thank you so much, Magnolia. Somehow, we changed the topic. You saved my pride. Now it's like I had never asked him…that…at all.

"You have to watch your bank account though, Mr. Miyamoto. Chiharu and Shiori, they're rotten thieves. Rotten to the core. They'll buy their own personal limousines and jets and say it's all for Choice Giving. I told them I'd warn you," Kotone said, trying to act natural again.

"I don't mind." Miyamoto laughed. "Easy come, easy go."

Xanadu flashed a brilliant silver, bringing the conversation to a dead silence. "Incoming."

"You're kidding me!" Kotone exclaimed. "The last one was just days ago!"

"I'll call the others," Miyamoto said grimly, getting out his cell phone.

"This one's…heavy, or sharp, if you prefer," Xanadu said, his voice strained. "We're going to need everyone."

Kotone sighed and gave a longing look at her flowers. *Another fight. All I wanted was to spread warmth.* But…she also wanted to protect Mr. Miyamoto. He was helpless because of her. And…he hadn't said what his response would be when she *was* eighteen.

"*Coi*, Magnolia." Magic exploded through her body.

Chapter 10

"Got it. We're on our way." Shiori ended the phone conversation. "Rei, would you mind carrying me to the hospital?"

"Of course I don't mind," Rei said. The two of them were in their room, snacking on some onigiri Mother had made for them and doing their homework together while listening to music. It had been a peaceful summer day. Shiori wondered if she would ever enjoy peaceful days again.

"*Coi*, Awesome!" Shiori invoked. She was glad to see her armor had repaired itself magically since the last fight. She slipped open the window and looked around for nosy neighbors.

"The coast is clear," Shiori said.

"*Coi*, Onyx!" Rei invoked, and she was back into her gothic dress and violet chased butterfly wings. Rei wrapped her arms around Shiori's waist, and then they jumped out the window. For a brief moment, Shiori feared they were just going to plummet into the bushes. But Rei flapped her wings a few times, a powerful wind blew out beneath them, and they were soaring in the sky.

"Let's get high enough that at least no one recognizes our faces," Shiori shouted into the wind.

"Yes, sister," Rei said and soared upward accordingly. Rei didn't look strained, even though her magic was carrying both of them. Shiori supposed neither of them weighed *that* much.

Kotone and Miyamoto were alone, awaiting some new monster stronger than all the others. Chiharu couldn't fly, so she might arrive too late. On the other hand, her power suit could leap tall buildings in a single bound. Maybe she'd be fine. Chiharu was the key. Once they saw how well Kotone's magic performed with Chiharu's help, everyone had demanded Chiharu combine with them to make a new move. The results had been spectacular. If this guy was stronger than George Flint, only twin techs would suffice to take him down. Shiori couldn't wait to try out hers.

Shiori thought flying would be fun, but it was surprisingly normal. The fact that she was flying to a life-and-death encounter, where her and her friends' lives were on the line, made the flight impossible to enjoy. *If only we could cut off these dark Wyrds at the source.* The dark Wyrds were behind all the Dead-Enders. Without them, everything would return to normal. But she couldn't imagine any such way.

When they arrived, Kotone was already standing on the rooftop, with her ostentatious white dress and pink hair both flapping gently in the wind that always rushed on buildings at this height. She looked grim, like she had been chewing on licorice this entire time.

"Kotone!" Shiori waved. The two landed at a run, slowly breaking their speed.

"Shiori." Kotone turned to give her a big smile of relief. "Chiharu?"

"She's coming. I'm sure she'll make it in time." Of course, Shiori only said that because she *wasn't* sure

Chiharu would make it in time. But there was no point worrying about stuff that couldn't be changed.

The three stood quietly on the rooftop, watching the sun set. It threw off brilliant scarlets, pinks, and golds, dyeing the clouds with various impossible colors.

From behind, they heard a *shing-shing* of servos whirring and carbon landing on concrete.

"Looks like I made it in time," Chiharu said happily.

"Chiharu!" Everyone called out her name at once, suddenly feeling more confident.

"You heard this one was strong, right?" Shiori said.

"I heard," Chiharu said.

"I want your amplification first." Shiori begged with wide eyes. Chiharu never said no to her widest eyes.

Chiharu laughed. "Fine by me. Let's finish this in one strike, Shiori."

"After we talk things over," Shiori reminded Chiharu.

"Of course. After we talk things over." Chiharu agreed.

"It's strange, isn't it?" Kotone mused. "It's such a beautiful sunset." No one knew how to respond to her, so they just stood watching for the Dead-Ender's arrival. *The beauty around us never seems to seep into our souls.* It really was strange.

"Incoming," Cyan warned. A few tense seconds later, they could see the speck in the air. *Oh no. Why can all my opponents fly?* Shiori bit the inside of her cheek in frustration. The Dead-Ender flew close enough that everyone could see him clearly. The man was in the prime of his health, carrying a giant claymore with a blue gem embedded in the middle. He wore a full suit of plate mail, with gold chasings and lines, and a white heroic cape with gold decorations down his back. His face was un-helmeted, revealing a strong jaw, blond hair, and bright blue eyes. It looked like he had just stepped out of a picture book.

"My name is Shiori Rin," Shiori cried out to the flying man, making sure her voice would carry. Awesome translated her words into whatever language the man needed to hear. "I'm a Choice Giver. We don't want to fight. Please, if you have grievances, tell us about them, and we'll change whatever we can. If you're angry with us, or hate us, let's talk it out. If you think we're bad people, ask us any questions you like, and we'll try to answer them. If you're in pain, we can try to heal you." *There. That should cover all bases. And this time I didn't insult anyone's Wyrd companion or religion and get their backs up. This time it had to work.*

"Schoolgirls." The knight sneered. "I thought 'Captain Japan' was going to be my most ludicrous fight."

"Whatever you've been told, we *are* just schoolgirls. Chiharu and me, we have a softball tournament coming up. Kotone has a flute recital. Can't you just leave us alone? We only want to go to school and live out our lives in peace." More and more, Shiori ached for the peace she had taken for granted just a month ago.

"Indigo has already told me all about you. You sound convincing, but there's no point lying. Indigo's scrying is perfect. No matter how someone looks or behaves, he can tell a Dead-Ender from a Choice Giver. Somehow or other, you three are going to bring about the destruction of the world. I'm the true Choice

Giver. Indigo's scrying says so. And I have come to free the world from your dead end. Prepare yourself, Shiori Rin." The knight lifted his claymore.

"Stop! Please!" Kotone cried. "Your Wyrd is lying to you! All of our Wyrds say we're Choice Givers, and *you're* the Dead-Ender. Free yourself before it's too late!"

"Listen to yourselves. By the same logic, why couldn't all of *your* Wyrds be lying to you and *mine* be telling the truth?" the knight shot back angrily.

"Because Awesome couldn't lie his way out of a paper bag!" Shiori retorted angrily. "If you're so confident we're being deceived, convince us. If you're a real Choice Giver, show us a better way. Is violence the answer to everything? If your soul is full of light, share a little of that light with us, and open our eyes! I've told you my name, but you won't even give your own! We aren't people to you, just firewood to be chopped up. Is that what being a Choice Giver means?"

"If you want to know the name of your executioner so much, so be it. I am Claus Reinhardt. And it's useless to pretend. Indigo has already told me that scrying is absolute. He can foresee the future. Dead-Enders don't change," Claus said.

"You couldn't be more wrong!" Shiori shouted. "People can change! They can change from night to day, if you ever reach out to them! The future isn't set, and it isn't a flat line. It's full of infinite possibilities! Wyrds can't scry the future of people's hearts, only the consequences of their present heart's trends. They can't foresee free will!"

"More lies! Why should I risk the fate of the world on useless, sappy lies like these!" Claus Reinhardt roared.

"And what if you're risking the fate of the world by *not* listening to me? Claus Reinhardt, is the world normally saved by chopping up little girls?" Shiori challenged.

Claus gave her an agonized look, his sword lowering. "No! No! I cannot pity you! I have a five-year-old girl at home. Her name is Claudia. And she is counting on me. If you wanted pity, you should have taken pity on her before you plotted to kill us all! I will protect my children from this insane world!"

"Crown of Glory!" Claus shouted. Shiori clenched her fists in frustration. Again and again, she couldn't reach them. Again and again, she failed.

Eight sparkling balls came into being, glowing a white-yellow and sending out flares and forks of electricity in all directions. All four girls scattered, two taking to the air. Claus wasn't going to talk anymore.

"Strike them down!" Claus pointed, and the ball lightning scattered, two to each of them, creating a high-pitched whine as they tore through the air.

"Chiharu!" Shiori cried out, her boots giving her enough speed to sprint to the side as the lightning whooshed by.

"Go!" Chiharu called, her power suit letting her leap over the lightning headed for her.

"Super Move!" Shiori cried out, emitting more and more of Awesome's light from her forehead tiara.

"Amplify." Cyan started glowing in unison from Chiharu's chest.

"Firestorm!" Shiori yelled, and her normal firefly came out as an enormous torrent of flame.

Claus Reinhardt was fast. The plate armor didn't seem to weigh anything. Even though she had tried to cover the whole sky around him, he was still zipping out of the way.

"Deflect!" Chiharu shouted, and suddenly the fire-storm took a right angle turn and slammed right into a startled Claus.

"Shiori, behind you!" Rei cried out. Out of instinct, she jumped as high as she could. The lightning from Crown of Glory hadn't faded out when it missed. They were still homing in on her, turning around for a third pass. Everyone had to occupy half their energy just dodging the stupid things every pass. Shiori looked up in frustration. Hadn't they hit him dead-on? So how was his lightning still going?

When the smoke cleared, Claus stood smiling, his Claymore held in a guard position in front of him. He started to laugh. "As expected, Shiori Rin, you are a fine opponent! But the light always triumphs over the dark-ness. That is why I am the strongest." Claus whipped his sword toward her, and a shockwave shot through the sky.

"Stasis shield!" Rei cried out, freezing the energy wave right in front of Shiori. Two lightning balls slashed through the air after her.

"Ah, moooh!" Shiori yelled, cutting the line of her body left and right to weave back through the inces-sant attacks.

"Chiharu, let me try!" Rei cried out.

"Ready when you are." Chiharu agreed, ducking under her lightning hounds.

"Super Move." Rei's butterfly wings became thicker and thicker.

"Amplify." Chiharu concentrated Cyan.

"Eclipse!" An enormous dark lance of erasure shot out of her toward the target.

"Aegis Shield." Claus Reinhardt invoked, and a giant golden light slammed down to protect him.

"Counter!" Chiharu cried. But nothing happened; his spell brushed hers aside like she hadn't even tried. The lance slammed into the shield, and after a few dizzying seconds of magical forces vying for supremacy, all of Rei's darkness spread out into motes and floated away.

"You've got to be kidding me!" Chiharu exclaimed in frustration.

"Royal Verdict!" Claus Reinhardt called, and a bolt of lightning came out of a rift in the sky and struck Chiharu dead on.

"Chiharu!" Shiori cried out.

"Eternal Zero." Rei cast, but Claus kept darting about, and the zone she froze was always a few seconds too late and behind where he was. With Crown of Glory making *her* dodge half the time as well, the spell simply couldn't hit.

"Sting Snipe." Kotone cast, from high above all the other combatants. A rain of needles pinged off of Claus's plate armor. The man started laughing again.

"Good! Keep struggling, Dead-Enders! The end is nigh!"

DEAD ENDERS

"Flaaame—Geyseeeerr!" Shiori turned, channeling fire through her leg in a sweeping roundhouse kick. The two ball lightnings exploded against the edge of her kick and ceased to exist. She was at Chiharu's side in an instant, her leg still on fire. When the balls came in for their next pass, she smashed them into puffs of air.

"Chiharu, say something!" Shiori said, grabbing her and shaking her.

"That hurts, Shiori," Chiharu complained. "Do you think…this power suit…is for show? Losing to…an attack like that?" she muttered, trying to stand back up.

"Chiharu, we need something stronger! What's stronger than Eclipse?" Shiori asked her. The battle between the three flyers raged above them.

"I guess…if a twin tech fails, there's always triple techs?" Chiharu said.

"Tell me what to do!" Shiori encouraged her, pulling her up to her feet.

"Just stand here for now. Kotone, we need gas number three! All you can make!" Chiharu shouted.

"Magical miracle carbon monoxide." Kotone waved her wand, white light glowing brightly from Magnolia in her right glove. "That's it," Kotone cried, dodging a shockwave of Claus's sword and two lightning balls besides.

"Good! Keep it up!" Chiharu yelled encouragingly. "Amplify." Cyan started glowing brightly again in her chest.

"Rei, get out of there, but keep him occupied!" Chiharu shouted.

Rei nodded and shouted, "Blackest Night!" with black lances stabbing at Claus from behind. Claus's plate armor couldn't stop erasure, so he at least had to pay attention to her.

"What is this? Are you trying to make me dizzy? Carbon Monoxide is useless in the open air." Claus sneered.

"Just stand there and see!" Chiharu challenged him. "Shiori, one more time!"

"Fire!" Awesome flashed brilliantly.

"Amplify." Cyan pulsed in synchronization.

"Storm!" Shiori shouted, her fist punching a cone of flame into the sky.

"The same stupid tricks…" Claus sneered, lifting his claymore, which was glowing with blue-violet light, to block.

Then the entire atmosphere around him ignited as Shiori's spark hit Kotone's super-saturated, flammable gas.

"It's not over yet!" Chiharu shouted. "Deflection!" Cyan's light poured out of her, and instead of an explosion outward, the explosion warped back around into the target, right into the core where Claus stood.

Rei took the opportunity to erase the four remaining balls of lightning, and everyone held their breath.

Claus dropped from the sky and landed in a heap against the ground. But the blue-violet light kept flickering around him, trying to regain its strength. Everyone stared, disbelieving.

"Get down there! This is our chance! Finish him off!" Chiharu shouted, jumping straight off the building to heed her own advice. Shiori yelped. Whatever Chiharu's power suit was made of, if Shiori tried that, she would become a flesh puddle at the bottom. She turned to the roof's door and broke it open, running down the stairs.

"Magical miracle oxidization!" Kotone cast from high up in the sky, determined to get him out of his plate armor so her Sting Snipe could strike home. The man stood up, laughing, swinging his claymore back over his shoulder, even as his armor started rusting and falling off him in enormous chunks.

"Is that it? Is that the full power of darkness?" Claus roared up at them. "It ends here. Royal Verdict!" The sky split, and lightning struck all three girls within his sight. Chiharu slammed into the ground, landing sideways instead of on her feet like she'd intended. Rei flapped a few times, trying to break her speed, and fell into the pavement with a painful smack. But Kotone was too high up. She started to fall faster and faster toward the earth.

"Kotone!" Shiori screamed, willing more and more power into her boots. *I'm faster than anyone,* she reminded herself, and her footsteps started pounding holes into the ground. A cloud of dust shot out behind her as she sprinted under Kotone then jumped, snagging her out of the sky and into her arms.

"It is finished!" Claus yelled triumphantly, cutting a vicious arc with his claymore. The shockwave thundered toward her, and Shiori was still in midair, completely incapable of changing her trajectory. *I have to shield Kotone!* Shiori bent double around her, willing her armor to do something. The shockwave hit, and then it passed through her body and was gone again. It didn't feel like a thing. Had the attack been an illusion? No.

Shiori landed, her face bright. "Miyamoto!" And there he was, floating in the air, and Xanadu was gleaming from his scabbard, his sword glinting with its own silver light.

"Yo." Miyamoto managed a smile. "Having some trouble?" He fell a few meters in the sky before Xanadu's light picked up again and caught him. His face grimaced in pain, but he held his sword with the same determination as ever to protect the Choice Givers. That was all.

"Finally the ringleader emerges." Claus glared. "Indigo says you're the darkest—you and this girl. No matter. This sword will see you all dead."

"Not if I can help it." A voice came out of thin air. And then a spear sprouted out of Claus's chest, straight through his heart.

"I am Isao Oono." A boy phased into view, draped in a classical ninja look of pure black clothes that covered everything but his eyes. "And that"—Isao suddenly tore his spear back out of the man's chest, letting the Dead-Ender fall to the ground—"was for my friends."

Shiori woke up to her alarm clock. Rei's long hair was tickling her face. She wondered how long-haired people didn't choke to death in their sleep, with it constantly getting in their face like that. Short hair was definitely best. She was still lying in bed, trying to gather up Rei's hair and stick it behind her head instead of in front of it, when Rei opened her eyes. Shiori smiled, staring straight into her sister's eyes.

"Good morning, Rei," Shiori said.

"Good morning, Shiori." Rei gazed back at her for a full three seconds before blushing. She looked away and sat up, which caused a stuffed chicken to roll off the bed.

Shiori sat up and kicked their sheet down to the bottom of the bed"Does it hurt?" Shiori asked as Rei rolled out of bed.

"My old cuts and bruises? Or the new ones I got landing on the pavement? Or the lightning burns?" Rei asked.

"Anything," Shiori said.

Rei smiled, giving her a quiet thank-you with her eyes. "No. Nothing hurts. None of it hurts at all." Rei started undressing, and Shiori lunged to stick her pillow on top of Awesome. Even though Rei said that, her back and hip looked like a mess. Shiori winced just looking at it. *I have to get dressed and brush my teeth and eat breakfast.* Today was an important day for Project Heal Rei. It was finally the first day of the softball tournament. Rei had promised to cheer in the stands with Mother and Daddy. Shiori just *had* to win and make Rei proud. She couldn't do anything for Rei's body, but she could win a softball game for Rei's spirit.

Shiori Rin got out of bed and started dressing, her back turned to Rei Rin, both of them buttoning up their school uniform with practiced efficiency. It had been a full week since Claus Reinhardt's attack. Shiori had finally been able to relax in class and assume they wouldn't always be under assault again. Now it almost felt like those fights were a dream, and school life was the only reality.

Shiori noticed Rei standing in front of the full-length mirror, brushing all of the tangles out of her hair that sleeping had created. Then Rei tied a short pony-tail and a long ponytail on the same side, one stacked upon the other.

"That's so gorgeous!" Shiori said. "I wish I had long hair." Short hair was so awful. You couldn't do anything with it.

"This is an important day for my older sister," Rei Rin explained. "What will she do if she looks around to take heart from my cheering, and I don't look pretty in the stands?"

Shiori tackled her in a hug. "I'd just throw foul balls—four balls against every batter. They'd beat us by a thousand points."

Rei Rin grinned, her face clearly visible as a reflection in the mirror. "A good thing I thought ahead, then." It had never occurred to Shiori that Rei might have been thinking how to help *Shiori* today. It made her fill up with so much love that she didn't know where to put it. *If I'm constantly trying to make her happy, and she's constantly trying to make me happy, we're going to get so hopelessly confused. We won't know who is who anymore.*

"Awesome, you can come out now. You're unusually quiet this morning. I hope you're not plotting anything." Shiori gave him a suspicious scowl.

"Me? Plotting?" Awesome blinked.

"So you *are* plotting something. What is it this time? " Shiori asked.

"I'm just thinking about something," Awesome said.

"Thinking and plotting are the same thing," Shiori said.

"Aren't you going to eat breakfast? This is an important day. Stop dillydallying," Awesome said.

"For your information, bonding with my sister *or* my Wyrd is not a waste of time. It's my favorite time out of every day. But, yes, I am a little hungry. So you can keep your secret—for now." Shiori scooped Awesome up and tossed him into her school bag.

"Onyx," Rei called, and the dark Wyrd floated out of the closet and into her bag. Shiori and Rei stopped over at the bathroom, brushing their teeth together, and then they were finally ready to go down the stairs.

"Good morning, Daddy. Good morning, Mother." Shiori ran up to each of them and gave them a hug. She grabbed the bento left out on the counter for her and packed it into her school bag.

"Good morning, Shiori. Your father is getting out of work early just to watch your game, so you had better win." Mother waved the rice serving ladle at her warningly.

"Rei Rin, you look positively beautiful," Daddy marveled, setting down his cup of tea.

"Thanks, Daddy." Rei blushed, trying to sidle quietly into her chair and eat the breakfast already laid out in front of her. Both Shiori and Rei gave a proper "*Itadakimasu*" before starting their meal.

"If it's softball, we have to eat hot dogs and nachos. Do you think they'll be serving hot dogs and nachos?" Daddy asked pleasantly.

"Daddyyy," Shiori said. "This is middle school. Where did you think we were playing, Koshien?"

"Baseball requires certain food. Those are just the rules of life," Daddy insisted. "You agree with me, don't you, Rei?"

"Umm…yes, Daddy," Rei said, her chopsticks making quick work of her rice and eggs.

"I'll see what I can cook up." Mother sighed and rolled her eyes. "But *only* because we're going to be watching with Rei."

Rei couldn't help the smile that crept across her face, even though she kept her face pointed as far down as possible. Shiori felt a thrill in her heart. *Way to go, Mother! You got her that time.*

"I don't want to keep Kotone waiting." Shiori got up. "Thanks for breakfast. Let's go, Rei." Shiori kicked off her indoor slippers and sat down to put on her shoes.

"Coming." Rei placed her plate in the sink and then grabbed the bento Mother had packed for her and stuffed it into her school bag.

"Then, Mother, Daddy, we're off." Rei waved to them.

"Have a safe trip," Shiori's parents said. And the two of them were out the door.

They walked through the streets, the sun still low in the sky, with birds chirping everywhere and car motors constantly zooming by.

"Do you really get to eat nachos?" Shiori asked. "I wish I got to eat nachos in the stands."

"If you weren't pitching, none of us would get to eat nachos, including you," Rei said.

"Oh. I hadn't thought of that," Shiori confessed.

"Honestly. I *know* you're intelligent, Shiori. You say the most amazing things. So why are you so airheaded the rest of the day?" Rei asked.

"I have to recharge between wise sayings." Shiori stuck her tongue out at her younger sister.

Rei laughed. Then she spotted Kotone waiting for them up the hill and waved. "Good morning, Kotone!"

"Good morning, Rei!" Kotone waved back. She was in high spirits. "Good morning, Shiori."

"Good morning, Kotone," Shiori responded warmly. The two caught up to her quickly, and they all three started walking in line.

"Today's the game, right? I'll definitely be cheering you on," Kotone promised.

"Thanks, Kotone." *Please, all my ancestors and all the gods of this town, let me win this match. Everyone's relying on me.* "How are you?"

"Oh, that lightning bolt? Don't worry, don't worry. You caught me before I landed, right? It's not like it had the full force of a natural lightning strike. It just sort of numbed me and stung a bit." Kotone waved her hand dismissively. But Shiori had seen Rei shirtless. The lightning had looked every bit real to her. That fight had been close. It had been really, really close. *If everything hadn't gone right*— Shiori shook her head. Everything did go right, and that was that.

"I bundled Miyamoto straight back into his hospital bed and lectured him for thirty minutes about reopening stitches," Kotone said. "Really, the nerve. The man could barely walk. At least that Oono boy agreed to watch after Miyamoto until he was fully recovered again."

"He saved my life, Kotone," Shiori pointed out.

"But can't he save us without endangering his own life, just once?" Kotone complained. "I would like for him to *someday* emerge from that hospital."

Shiori smiled. If she didn't know any better, she would have thought Kotone was in love. But they were only thirteen years old. It was far too early to be thinking about boys. Plus, Miyamoto was like, fifty years old. *If I had to choose a guy, I'd choose Isao Oono. He looks super cool in that ninja outfit and talks like a total badass. Even so, Miyamoto was an impeccable gentleman. I need to thank him again. Well, he was going to stay in that hospital bed forever, since he reopened all his stitches. No matter how long I put the visit off, he'll still be there waiting.*

"Even though it feels like a long time, school only started two weeks ago. He's only mortal. Wounds like that don't just heal overnight," Shiori said.

"Has it really only been two weeks?" Kotone asked wistfully.

"Less than two weeks for me," Rei murmured.

"That's so weird," Kotone said. "Oh! Rei, that reminds me. I'm inviting you over to my house this weekend. Please say you'll come."

"Just me?" Rei sounded nervous.

"Oh, I don't need to ask Shiori or Chiharu. I'm just ordering them to come." Kotone smiled.

"Then, I'll come." Rei agreed. Shiori groaned.

"What? What's wrong?" Rei asked, her eyes widening.

"She's trapped you. And now that she's trapped you, she's trapped us too. It has to be *that*," Shiori said.

"What?" Rei asked worriedly.

"An anime sleepover!" Kotone announced triumphantly. "We start as soon as we can and watch anime all the way into the night. Then we crawl into our sleeping bags and talk about everything we saw until we fall asleep. It's like…like the happiest experience possible in life!"

"Anime is boring. No one acts believably at all. And the girls are always half naked," Shiori complained.

"Anime is the highest art form known to man. Everyone acts as they ought to, even if we fall below the excellence of their moral standards. And all the girls are full of personality and vigor. They are *not* just eye candy," Kotone answered back.

"Is anime really that good?" Rei seemed dubious.

"You just haven't seen the right series," Kotone said, grabbing Rei's hands. "Under my expert care, I promise you'll be happy."

"Then I'd love to come over and watch anime." Rei bowed.

"Let's at least make part of the day fun and eat crepes and ice cream for dinner," Shiori pled.

"I don't know how you stay thin," Kotone complained.

"Hello? Softball tournament starts today?" Shiori pointed out.

"Pshh. Like pitchers do any running." Kotone tossed her hair.

"I bat too, you know!" Shiori protested.

"If you simply must have crepes no matter what, we'll get crepes. But we're going right back to my place to watch more anime afterward," Kotone said.

"Fine, fine." A sleepover was a perfect addition to Project Heal Rei. Kotone was so sweet to think of this. *Everyone I know is so great.*

When Shiori arrived at the school gates, they told each other, "See you again!" and each split off for their own classroom. They'd all meet up at the roof for lunch. *Knowing Mother, she filled my bento with meat from top to bottom, to give me energy for the game.* Shiori couldn't wait to open it and see. Kotone was right. It was a wonder she wasn't a blimp.

Chiharu signaled a time out to the umpire and walked up to the mound. "What's wrong? Those two balls weren't nearly close enough to force her to swing." The game had remained tied, 2-2, all the way to the ninth inning. But Shiori's pitching was getting erratic, and Shifuto Gakuen had a runner on second and first base with only one out. They absolutely couldn't let Shifuto get to third base with two outs left, because then a fly ball could give a free run to the man on third base with an out to spare. Shiori had to strike this person out. But it was three balls and no strikes so far.

"I'm just…so tired." Shiori wiped her forehead. "What is this now, one hundred and thirty pitches?" Shiori asked.

"Stuff and nonsense. You've thrown eighty pitches, tops," Chiharu lied.

"Oh…well, okay then." Shiori fiddled around with her cap.

"This batter doesn't have perfect form. If you throw to the inside, she'll strike. Three pitches, Shiori. That's all I need from you. Three pitches to the inside."

"But if I throw them all to the inside, she'll figure the pattern out and hit," Shiori complained.

"Not if she's so stressed out about winning a 2-2 tie game for her team that no matter how hard she tries, she lets her bad habits take over," Chiharu said. "Of course, there's no way *you're* stressed out about winning a 2-2 tie game and losing control of your pitches. I know you better than that."

"Of course. Hehe. Of course I wouldn't do that." Shiori gave her a look of wide-eyed innocence.

"Three pitches to the inside. Let's send these girls home in tears," Chiharu said. Then she held out her left, ungloved hand. Shiori nodded and slapped her a hard high five. All the fire was back in her eyes. *That's my Shiori.*

Shiori gave a hawk-eyed look at her batter then wound up and pitched. *Thwunk.*

"Strike!" the umpire called. The batter had cringed backward when she saw the fastball heading near her. Chiharu smiled and tossed the ball back to her best friend. That pitch had been as fast as the first inning.

"Go, go, Shi-or-i! Go, go, Shi-or-i!" one half of the stands started chanting.

"Hey, pitcher! No control! Hey, pitcher! No control!" The other half started yelling back.

Shiori wound up and slashed her arm sideways for a slider. *Thwunk.*

"Strike!" the umpire called. Their school's side erupted in cheers. Chiharu shook her head and tossed the ball back. *I ask for three nice, simple fastballs to the inside, so she does a special pitch that just barely enters the strike zone like some sort of pro.* It was enough to give you gray hairs.

Shiori caught the ball and paced a few steps back and forth, giving her shoulder every second of rest she could. Then she got into her stance, wound up, and pitched again. It was a beautiful fastball to the inside. The batter swung well over the ball. *Thwunk.*

"Strike three! You're out!" the umpire called.

The next batter took up position, holding the bat farther forward so she could swing it faster and connect with the center of the bat to inside pitches. *Like I'd let you.* Chiharu positioned her glove to the outermost corner of the plate. This Shiori could stay within the strike zone. Her eyes were on fire.

Shiori wound up and pitched, and the batter caught it with the edge of her bat, completely surprised. Chiharu walked underneath the ball and waited for it to come down, catching it snugly into her glove and showing the umpire.

"You're out! Three outs! Switch sides!" The umpire signaled dramatically.

Shiori jumped up and down, waving up at Rei, Kotone, and her parents, who were all jumping up and down and hugging each other. The entire crowd was chanting her name. Chiharu just smiled and started taking off her catching equipment. As it so happened, it was also Shiori's turn at bat. Shiori was last in the batting order, and Chiharu was first, which meant the two of them would have the chance to seal the game. *Shiori's thrown one hundred and forty-five pitches now. I can't let this game stay a tie. If it goes to extra innings, it might injure her permanently.*

Shiori rushed over to put on her batting helmet. "I'll get on base, Chiharu, so send me home!" Shiori ordered. She refused to even take a sip of water and just went out to the batting area, practicing her swings.

Chiharu didn't mind the irresponsibly optimistic order. She had planned to do so already. She just wanted the bat in her own hands already and watched Shiori with impatience.

After two balls, Shiori tried her first swing and missed. Then there was a third ball. Then a foul ball, which counted as a strike. A full count. The entire crowd went silent in agonized anticipation. Chiharu bit her lip from the tension. *If you strike out, Shiori, I'm going to kill you.*

"Ball four! Walk!" Shiori sighed and dropped her bat. No doubt she had wanted to at least get a hit in sometime during the game. But it didn't matter. Only results mattered. Shiori was on first base. The other pitcher was tired too. That's why she had thrown four balls.

Chiharu stepped up to the plate, wondering how to win the game. Only a home run could reasonably win it from here. *Should I bunt, and at least get Shiori to second? But who can I trust to get her home if not me?* No one had shown any ability to hit this girl's pitches consistently.

Chiharu simply watched the first ball go by, trying to feel the strength of her opponent out. *Could I have hit that for a home run? No way. It had still been too fast and too low.* The Shifuto pitcher wound up again, and halfway through her release, Shiori started running. Chiharu stood still and watched as the changeup slowly passed her by. *Shiori, you genius. You read the other pitcher's stance and decided to steal. That is a terrifying skill.*

The opposing catcher snagged the ball out of the air, stood up, and threw as hard as she could. But Shiori was already sliding—without trying to protect her pitching hand at all!—and the field referee quickly made the call. "Safe! Safe!"

"Great, Shiori!" Kotone yelled, and the crowd started applauding again. Of course, her fool stunt had meant Chiharu just got another strike. Next time, she'd have to bet everything on a swing. Unless…Chiharu desperately went through the calculations.

How fast was Shiori? I can't reliably hit this pitcher. So what if I don't try to hit? What if I only try for a fly ball? Sure, I'll be out. But the ball will be so far into the outfield that maybe…just maybe…

The pitcher wound up and threw. The pitch wasn't easy at all. Chiharu did everything she could to just get under it and give the ball lift. Chiharu didn't even bother to start running. It was an out. A two-year-old could catch that ball. She just yelled out to Shiori.

"You can do it, Shiori! Take us home!" Shiori nodded back at her with a grim look as she waited on the plate for the ball to be caught. It looked like she was taking energy from all of her muscles and slowly eating it, absorbing it into her mind, and passing it down to her legs.

"Out!" the umpire called. The outfield had fielded it. And then the race was on. Shiori bolted for third. Everyone in the benches started yelling at her, screaming for her to run faster. The outfielder threw it to the infielder. The ball hung in the air as Shiori rounded third base and ran for home. She never looked back to see where the ball was. She just leaned into the air and pumped her arms like daggers directly in front of her body. The ball reached the infield, and the girl turned expertly and launched it for home. No one could outrun a ball. The ball was going to get there first.

Shiori dived headfirst for the plate, angling as far away from the Shifuto catcher as possible, so only her hand was within reach of the scoring plate and her body as far away from being tagged as possible. The catcher caught the ball, turned, and dived for Shiori. The two collided into a heap of dust.

"*Safe!* Safe! Game over! Reika Gakuen wins!" the umpire called.

Shiori screamed and jumped into Chiharu's arms. Chiharu fell over from the weight, hugging her and pelting her on the back, the shoulder, anywhere her punches could land.

"We did it! We won! We won!" Shiori kept repeating. And then the whole team was piling on top of Shiori and Chiharu. They were so heavy, she couldn't breathe. It was softball. It was the stuff of life.

Chapter 11

"Neh, Awesome," Shiori said, holding her knees upright with her arms and resting her chin on top. They were sitting at the park outside the library, on standby. If all went well today, no one would have to fight. The Dead-Ender had seemed eager to argue her case to anyone who would sit and listen, and so in a gesture of good will, they had let Chiharu argue the case out peacefully one-on-one. Hopefully she would have time to call them and ask for help before fighting broke out. They were in the same park, and it wouldn't take long to reinforce her friend. But it was important to repay the stranger's trust with trust. Good people didn't use other people's goodness against them. Everything had a price. Saving someone without a fight meant risking Chiharu alone with her opponent. They had all agreed it was a price worth paying.

"What is it, Shiori?" Awesome replied.

"When Cyan scries Chiharu, he sees a field of blooming flowers. When Magnolia scries Kotone, she sees a waterfall that keeps splitting and falling down a boundless cliff. But you've never told me what you see when you scry me," Shiori said.

"True," Awesome said.

That stubborn Wyrd would *make me beg.*

"What do you see when you scry me, Awesome?" Shiori asked.

"A web of light," Awesome said. "The web is vaster than I can see. Along the web, pulses of light shoot from nexus to nexus along endless filaments. Sometimes the light cascades in a wave all in one direction. Sometimes the pulses all travel freely, all on their solitary missions, each in their own direction. But the flow of light never repeats, and it never goes out."

"Is it beautiful?" Shiori asked.

"More beautiful than you could ever dream," Awesome replied.

Shiori smiled. "I'm glad, you know."

"Hmm?" Awesome asked.

"That it was you," Shiori said.

"I know," Awesome said. The two sat quietly for a while.

"I chose you before we even met," Awesome confessed.

"I know," Shiori answered just as simply.

"Shiori, now's as good a time as any," Awesome said.

"To tell me your plot?" Shiori asked.

"To tell you my plan." Awesome blinked sternly. "You should realize by now how hopeless this fight is. The dark Wyrds will keep coming. Even if they didn't, the sheer vast mass of Dead-Enders on this world will crush out the light of good souls, sooner or later. I thought our coming here would help, but…we've probably just made it worse. Wyrds probably made Earth's fate all the more sealed."

"Listen to you, talking about fate to a Choice Giver," Shiori chided.

"Probable course, then." Awesome blinked. "The point stands. Every time I scry, there are fewer Choice

Givers. Dead-Enders aren't only targeting us. Maybe someday it will just be us—just us against all the evil of two combined worlds. Maybe someday Kotone will die in battle, or Chiharu. Maybe someday it will just be you and me, Shiori. You and me against all the darkness in every living soul."

Tears emerged unbidden in the corners of Shiori's eyes. "I don't want that."

"What if there were a way to escape all this? What if we could take everyone and everything we care about, and journey to another world? The dark Wyrds can't hurt us if they can't find anyone who will contract with them. The Dead-Enders can't chase us beyond space and time to a world ruled by Choice Givers, who we know won't go wrong. A population of followers or emulators, who would never turn on their shepherds. How wonderful would that world be? Most of all, it's somewhere safe for all of us. Kotone and Magnolia. Chiharu and Cyan. You and me. I won't have to watch the people I love die. I won't have to watch your web of light go out," Awesome said.

Shiori shook her head, tears falling down her cheeks. "Awesome, you've studied our religions. So tell me, did you ever read the parable of the lost sheep?

"I…may have," Awesome admitted.

"Did you ever read the psalm of David?" Shiori pursued, summoning up the memorized lines Daddy had once recited to her when she had had a particularly bad fever at age five.

"I read it," Awesome said.

"Then you know why I have to stay and fight," Shiori said.

Awesome flashed a deep red again and again. "I… guess I did know… I just didn't want to admit that I knew."

"That's why you're such a child." Shiori sniffed, wiping at her eyes.

"I'm thousands of years old," Awesome complained.

"It doesn't matter. All Wyrds are spoiled children. Your lives are too easy. That's why you say things like, 'Let's run away and abandon the weak and the lost to their fate' the moment things gets tough. And that's why Onyx says things like, 'Let's destroy other worlds because it just isn't fair.' Wyrds or humans, it doesn't matter, we only mature by building relationships and overcoming obstacles. Until now, Wyrds have never faced a difficult obstacle. Judging by you and Magnolia, Wyrds never get past first base either. If no one dies, there's never any urgency to live. And so none of you grew up at all," Shiori lectured.

"Choice Givers are insufferably impossible to win arguments with." Awesome glowed angrily.

Shiori smiled. "Then I pity whoever's trying to argue things out fair and square with Chiharu."

"Before we begin, I need to ask some questions." Chiharu poured Phyllis Landstrum some tea. Cyan was magically translating for her. The two of them sat together at a picnic table. Phyllis was newly out of college, eager to spread her message to the world about how everything should change. She would have looked young, except for the ridiculously serious-looking thirteen-year-old child she was facing across the table. Neither of their ages mattered. One was a genius Choice Giver. The other was one of the most ambitious, competent dark-Wyrd-contracted Dead-Enders in the world. Those were qualifications enough for either side to demand a fair hearing.

"Go ahead." Phyllis gestured politely.

"Do you know what being a Choice Giver means?" Chiharu asked.

"It means giving the world infinite possibilities," Phyllis said.

"Okay. And do you know what a Dead-Ender is?" Chiharu asked.

"It means ending all possibilities, flatlining into stagnation or extinction," Phyllis answered.

"Your Wyrd told you this?" Chiharu blinked in surprise.

"Sunglow chose me because we both like being honest and upfront. Our motto is: 'Fair and square.'" Phyllis smiled warmly at her floating companion.

"In that case, do you know I'm a Choice Giver and you're a Dead-Ender?" Chiharu asked.

"Yes," Phyllis said.

"That's…unconventional. And you're okay with this?" Chiharu asked.

"Have you ever really thought about the meaning behind those terms?" Phyllis countered.

"I've certainly tried," Chiharu responded.

"Then did you ever consider that 'infinite possibilities' could just be another term for chaos?" Phyllis asked.

"I—no." Chiharu frowned.

"How about Dead-Enders then? Did it ever occur to you that perfection is a flat line? Any deviation from perfection, up or down, left or right, any change from perfection in any way, would just make the world worse. Therefore, perfect things are immutable. If the world ever reached perfection, it would stop changing. A Dead-Ender, then, is someone who wants to perfect the world. Choice Givers are those who want to throw it back into chaos. So long as Choice Givers live, we can never reach perfection. You are a destabilizing force—you foil everyone's hopes and dreams. Your very existence radiates chaos. That's why I had to come here and, hopefully, convince you to change your ways. I know Choice Givers can become Dead-Enders whenever they please. I want all of you children to join me. My cause is just. My path is a straight, flat line to utopia," Phyllis explained.

"Well." Chiharu took a sip of her tea to gather time to think. "And if we don't join?"

"We'll fight it out, fair and square." Phyllis shrugged.

"So what if I convince you to give up on being a Dead-Ender?" Chiharu asked.

"Fair is fair. We'll both try to convert each other, here and now. I'll listen to your arguments if you listen to mine," Phyllis said.

In twenty minutes it was all over.

"It's my complete defeat." Phyllis stood up, bowing ruefully. "I'm going home. I'll tell my college friends. Love, beauty, truth, *and* a citizen's dividend—Communism doesn't go far enough. This time, I'll redistribute them all."

"Call me or write me any time," Chiharu Sakai said encouragingly, holding out her hand.

"I will." Phyllis Landstrum shook it.

It had been a good fight.

Like usual, Isao Oono was with Masanori during visiting hours. The first few times Isao had visited, they had caught up on all of their recent fights. Isao had mocked Masanori for losing to a tree man, and Masanori had praised Isao for another successful run-in with North Korea. But the conversation had quickly turned to their lost friends. Isao talked about all the conversations they had had together, even the stupid ones that really hadn't meant anything. They traded inside jokes Masanori, Isao, Nao, Hisoka, and Ryo had shared. A lot of conversations started with, "Do you remember when…?"

Masanori always remembered when. That was a solace. Sometimes Isao thought he might be a little morbid company and would try to turn the conversation away from his memories. But he couldn't. Somehow or other, he always found himself asking, "Do you remember when we first met Nao? She was singing on a sidewalk, with just her acoustic guitar and a tin can for tips. I don't think she even had a place to sleep until we invited her back to base…"

And a few minutes later, he was suddenly starting a new story. "Do you remember when Ryo asked Nao to be the heroine's voice actor for his series? She refused, saying she was a singer. Then Ryo called her stupid and elitist. She stormed out of the place, and he chased her down. They were yelling at each for hours, but at the end, they were a couple, and she was playing the voice of his heroine's role. I wonder what Ryo said to her. I mean, that's pretty sly, don't you think? Nao was furious with him, storming out of the place, and in the next two hours, he had a girlfriend, and his heroine's voice actor…" Isao laughed, but his eyes wanted to cry.

Masanori laughed with him, wishing he had Ryo's luck with girls. Then he would tell about Hisoka with his Captain Japan shield, white with a red sun in the middle, that could break through or block anything, and how only Hisoka could have imagined both his strongest weapon and strongest armor into a single object. Hisoka had always been frustrated with Masanori and Isao.

"Why was your magic so creative? I can't fight you min-max exploiters. One cuts off the universe around me and sends me into the void. How do I block that? And Isao, what the hell, he walks up and stabs me whenever he wants, and I'm dead before I know I'm in a fight. It makes my shield look ridiculous."

They promised him his shield looked great, even though it did look ridiculous. They both started laughing over that. Hisoka had liked going out in his costume and fighting crime. Isao kept wondering if any of them blamed him for being gone. He kept wondering if Ryo, Hisoka, Nao, and he together could have defeated Claus.

"No, you would have died with them," Masanori answered.

"I could've gotten a hit," Isao stubbornly insisted.

"With Indigo's barrier and his full plate still on? And with him still flying?"

"With flash move…" Isao suggested.

"What's stronger? Flash move or firestorm into carbon monoxide gas, deflected back into an implosion? And Claus *survived* that. You know full well you exploited an opening that no one but those girls could have created for you," Masanori said.

"I could have tried," Isao insisted.

"Yes, you could have tried and died. And then Claus would have come here and killed all of us too, and that would be the end—the end of everything. Isao, I thank the spirits you were in North Korea. It was divine providence that kept you out of harm's way. If you feel guilty for saving the world, I will punch you in the face," Masanori said.

"Go ahead and try, old man. I was always quicker than you." Isao grinned.

"Short spears stab faster than katana, but they can't parry." Masanori sneered.

"Like I've ever had to parry someone." Isao laughed, but it was not about his spear. It was about his realization that Masanori was right, and Isao had been exactly where the gods wanted him to be and where the gods had directed him to be. The guilt would go away; he had avenged his friends, he had protected the light of the world, and that was surely enough. But the loneliness wouldn't stop. He missed them so much. It's like he could see them all here again, right beside him, whenever he closed his eyes.

They were alive just a week ago. Just one week ago, they had all been real, not figments of my imagination. They were warm, tangible, living, breathing friends who would laugh with him, spar with him, and eat instant ramen with him in front of the TV. They were people he could share anything with and never feel afraid. Now it was just down to Masanori. Masanori and Isao were the only two people who really knew these people ever existed. They were the last two carriers of these people's existence left in the world. Isao wouldn't let the Dead-Enders take Miyamoto in his injured state. The assassinations would just have to wait. Masanori was his only remaining friend.

That was when Isao's cell phone rang, which was strange, because the only person who should know his number anymore was Masanori. He answered it, expecting some stupid, computerized advertisement.

"Hello?" Isao said.

"Hello, Oono? This is Kotone Nakano speaking. Um…you may not know me." She sounded nervous.

"Sorry, I don't. But you seem to know me," Oono replied.

"Well, see, when you stabbed Reinhardt, Shiori overheard you talking like…well….like Inigo Montoya from *The Princess Bride*…and you happened to mention your name," Nakano confessed.

"Oh! I'm sorry. You must be one of the girls." Isao Oono's voice became much more friendly.

"Right. I'm the one who rusted the armor away. I like to think it helped," Nakano said nervously.

"It did. I couldn't believe my good luck when it happened. There's no telling how strong the strongest Dead-Ender's strongest armor was. My spear probably would have just smushed against it without you." Isao thanked her.

"Thank you. That… I'm glad. It's so hard keeping up with Chiharu and Shiori. I'm always worried…that I'm second tier or something…" Nakano trailed off.

"From what I saw, you were the most valuable player of that fight. You helped the attack while dodging lightning and sword slashes, keeping his eyes off the true threats the entire fight. That's not second tier, Nakano. If anyone's second tier, it's me. I just sneaked up on a guy from behind and stabbed him. I can't even fly."

"You just sneaked up and stabbed him? We were at our wits end trying to hurt him. He always had time to block or dodge our attacks, but you finished him in seconds. That's second tier?" Nakano laughed. Isao smiled to himself. Okay, so maybe he had done his part during that fight too.

"So what's this call about?" Isao asked.

"Right, well, we're having a party at my house this weekend. And I thought, 'Maybe Oono would like to come.' And then I thought you simply *had* to come because you didn't give any of us a chance to thank you for that night. I was unconscious at the time, so I can't even put a face to your voice," Nakano said.

"Well technically no one's seen my face because I was in a ninja veil," Isao corrected her.

"All the more reason for you to come over. I…I don't normally call up strange boys. Please say yes," Nakano said.

"Before then, how did you get this number?" Isao asked.

"Mr. Miyamoto told me, of course," Nakano answered. Isao glared at the man sitting in bed who held up his hands innocently.

"Was this his plan, some sort of 'Let's cheer up Isao' party?" Isao asked her.

"No, we just wanted your number so you could keep in touch. All for one and one for all, you know?" Nakano asked.

"Ah…I guess that is a good idea," Isao admitted.

"This party is my plan. Inviting you was all my plan too. So if you say no, you're rejecting a thirteen-year-old girl who will cry and cry and cry because the first time she asked for a date with a boy, she was turned down," Nakano said.

"So now this is a date?" Isao's eyebrows went up.

"It is if you want it to be." Nakano laughed. "It's also a sleepover party with friends if you want it to be. Or if you just want it to be some sort of formal tea ceremony where we all just glare at each other and walk in slow motion, we can do that too. We all want to thank you. We owe you some gesture, so…"

"I'll come. But it will only be a date if you're pretty." Isao agreed.

"Then it's a date," Nakano replied confidently. "And be sure to tell Mr. Miyamoto that."

"Why?" Isao asked, confused.

"Just be sure to tell him," Nakano insisted.

"Okay…" Isao agreed.

"My address is one four seven three Iza Street. Look up directions on Google. We start at twelve noon this Sunday. Don't stand me up," Nakano ordered.

Isao finished writing down her address. "Got it. See you then." "See you then." Nakano agreed happily and ended the call.

"What was that?" Miyamoto asked.

"I'm going on a date with Kotone," Isao said bemusedly. "She told me to tell you."

Miyamoto beamed happily. "Clever girl."

"Why? What's this about?" Isao asked suspiciously.

"Call it a bet—a bet between the two of us," Miyamoto said.

"Who's winning?" Isao asked.

"I don't know." Miyamoto shrugged it off casually.

Chapter 12

Mastermind was a man who would soon become a Wyrd. Of course, he had no intention of turning himself into one of those silly floating gems that had to follow a human's orders. No, he was going to become a *real* Wyrd, the ones the Wyrd council talked about and the ones who spanned solar systems, traveled between galaxies, fed off the very atmosphere, lived for eons, and had at their fingertips all the power and all the knowledge of the universe. The moment his Wyrd, Lust, had told him about the plane he had come from, Mastermind had known what he wanted most in life: to shed his human form and transcend and to become a higher order being that was akin to a god. The Wyrds complained that their magic would run out in a "mere" two hundred years. And yet, that was already over a hundred years of additional lifespan, all in perfect health. A place without annoying human needs like the digestive tract. Without having to work to earn your food. Without worrying about what temperature it was. Without insects. Without disease. Without everything that was disgusting and frustrating about this world. Up there, somewhere in the higher dimensions, was Mastermind's destiny.

The only problem was that Wyrds had discovered no way to fold *up*. They considered the act impossible. But what did Wyrds know? There must be a way. And that was why the magic that he had manifested was centered entirely on teleportation. He had attempted to immediately teleport to the etheric plane, but it had failed. Then he had built a machine to amplify his magic and tried it again. That, too, had failed. He added to the machine; he improved it further and further. He tried again and again, and always it had failed. That was when he had heard about the Choice Giver Masanori Miyamoto. He was a thorn in the council's side. He was always showing up and dispatching their foot soldiers. He was always saving other Choice Givers at the last moment. And there was one other thing they said about the man: He was a master of folding.

Mastermind had instantly scrapped his old designs and restarted with new ones. The first trick was to find someone with compulsion magic. Her name was Tien Feng. He had no illusions of trying to convince Miyamoto to help cast the teleportation spell. The machine required a good deal of energy to fold a human up into the form of a Wyrd. To be precise, once the reaction started, it would suck up all the energy of the universe in a microsecond. But who cared, if it could get Mastermind up there? What use did he have for this lowly plane, now that he knew there was another better one waiting out there? Convincing Miyamoto wouldn't be a problem. Whoever Tien Feng compelled would do whatever she said, so long as she lived. To get her on board, Mastermind had to share his plan, his dream of becoming a Wyrd, with her. The machine might support the transcendence of them both—who knew? Mastermind had programmed the computer to provide him all the energy necessary, and her whatever was left. He could be magnanimous, so long as it didn't interfere with his dream.

The next step had been when he met Robo. He didn't know Robo's name and had just started calling him that for convenience. He didn't even know if Robo was really a robot. What he did know was that Robo would follow his orders unquestioningly and would never betray his trust. This was of vital importance, because Robo had the one magic technique Mastermind needed to complete his plan.

Miyamoto was being protected by an enormous gathering of Choice Givers—more than Mastermind had any hope of defeating alone. The council had its own plan on how to deal with this gathering of Choice Givers. After Reinhardt's failure, they had given up on direct confrontation. The Indigo-Reinhardt pair, after all, had been their trump card. Losing him had shaken the council deeply. Now they talked of a much more patient plan to keep recruiting more Wyrds from the etheric plane and collect enough Dead-Enders that there was no possibility of defeat—a hundred magically contracted Dead-Enders or a thousand. But those kinds of numbers might be years in the making. So far, Mastermind had only been given an army of six. Plus, despite what the Wyrd council thought, Mastermind had no intention of leading such a fight. A fight like that might kill Miyamoto. And if Miyamoto died, Mastermind's folding machine wouldn't work. He would be stuck in this fleshy form forever.

No, Mastermind didn't want an army that could go kill the gathering of Choice Givers that was guarding

Miyamoto. What he wanted was a quick, surgical strike. He wanted to get in, compel Miyamoto, and get back to his machine where he could begin the magic ritual. If only those other Choice Givers ever dropped their guard! Their Wyrds constantly scryed for both each other's location and the location of any Dead-Enders who might approach them. Mastermind had been at this maddening impasse ever since he had heard of the samurai. Robo was the breaker of this impasse.

Robo had a simple technique; he could create a large block around a person. No magic or physical objects could get out of, or into, the block. You could talk to people in the box, and air could go in and out, but anything else was stopped cold. It was a useless technique in terms of combat. To make matters worse, the box lasted a day but could only be used once a week. But it was the spell Mastermind needed. It was a way to capture Miyamoto without harming him, and it was a way of escaping Miyamoto's friends without being harmed. The fact that Robo's magic was practically made-to-order was as suspicious as the thing's complete loyalty. But Mastermind didn't care how or why this convenient tool had been given to him. All he cared about was that it worked.

At last, with Robo, Tien Feng, Miyamoto, his lab machine, the physical energy of the universe, and Mastermind's teleportation magic, he would become a Wyrd. It had been a long trip, but transcendence was worth it. He couldn't wait to witness the world of the Wyrds firsthand.

Kotone had worked with Mama for over an hour to pick out the perfect outfit for her date with Isao. She could call him by his first name now, since they were going on a date, even if that date meant watching anime together with all of her friends. It was the feelings that counted. Halfway or so through her conversation with Isao, she had realized he wasn't just a cool guy. He was also a nice guy. At that point, she had begged him for a date.

After Miyamoto had rejected her, she had thought about why. She already knew she was too young; that's why she had asked him to wait for her. But he had rejected that idea too, which meant it wasn't just her age that was the matter. It was something she was supposed to gain in-between now and age eighteen. In short, it was experience. How could she talk about long-term love when she had never been in love? How did she know Miyamoto was the right man for her when she hadn't even met any others? How did she know she could handle a real relationship without ever being in one? How did she know she'd still like men like Miyamoto if she'd gone through a lot of life-transforming experiences between now and then? Without experience, whether she was eighteen or not, Miyamoto would still reject her, and it was for good reason. Without answering his doubts about whether he was really her top choice, and not just a crush by a naïve girl, about whether she could truly love someone, and not just think she did, she would be just as useless at eighteen as she was now at thirteen.

The problem was, Miyamoto was a Choice Giver, as was she. After being used to having so many Choice

Givers in her life, she really didn't want to trade down to ordinary mortals. She knew how good these people were. They were the best people on Earth. So a question like "How do you know I'm the right boy for you?" was very difficult to answer unless, of course, she could date another Choice Giver. Isao Oono was the perfect selection.

This didn't mean she intended to shortchange Isao. If they fell in love, if they got along perfectly, if they formed a lot of happy memories together, if they learned everything a couple needed to learn, then that was fine too. But Kotone had made a bet. She was making a bet that at eighteen, she would still want to be with Miyamoto. And she was making a bet that at eighteen, Miyamoto would for the first time want to be with her. It was just a wild girl's fancy, but there it was. When Kotone had seen the opportunity to inform Miyamoto of how admirably she was fulfilling his expectations, of how well she was taking his rejection, of how dutifully she was trying to overcome his objections, she had taken it in a flash. She was sure Miyamoto had gotten the message.

Kotone had finally settled on a tie-dye T-shirt and a black skirt. She thought black was suited to a date with Isao. She had kept her hair loose, except for a heart-decorated hair clip to keep her bangs out of her eyes. After a long check in the mirror, she smiled and decided she would definitely pass his "pretty" test. She was anxious for the clock to reach noon, and she was already ebullient though nothing had happened yet.

She had gone over her entire anime collection, trying to find something suitable for Rei Rin. It couldn't be anything sad, not with Project Heal Rei still underway. It couldn't be about fighting, not when they were all girls and had plenty of fighting in their own lives. Romance was unsuitable, since they were too young to really relate to it. Her first date with a boy who would probably journey all over the world after this and see her maybe once a month did not qualify as "able to relate to romance." And even this thin reed she could lay claim to was no use for Rei.

The anime, of course, had to be one of the best ever made. That left *K-On!* and *Working!!* Kotone decided *K-On!* appealed more to men than women, and the selection was finally done. They would watch *Working!!* from start to finish in an anime sleepover marathon. And Rei would laugh out loud from beginning to end, to the point that all the sad things in her life were completely forgotten, and all she could remember was the here and now. Once Rei had tasted the forbidden fruit, she could always show her *K-On!* next. And from there, the world. Each and every time, pulling her away from her painful past and toward a totally different, totally pristine mental plane where all anime fans dwelled. It was heaven on Earth—a place they could all retreat to, no matter how bad the real world became. Rei, of all people, should appreciate that most of all.

When the doorbell rang, Kotone's heart jumped. She didn't know who at the door would make her more nervous, Isao or Rei. But she knew she would be a proper host to them both, and spread the warmth to both their troubled hearts, because that's what she had decided it meant to be a Choice Giver.

Rei Rin took off her outdoor shoes and put on the indoor slippers Kotone's family had provided for them, formally stating, "Sorry to intrude." Kotone hugged her immediately then took her hand and started pulling her toward the television in the living room.

"This makes everyone," Kotone said, surveying her friends like a particularly good day's catch of fish in her net.

"And now, introductions. Everyone, this is Isao Oono. He's a fifteen-year-old Choice Giver, a good friend of Miyamoto's, and an assassin of evil dictators all across the world. His magic is invisibility, and his Wyrd is Black. Oh, and as of ascertaining that I was pretty upon my opening the door, Isao also became my boyfriend." Kotone smiled proudly.

Everyone clapped, and the girls all bowed and said, "Pleased to meet you. We'll be in your care from here on."

"Now that we're all here, I wanted to tell Isao something important. It turns out that when Chiharu and I were unconscious, Miyamoto was weak as a newborn babe, Rei was a complete mess of injuries, and Shiori was the only one left standing, Isao Oono gave Claus the finishing blow. Maybe Shiori could have somehow handled it from there. I don't know. But I, for one, would like to formally thank Isao for coming to our rescue. Isao Oono, thank you for rescuing me and my friends."

Kotone bowed deeply. The others were quick to bow and thank him too. He looked a little embarrassed.

"Now, Isao, pay attention, because these are your new friends. The short girl with the long hair is Rei Rin, a reformed Dead-Ender. She wields negative energy, and her Wyrd is Onyx. It's the same color as yours, only a much prettier name." Kotone teased him. "Be nice to Rei, or I'll never forgive you."

"Next to her is Shiori Rin, her older twin sister. Never mind that they look nothing alike. Shiori Rin is Rei Rin's older twin sister. That's our story, and we're sticking to it." Kotone glared at Isao as though he had tried to raise an objection. "Shiori has short hair and likes to eat too much."

"Hey!" Shiori protested, covering her stomach protectively with her hands so no one looked.

Kotone laughed. "But she's also the best friend, best sister, best fighter, and best counselor in the world. I love her. Anywhere she goes, the room brightens up. Whenever she leaves, she takes a part of my heart and my happiness with her. Walking to school with Shiori and Rei is the happiest part of my day." Kotone went on, like usual, refusing to be embarrassed, projecting the confidence that let whatever she was doing be what was normal.

"Shiori wields fire magic and puns. Shiori was a firebug even before she got her Wyrd. You should have seen her when we went camping." Kotone smiled. "But now she's much worse. She solves all the problems of the world by burning them up."

"I do not!" Shiori blushed fiercely.

"I think Shiori likes you, Isao, so if you want to dump me for her, I'll understand. But do it quickly or you'll hurt my feelings, because I have no intention of dumping you," Kotone said.

"Enough about me, Kotone!" Shiori said.

"Shiori's our brightest Choice Giver. She probably gave us our sparks too." Kotone ignored Shiori's wishes. "She's so bright, it ended up taking three of us just to carry the load. Her Wyrd is Awesome. He's the best scryer among all the Wyrds and was the first to discover this world. He discovered it by finding Shiori. The contact was so shocking that Shiori fell down during softball practice, and Awesome refused to contract with anyone but her. " Kotone grinned.

"Sitting over there with the shoulder-length hair— don't flinch away from me, Chiharu. My introductions have been entirely complimentary, unless there's some shameful secret eating away at you that you don't want me to expose?" When Chiharu said nothing, Kotone resumed.

"As I was saying, sitting over there is Chiharu Sakai. She's our smartest Choice Giver. Her magic is redirecting vectors. Her Wyrd is Cyan, who is a perfect fit, because they're both unflappable elitists who always watch the world as though it's only on TV and never actually affects them personally. Cyan's already begged Chiharu to marry him," Kotone continued.

Cyan spluttered, "Lies, all lies!"

But Kotone went on like she hadn't heard. "From her aerie perch, Chiharu commonly descends to give us guidance on schoolwork, philosophy, how to win battles, or how to organize our days off together. I would be helpless without Chiharu, concerning everything. I love her so much." Kotone smiled warmly at her. She then turned to face Isao Oono directly and took a deep breath, looking into his eyes.

"I'm your last friend that needs introducing and hopefully your first girlfriend, Isao. My name is Kotone Nakano. I'm a Choice Giver, just like these two, but I don't do it by acting on instinct, like Shiori, or giving advice, like Chiharu. All I do is follow the warmth. I think that there's love and kindness everywhere, if we just open our hearts to it. And I think that if we weren't so afraid, we could love others freely and earn their love in turn. That is why I can bare my heart to you like this, right off the bat. I trust everyone up until the very moment they betray me, so please don't cheat on me. I'll never suspect it, I'll have no mental defenses against it, and it will tear me apart." Kotone gave Isao a pitiful look.

"My magic is a great reflection of my character. I am a poisonous, acidic, plague-bearing bug master. My Wyrd is Magnolia, who is great at explaining things and gets along well with everyone. Everyone says I'm beautiful, but Magnolia sees into my heart, and she says they don't have the first idea how beautiful I really am. I still like it when people compliment my looks though, so feel free to praise me as often as you like." Kotone smiled hopefully.

"We know you lost all of your friends in just the last few days. But we're here for you, now. We can't be your old friends, but we could be completely new ones who love you just as much, if you let us. I can't say I've suffered any great sorrows, though I can tell you, lightning *really* hurts. But just imagining how I would feel if I lost all my friends, it hurts enough to make me cry. So, I think I can understand you, if only a little. I think we can all understand you. Don't imagine you're alone and no one can ever understand you anymore. You're here today, and we're watching a funny anime, and you can laugh along with the rest of us. If Rei can laugh, so can you. None of your old friends will hold it against you." Kotone concluded her introductions.

"Today, we're watching *Working!!* We're also eating crepes and ice cream for dinner. And we're pulling out sleeping bags and falling asleep on the carpet of this very living room when night falls. We're also talking about anything and everything. I'm turning on the subtitles, so if you're bored with what people are saying, just follow the anime and zone us out. Don't be a cad and demand we all be silent for your exclusive benefit. This is a free-talking zone. Shushers will be escorted out of the environs.

"I'd also like to take a walk with you alone, Isao, just to stroll the neighborhood. It…well, it's about as daring as I'm willing to be with you, and it's as daring as my parents will allow me to be anyway, so it will just have to suffice. I hope you didn't come here with any evil designs?"

Isao lifted his hands up palms open and shook his head.

"Good. Because all of our Wyrds can see you're a Choice Giver. So we expect exemplary behavior from you. All men are supposed to follow or emulate your choices, so if it turns out that includes taking advantage of little girls…" Kotone shook her finger at him.

"It won't! It doesn't include that! You're the one that insisted this was even a date!" Isao protested vociferously.

"So, would you like to take a walk with me around the neighborhood, after, say, we finish our crepes, and that's all?" Kotone asked hopefully.

"Yes, I'd love that," Isao agreed, wishing the spotlight would finally leave him.

"Okay, everyone, I'm your hostess for the day. If you need anything or have any questions, just ask me. I've already prepared everyone tea, so I'll be fetching that now." Kotone bowed, her face full of nervous happiness, like she didn't know what to do with her feelings anymore.

"Don't trip! 'Waaaagh!'" Shiori squealed. Chiharu laughed while Kotone blushed, and Isao and Rei looked on, bewildered.

"This is the problem with making new friends. They don't have all of our inside jokes yet." Chiharu kept laughing and started explaining Kotone's hospital visit to see Miyamoto. "And then, 'Waaagh'!" Chiharu started laughing again. "Ah, you just had to be there."

Rei smiled. Even though she hadn't been there, it was still funny. She gave out a real giggle at the idea of Kotone falling straight onto her nose and dousing a guy with vase water.

"Two girls who will go unnamed are not getting their tea," Kotone said fiercely, putting steaming cups from her tray in front of the others.

"Forgive me, Kotone. Give me tea too. You called me fat." Shiori begged.

"Oh very well, since this is a day of good cheer." Kotone smiled and served her best friends.

"And now, let the anime begin!" Kotone excitedly pressed play on her DVD player and then rushed over to sit next to Isao. They were not touching but just close enough to exchange glances whenever they liked to feel like they meant something to each other.

Rei Rin tried to soak it all in with an open mind and nonjudgmental eyes, wanting to find whatever Kotone found so wonderful in this series and wanting to follow the warmth that Kotone was trying to give her. It was a story about eccentric people hanging out and talking during and after work at a café. They didn't stand around making jokes; their entire existences were jokes. And whenever two of these people collided, something ridiculous was said or done, like how a particle was created whenever two fields collided in physics. It was inevitable, and it was incredible. Rei started laughing out loud. After a bit longer, even Shiori gave in and started laughing. No one had seen anything like this. Maybe Kotone was right; maybe it was just about finding the right series.

After everyone had calmed down, they did start to chat. Kotone brought out some rice crackers and pocky to snack on.

"It's such a shame though. I wanted to win the national tournament and give Rei the trophy." Shiori sighed.

"Our goal was one win, not winning the nationals." Chiharu threw a cracker at her.

"But seven to nothing?" Shiori sighed again.

"It can't be helped. You're such a terrible pitcher." Chiharu shrugged.

"I am not! I was just tired from last game," Shiori protested.

"I don't mind, sister," Rei quickly interposed. "I have so many happy memories from that first game, it's like I didn't even see the second. I wouldn't care even if you lost a million to zero."

"I think they'd call the game before that point," Chiharu remarked judiciously.

"Rei, you're even worse than Chiharu! Do you really think your sister could lose a million to zero?" Shiori's wide eyes looked like they were going to cry.

"I didn't…!" Rei panicked. And then everyone laughed, and she realized Shiori was giving her a triumphant "gotcha" look. Was it so impossible for them to be mad at each other that anything mean *had* to be a joke? And yet, it seemed that was the case. *I have so much to learn from these people.*

"Chiharu, tell me how you converted 'fair and square' girl." Kotone was brimming over with curiosity.

"Oh, it was nothing. Phyllis was willing to listen fairly to what I had to say, I'm always right about everything, and so of course she walked away a convert," Chiharu said.

"That can't be the entire story!" Shiori interjected.

"Okay, well. Hmm. Actually Phyllis did teach me something important. When I asked her why she was okay with being a Dead-Ender, she said something interesting. She said that perfection was a straight line that never deviated in any direction. A Dead-Ender was just someone aiming for a perfect world. She was proud of her title. She thought we were the ugly ones because we kept creating so many possibilities, and we kept adding so much change and chaos to the mix, that the Earth could never settle down into its one ideal shape," Chiharu said.

"Is that true, Awesome?" Shiori asked.

"It could be," Awesome said. "Our scrying can only see if a person's choices lead to stagnation or extinction. If that stagnation were an ideal utopia, or a horrible dystopia, we couldn't tell the two apart."

"But from our point of view," Cyan was quick to add, "stagnation is a horrible, ugly ending, no matter where things stagnate. There's no such thing as a stagnant utopia. There's always got to be something better, just a bit further ahead, that we should be striving for."

"I tend to agree with Cyan," Chiharu said, sipping her tea. "But it got me to thinking about the true nature of Dead-Enders. Their secret identity, if you like. If you look back on all the people we fought, they all shared one essence. Whether in this world, or in some fantasy 'next world,' they all wanted to impose a universalist utopia. They knew what this world needed, they had everything figured out, and it was okay to impose it by force. Whatever prize they had in their eye, it was so blindingly bright that it was worth any cost—even sacrificing everything else that anyone else might think is good about life. If the utopia could be reached, the rest didn't matter. This is why they cut off all our possibilities. They force us all into their single mold. George Flint probably wanted a bunch of growing trees, for instance. And so everything else, in the way of trees growing, had to go. Rei wanted a perfect, still, quiet zero, where no one would have to suffer anymore. And so everyone had to cease existing so the zero could be put in place. Phyllis wanted perfect equality, even if it meant sacrificing freedom. Mahmut wanted Allah to rule the world, even if most people would suffer under Him. Claus wanted his daughter to be safe, even if we had to be killed for it. They always take some narrow good, balloon it up, and then imagine they've fulfilled the highest potential of mankind. They always leave so much good on the cutting board that will never be fulfilled anymore. And that is why they always lead to dead ends."

"So what does that make a Choice Giver? Someone who doesn't believe in utopia?" Isao asked, dissatisfied.

"No. If it were that easy, there'd be more than fifty of us on Earth or however many of us there are left now. It's more like Choice Givers are the people who really *could* reach a utopia. But our utopia is different from theirs. It's open-ended enough, it is particular and local enough, that it never narrows the full spectrum of good's expression. For instance, this sleepover here, now, is a utopia. It is a utopia for everyone in it. Am I wrong?" Chiharu looked around the gathering. No one thought she was wrong.

"Choice Givers are people, if emulated or followed, who really can give life the full appreciation it deserves.

If everyone were like us, they could all create their own little utopias, each suited to their own needs. And those little utopias could be woven together into a tapestry, seamlessly flowing into one another like small trickles flowing into a river that empties into the ocean—only the ocean the waters of life empty out into is the ocean of stars. Trillions of utopias, utopias like this gathering of friends, circling around trillions of shining stars, across the entire multiverse. We, uniquely, have a dream as big as life's possibilities, and we are taking the right paths to get there. That's what our Wyrds are telling us. That's what we somehow need to tell the world."

"See? What did I tell you about Chiharu explaining philosophy for us peons?" Kotone grinned at Isao.

"I believe you. That…was astounding," Isao said, shaken.

"I wish I could convert a Dead-Ender, like you and Shiori." Kotone sighed.

"You will!" Shiori assured her. "You're a great speaker, Kotone!"

"I hope so." Kotone sighed. "Maybe all my poison and acid is trying to tell me I'll never measure up."

"And maybe you're an idiot," Chiharu said. "I won't let anyone talk badly about you, Kotone, even you."

"Err…but you just…" Isao started to point out in confusion.

"Oooh. Isao's coming to Kotone's rescue! Oooh." The girls all turned on him with expectant eyes.

"That is… Kotone! Let's go on a walk!" Isao grabbed her hand and pulled her up. Kotone looked at the crowd and then started blushing furiously. For all her embarrassment, though, she didn't let his hand go for as long as Rei could see them.

"Shiori, wake up." Awesome flashed urgently. "Dead-Enders, three of them, are heading for Miyamoto's hospital. We have to hurry."

"Mmm? Awesome? Tell me in the morning." Shiori tried to close her eyes.

"Wake up, you stupid baby!" Awesome rammed into her forehead.

"Ow!" Shiori woke up, rubbing her forehead. "What did you do that for?"

"Three... Dead-Enders... heading... for... Miyamoto." Awesome repeated, flashing to accentuate each word.

"Not again." Shiori moaned. "Everyone, wake up. We have to go save Mr. Miyamoto. Again."

Chiharu yawned and rolled up from the floor. "What is this, the third time?"

"This time, I'll definitely convert one through talking." Kotone looked determined.

Isao just got up. "Let's go, Black." Rei sighed and squeezed Onyx to her chest.

Awesome blinked. When did three Dead-Enders together stop being a serious threat? These girls were getting to be ridiculous.

Chapter 13

Everyone arrived at the base of the hospital with time to spare. Isao went invisible. Shiori curled up on the grass to go back to sleep. Kotone practiced speech lines, hoping for the exact right introduction that would finally convert a Dead-Ender. It was annoying when Dead-Enders attacked in the middle of the night, but at least that was better than attacking during school hours. Chiharu suppressed a yawn and sighed. School was coming up in just a few hours. After the fight, there probably wasn't even time to get back to sleep.

Miraculously, Shiori had no problem falling back asleep. Chiharu supposed it was like in those soldier stories. Soldiers eventually figured out that any downtime was time to sleep, and they slept accordingly, or maybe she was just too fearless for her own good. Or maybe she trusted Chiharu to kick her awake before the fight started. Well, that could be arranged.

I wonder what they'll hit us with this time. They had never fought a party of Dead-Enders working together. But then again, none of them seemed as dangerous as Claus Reinhardt. In fact, all three of them together didn't seem as dangerous as Claus Reinhardt. As far as Chiharu was concerned, they were just throwing away valuable pieces. If the dark Wyrds ever thought to attack with ten or twenty at once, instead of all of these piecemeal nuisance raids, what would they do then? *Maybe we should give up on living in Japan and go search out the other Choice Givers around the world, and make a full-scale army. Maybe we should start hunting down them and killing dark Wyrds the moment they appear.* But if Chiharu did that, she knew she would never enjoy her life again. It would just be battle after battle, forever. I don't want that. *I want to enjoy my life with my friends— my normal life with my family, with Saki and Aiko.* Maybe it was stupid, but there it was. There was no point protecting her life through a route that would itself make it unlivable.

"Incoming," Cyan told her. Chiharu stepped over and nudged Shiori with her foot.

"Nnn. I'm up." Shiori sighed, getting back on her feet.

"Let's let Kotone lead the conversation with the Dead-Enders," Chiharu suggested. "She's feeling left out."

"Fine by me. Just tell me when to firestorm." Shiori held a hand over her enormous yawn.

The three Dead-Enders appeared. They were all flying. Chiharu sighed. Everyone just loved to fly these days. The one in the middle had some sort of crazy silver skinsuit with pretend atoms orbiting around him. To his right was a white cloaked and hooded figure with a metallic mask, keeping himself, or herself, aloft with a jet pack. To his left was a girl wearing a Chinese-style dress with devil horns, bat wings, and a tail. That was pretty imaginative. At least that Dead-Ender seemed to realize she was a bad guy through and through—or maybe she just thought it was cute.

"I'm Kotone Nakano, a Choice Giver." Kotone started, nerving herself up for the best speech ever. The hooded figure started making weird hand signals. Chiharu bit her cheek and readied a counterspell. Their resolution had been to keep talking even if they had to dodge attacks, as long as they could. She had to give Kotone this chance to shine.

Suddenly, a transparent, yellow box appeared around the group. Chiharu let loose a counterspell, but it fizzled upon touching the wall. Deflect fizzled too. Everything fizzled on contact. Isao reappeared touching the barrier, looking startled. The entire group was trapped.

"What…?" Kotone looked around, holding her wand uncertainly.

"Our business is not with you children," the atom-orbiting man said. "Don't worry, the box won't do you any harm. It's just that you can't leave it for the rest of the day."

"Who are you? What is your objective?" Kotone challenged the man.

"I am Mastermind. Our objective is simple. The world the Wyrds come from is superior to our own. Therefore, we will fold up. It is time for this cross-cultural contact to stop being so one-sided. With the help of Masanori, we will become Wyrds," Mastermind happily explained himself.

"*Coi*, Xanadu!" Sparkles appeared around the hospital window of Miyamoto's room. And then the man, weak as ever, walked into the air with sword ready. "You're a fool if you think I'll help you with anything."

"Of course. I would be a fool, *if* I thought that." Mastermind smirked.

And then Miyamoto's face went slack, and he lowered his sword.

"By the way, I am Tien Feng. And that was *my* magic. Remember me, mortals." The devil flapped her wings. "For next time my name is spoken, I will be a god."

"Stop! Wait!" Kotone yelled, flying into the box's yellow wall and bouncing off.

"Come, Miyamoto." Tien Feng smirked. Chiharu had to shake her head. The girl had the suit of a succubus and used compulsion magic of all things. *Now that is a girl who knows what she wants.*

"Yes, mistress." Miyamoto flew to them.

"Robo, carry the man. He'll never make it back to base in that condition," Mastermind ordered.

Robo didn't say anything but just flew over on his rocket pack to pick the man up easily into his arms. It was almost comical to see a man in a princess carry-hold like that. Robo's suit was certainly strong enough. In just a minute, the entire Dead-Ender force had flown away. Chiharu sighed and sat down in her powersuit. They had been well and truly had.

"What do we do? They've taken Miyamoto away!" Kotone wailed, kicking the wall of the box.

"We wait a day." Chiharu shrugged. "Mastermind said they needed him to fold up. We can only hope that they'll need him for more than a day. What a sick technique. Anti-magic barrier plus anti-physical barrier? At least they couldn't finish us off." Chiharu sighed.

Could she have foreseen a move like this? How? No other Dead-Ender had cast anything remotely like it. The world was indeed vast.

"Awesome, are you okay?" Shiori asked worriedly. All Wyrds needed continuous supplies of magic to survive.

"No problem. The box is active in this dimension. My conduit is hyperdimensional." Awesome sighed. "But I do feel like a fool."

"Is it possible?" Shiori asked. "Can people fold up?"

"No, it's impossible. The energy needed for that sort of reaction…would devour the entire cosmos in a microsecond…" Awesome trailed off.

"Which isn't a hindrance at all to a Dead-Ender," Isao said.

"Even then, Wyrds have already done the math. There's no known way to fold up. We knew that when we came down here, it was permanent," Awesome said, regaining his confidence.

"Mastermind sounded confident it could be done. It's not like Wyrds have been studying folding for a long time. From what you told me, you only started worrying about the question a few weeks ago, right? Plus, Wyrds only have their own magic to work with. They never considered what magic might emerge from Wyrd-human contracts," Chiharu said.

"Then it's over. We're going to sit here in this box until the universe explodes, and Mastermind achieves all his dreams with Miyamoto as his helpless accomplice." Rei Rin sat down, sighing.

"It's not over. We have no idea how long Mastermind's plan takes. We don't even know if this box will really last as long as he said it would. We'll track them down and take Miyamoto back," Shiori said, patting Rei on the shoulder. Rei offered Shiori half a smile, as though she knew Shiori was just trying to cheer her up but appreciated the gesture anyway.

"If Mastermind can interact with the Wyrd world, then so can we," Shiori said. "Awesome, you said your conduit is still connected. When you suck in more or less magic from the etheric plane, that's interacting with the Wyrd world, isn't it?" Shiori asked.

"Well, sure, I guess," Awesome said. "But I already said, there's no way we could fold up, even if Mastermind and Miyamoto can. If you thought I could somehow transport us up my tube—"

"No, who cares about that? Tell me, is anyone watching your conduits to see how the Wyrds connected to Choice Givers down here are doing?" Shiori asked, an idea clearly forming in her head.

"Sure. If a Wyrd on duty dies, the conduit will disappear, and then they'll know to send another Wyrd replacement to his or her Choice Giver. That and scrying are about the only two things the Wyrd world can see about Earth," Awesome explained.

"Then would they notice if your conduit suddenly turned off?" Shiori asked.

"Umm, are you angry with me, Shiori? Turning off my conduit would kill me." Awesome flashed worriedly.

"Not if you were at absolute zero. Without a metabolism, you won't need any magic." Shiori smiled.

Everyone looked at Rei.

Awesome flashed his light, still not content. "So why would you want to turn me off? It's not like any new Wyrds, even if they did arrive in the hopes of replacing me, could penetrate this box. We're just weak floating gems down here."

"I'm not going to turn you off. I'm going to turn you off and on, over and over. With just an 'on' and an 'off,' we have a binary code: one and zero. Humans call it Morse code, 'dot' and 'dash.' Surely Wyrds, in your great wisdom, have developed a binary language with just two letters to work with?" Shiori asked excitedly.

"I, yes…I suppose we have." Awesome looked flummoxed.

"Then we've won." Shiori clapped her hands together. "Gods, we could have thought of this at any point. I can't believe it took Mastermind to tip me off."

"Tip you off to what?" Chiharu asked, jealous that Shiori was somehow two steps ahead of her.

"I've been wishing, hoping, for some way to turn off the spigot of dark Wyrds that keep coming from your plane to go haunt ours. It just sounded like a dream, until now. Now I see that we've had all the pieces in place to do this since forever. We can send any message we want, right? What do you think would grab their attention up top? We need to get them to realize your 'death' and 'non-death' is spelling out a coded message.

"How about 'dark wyrds'?" Cyan flashed helpfully.

"Okay, we have a day to sit around in here." Shiori started ordering them around. "Cyan, you don't have to teach Rei the language. Just tell her when to turn on and off Eternal Zero. Start spelling 'dark Wyrds' with Awesome's conduit over and over again. Meanwhile, Onyx, you're going to tell us the location of the dark Wyrd's base, the identities of all your friends, where you've hidden your folding device and your folding device backup plans, and anything else we need to know. And once you've told us, you're going to tell the Wyrd government, in binary."

"Why should I?" Onyx flashed petulantly.

"Because if you don't, Rei will cry," Shiori said.

Onyx tried to blink carelessly and villainously not care. "Rei…look, Rei, Mastermind is just doing what we always wanted. He's destroying the whole universe. Let's not cooperate with them. This is our win."

"Onyx, you can't fool me. You ceased being a villain ages ago. We're your friends. You were always my friend. You don't have to put up a tough front anymore," Rei said.

"I…I am a proud villain of the honorable dark Wyrd organization…" Onyx said; then everyone started laughing.

"'Dark Wyrd organization'? Do you guys really call yourselves that?" Kotone's asked.

"Err, no, we're the Wyrd council." Onyx blinked a wave of black embarrassment.

"You've already joined our side, or you wouldn't be using our terms, Onyx. Come on. We're all waiting on you. No one here will think less of you for being a good guy," Shiori appealed to him.

"Am I really not important to you, Onyx?" Rei asked pitiably.

Onyx sighed. "You're right. Somewhere in there, I started to care. You Choice Givers…are entirely too corrosive."

"If by corrosive you mean purifying, then, yes, we are," Shiori answered him smugly. "Now get talking. We have all day in a box to tell the Wyrds up top about this."

"But how will this help against Mastermind? You said we'd won," Chiharu complained.

"Don't you get it, Chiharu? If we can turn off the spigot, then this is our final battle. How strong will we be, knowing this is our last fight and one more victory means…means…everything? Our lives back. Our Earth saved. Just smack Mastermind in the face, and we can go home and do whatever we want! If you remember that, how strong will we be? I don't care what's waiting for me in his evil lair. I can already feel the weight falling off my shoulders! From here on, we can do anything. Beat Mastermind, and our lives won't just be restricted to endless fights. There will be infinite possibilities. We can all have a Christmas party and visit a New Year's shrine together!" Shiori enthused.

"You're really looking forward to Christmas, aren't you?" Chiharu smiled. Shiori's hope was flooding into her and lighting up her imagination.

"Of course!" Shiori shouted. "Our lives begin here, today. Today, our lives begin anew. Who cares about Mastermind? Who cares about the universe exploding? We'll tear down anything in our way and go celebrate Christmas together! This is their final hand," Shiori said.

"Their *gotterdammerung*." Chiharu grinned. "It's the twilight of the Wyrds."

Isao Oono grinned. "If only we could play 'Ride of the Valkyries' when we fly over to their base and take Miyamoto back."

"I could hum it." Chiharu grinned back.

"What are you two talking about?" Kotone asked jealously.

"Our first inside joke as new friends," Chiharu replied.

"All friends need inside jokes, Miss *Waaagh*!" Isao grinned.

Kotone tried to get angry then she just laughed. Rei was already signaling, "dark Wyrds." Trapped in a box, the world in peril, and Miyamoto a slave to a succubus, the group had never been in higher spirits.

Mastermind, Tien Feng, and Robo landed deep in the mountains of Japan, walking into a subterranean cave that housed his irreplaceable machine. Even with Miyamoto compelled, it's not like either of them knew how to incorporate their two teleportation techniques into the spark that would overload the machine. Somehow or other, their magic could cause a chain reaction. Mastermind *knew* it could. But it would take time, experiments, and a deep amount of focus to do so.

"Tien, bring Miyamoto. We're going to my lab. Robo, guard the entrance." The hooded figure turned and stood a silent sentinel.

"What is this, Mastermind?" Ajani Ngige intercepted him and complained. He was one of those despicable Dead-Enders with a petty dream—a drug dealer whose magic had manifested as the ability to create the perfect drug, without resistance building or side effects. Since to him pleasure was the sole purpose of life, Ajani had figured that distributing his drug would bring about his utopia. Mastermind sneered inside his head. *As though I would waste a mind like mine simply feeling good, when there was a whole universe just waiting to be explored above me.*

"We agreed not to make any moves until we had a decisive military advantage," Ajani complained.

"The situation changed. The Choice Givers have decided to attack us. At least this way we caught their strongest member." Mastermind gestured to Miyamoto.

"I don't like it. These guys beat Reinhardt…" Ajani mumbled.

"Are you a man or a coward?" Tien Feng sneered. "They're schoolchildren. They're thirteen-year-olds. If they come here, kill them. It's not that complicated."

"I don't like it either." Miguel Sores walked up to the entrance, with Genevieve Desmarais like always in tow. "We were supposed to outnumber them. You've acted too soon."

"By my count, there's seven of us and five of them. Four of them are thirteen-year-old girls." Tien Feng rolled her eyes. "I think we've fulfilled the conditions necessary to win. That is, if you three do *your* part. I've already defeated *my* opponent."

Miguel Sores was some sort of anarchist who wanted everyone to return to subsistence farming. Genevieve Desmarais was even worse. She just loved Miguel. Both of them made Mastermind sick. He was surrounded by pettiness. At least Robo was quiet and did what he, or she, was told. Mastermind could imagine that Robo was wise. Robo was a good talking companion. Mastermind could say whatever he wanted, and Robo wouldn't say anything stupid in response.

"I suppose they'll be coming here whether we like it or not." Miguel sighed. "But I'm bringing this up with the Wyrd council."

"Bring up whatever you want." Mastermind snarled. *Fool. The Wyrd council is going to evaporate into pure energy in the next few days. But go contact them all you want. This world is already dead to me.* "Tien, let's go."

"Cooooming," Tien Feng said fetchingly, winking at the Dead-Enders she left behind. Tien got the enormous joke being played on these losers. Tien wasn't bad company at all.

"Amethyst, come here. What do you make of this?" Taupe asked the other guard on duty.

"What?" Amethyst stored his phone away. He was watching the Bulls game while on duty. Well, it was an extremely boring duty. Taupe didn't blame him.

"Awesome—his conduit is blinking." Taupe pointed.

"That's impossible. If his conduit stops, that means he died," Amethyst explained.

"So what, he's dying and coming back to life hundreds of times, just for fun?" Taupe gestured. "Just see for yourself."

The two guards stared at the conduit turning on and off, from perfect health to complete silence, over and over.

"That…is weird," Amethyst finally granted.

"Moreover, look, the blinking isn't just on and off. Look at the time gaps between them. They aren't the same period," Taupe insisted.

"Long, long, short, short, long, short, long, short—" Amethyst started counting them.

"That isn't random. He's purposefully showing us something. But what? What can a blinking conduit show anyone?" Taupe asked.

"It can show anything. With two states, any amount of information can be conveyed," Amethyst replied, his mouth going slack. "By God, he's discovered a method of contact. True communication from the bottom up— as expected of our greatest scryer."

"What are you talking about? How can 'on' and 'off' say anything?" Taupe asked.

Amethyst hit a few buttons on his phone, summoning up the relevant data. "Here. The long-short code for our written language. I suppose it's a hobby only some of us learn. Now let me watch for a bit."

Taupe and Amethyst stared at the conduit sucking and not sucking, for longer and shorter amount of times.

"D-a-r-k w-y-r-d-s." Amethyst spelled out. Then there was a pause. "D-a-r-k w-y-r-d-s."

"That's not random." Taupe agreed.

"Awesome's trying to get our attention." Amethyst agreed. "Taupe, call the higher-ups. Actually, call everyone. Get the entire government here. They're going to want to see this."

Taupe agreed. His hand shaking, he dialed up his captain. "Sir, we have something you're going to want to see."

"Do you think they got the message?" Rei Rin asked, sitting on the floor of their box. Her voice was a whispered croak. Invoking Eternal Zero didn't take any real energy from the magical girl. The energy came from above, through the conduit. But just saying the words that many times, stuck in the box with no water, had made the experience miserable.

The night had turned to day, and a vast mass of Japanese were gathered around them, staring and pointing. Various people had tried to break through the box. Of course, it was all to no avail. Policeman had come to look at them, scratched their heads, and then left again. They were in a box. Sitting in a box wasn't exactly a crime.

Rei was glad they at least had all their costumes on. Hopefully they wouldn't be recognizable when they returned to school life. Rei envied Kotone's pink hair.

"They did. They had to," Shiori replied. "You did great, sister."

Rei smiled.

"Once the dark Wyrds are caught, they'll probably fold a Wyrd down here to tell us. We'll probably receive medals," Cyan promised.

"Great. I always wanted medals," Chiharu said sarcastically.

"Don't fight, you two." Magnolia pulsed.

"Hello, everyone! I'm magical girl Kotone! Have you hugged your neighbor today? Teehee!" Kotone posed and released little hearts from her wand. The crowd started laughing and applauding. Actually, Rei wanted to laugh too. Trust Kotone to turn this into a "spread-the-warmth" advertisement.

"Our teachers are going to kill us for skipping school." Shiori sighed.

"You do know Cyan has scryed out seven Dead-Enders, including Miyamoto, in that mountain?" Chiharu mentioned judiciously.

"Who cares? What's seven more? Just seven more, Chiharu," Shiori said, her eyes glowing. "If only this stupid box would end."

"What if Robo catches us in another box?" Chiharu asked.

"We'll spread out this time. Whoever isn't caught, beat Robo, and we'll be freed again," Shiori ordered.

"We are *not* fighting seven more." Kotone turned on them with a glare. "Miyamoto is being held captive. No one had better even be *thinking* of hurting him. He's injured enough as he is. Just take out Tien Feng, and Miyamoto will be free again."

"You're right. I'm just a little tired." Chiharu sighed. "We didn't exactly get much sleep last night."

"Box?" Shiori addressed the yellow rectangle directly. "I think you've lasted long enough. You've made your point. How about it, box? If you set us free, I'll love you forever and ever."

"You've gone—" Chiharu started to respond. But then the box disappeared. Rei stared in complete astonishment. *No way. It was a coincidence. Not even Shiori could do something like that. Could she?*

"Choice Givers make the impossible possible." Shiori had an extremely self-satisfied smirk on her face.

"You did *not* just do that. Choice Giving doesn't work that way." Chiharu glared.

"Uh-huh. Tell it to the judge." Shiori smiled. Then she turned to the others. "Kotone, Rei, can you carry us all, divided between you two?"

"No problem. Chiharu can amplify our flight if we need it. Amplified, I'm pretty fast." Kotone bragged, her boots sprouting wings and floating her a few feet off the ground.

"We'll never forget you, box!" Shiori called. And then the crowd watched the entire crew hold hands and fly away.

Chapter 14

When they came within sight of the mountain, Rei and Kotone split apart so they couldn't be boxed again. Sure enough, Robo was waiting at the entrance. He or she didn't say anything but just started spraying lasers into the sky.

"If Robo doesn't like talking, that's fine by me. Onyx!" Rei rasped.

"Let's do it," Onyx agreed cheerfully. Rei's butterfly wings started growing wider and wider.

"Chiharu?" Rei asked her friend.

"Got it." Chiharu grinned.

"Secret technique," Rei intoned, gathering up all her energy.

"Amplify." Cyan started glowing blue to her black.

"Abandon hope, all ye who enter here," Rei chanted. "Black Hole."

In a few moments, the mountain cave had become noticeably wider. Robo's jet pack hadn't saved him—or her or it. *I guess now we'll never know.* Rei sighed.

"Let's land," Chiharu said. "The rest of them are in there with Miyamoto. We don't want to suck him up with them."

Rei Rin nodded and flew her to the entrance. Kotone was delivering Shiori and Isao nearby.

"Rei, that was amazing!" Shiori shouted at her.

"Just one more fight." Rei rasped. "If it's just one more fight, I don't want to wait any longer. I want to go play with Melody."

"The Dead-Enders are all over the place. I can't give you anything specific," Awesome said.

"All right, everyone. Let's split up and hunt them down," Shiori ordered.

"Fine by me," Isao said, slipping into invisibility. "Just don't interfere with my target. Black, I need some speed. *Flash move.*"

A curtain of dust shot up from where Isao used to be standing.

Kotone, Shiori, and Chiharu all put their hands in a circle, and then they nodded. "One more time!" they all shouted. And then they split up into the innards of the cavern.

Rei tried to follow Shiori, but she stumbled. *That's strange. Magic isn't really that draining.* She tried to get up again. Her legs wouldn't move.

Shiori smiled and came back to her. "You've done enough, sister. Eternal Zero all day, flying here with another person, and tearing a mountain in two? That's enough. Rest here. I'm going to punch Mastermind in the face."

"Thanks," Rei whispered. "Good luck." Rei's part in this fight was done.

Isao walked silently within range of his target. He was a good-looking fellow in his twenties or so. His suit was radiating electricity. He was ready to fight, but it didn't really matter. Isao stabbed him through the heart. It looked like his part was done.

Chiharu sped through the caverns in search of prey, her laser gun ready. She met the exact person she had hoped for.

Tien Feng whipped her tail in the same gesture she had used before Miyamoto was caught, with a confident smirk on her face.

"Reflect," Chiharu cast. An invisible wave turned around and went back toward its master. There was a brief look of horror, and then Tien Feng had a dull, vacant look.

"Release Miyamoto," Chiharu ordered.

"It is done," Tien said listlessly.

"Become a good person," Chiharu said. "Actually, I'm not sure how well your brain can process that order. Okay, for starters, follow and emulate me. I'll see what new additions I feel like adding to your personality later."

"Sounds interesting," Tien Feng said, changing her pose, for some reason, to an extremely arrogant slouch.

Chiharu had to suppress the desire to tell Tien to become her footstool. This was just so ridiculously fun. "Obey me and my friends. Don't harm us. And don't harm yourself." Chiharu immediately resorted to the three laws of robotics. Asimov had tried to think of loopholes, but Chiharu doubted the magic would leave any.

"Let's go search for more prey," Chiharu said, shouldering her gun and beginning to sprint again.

Kotone faced off against a real-life angel. The blonde-haired girl had white angel wings and a flaming sword. Inside the cave, neither of them had much mobility. But that was okay. Kotone would *finally* convince this one last Dead-Ender. It was her last chance. After today, they were free forever.

"My name is Kotone Nakano. What's yours?" Kotone asked amicably.

"I... Genevieve Desmarais. I won't let you through." The girl brandished her sword.

"That's okay. I don't want through. I came here to heal you, Genevieve, not to go anywhere else. So tell me, why are you here?" Kotone flew over to a rock and sat down.

"All the governments of the world have to be abolished. We'll be happy if we just farm again..." Genevieve seemed confused, not knowing where to put her sword.

"Seriously?" Kotone asked. "You love farming that much? Where are you from? Genevieve is French, right? You flew all the way from France to Japan so you could kill me, because I was in the way of your farming?" Kotone asked incredulously.

"It makes sense when Miguel says it!" Genevieve snaps.

"Could you possibly be in love with Miguel?" Kotone asked.

"That's right. And he loves me too," Genevieve said hotly.

"That's a relief. I just had my first date with a boy yesterday. I specifically told him we couldn't do more than take a walk together. But he immediately grabbed my hand in front of everyone. I didn't want to make Isao lose face in front of my friends, so I bore with it. But do you think that was really loving of him? To completely ignore my stated wish on the *first* date? I bet Miguel would have been a *much* better gentleman," Kotone said.

"Well, it depends on the context," Genevieve said, sitting down. "Why did he try to hold your hand? Maybe you just said something so charming or cute that he did it without thinking. Wouldn't that be loving?"

"I think it was a reflex. Isao would never take advantage of me. He was just embarrassed because all my friends were teasing us, and he wanted to take me away. But really. He said I could trust him, and bam! He grabs me," Kotone complained.

"Well was it really fair of you to stick him in the middle of all your close friends on your first date? Maybe he was embarrassed because he felt outnumbered, and the whole situation was under your control," Genevieve replied.

"I hadn't thought of that," Kotone admitted. "I thought he would like my friends."

"I'm sure he does. But it's still awkward. They're your friends, so they'll always think he doesn't deserve you. That's a lot of pressure to act under all day long," Genevieve explained.

"What's it like to be loved? When I imagine it, if a guy loved me, he would want to protect me. He would protect me from the world, sure. He would protect me from any insult too. And he'd protect me from doing anything I'd later regret. I think he'd protect me most from my own weaknesses. He would be my strength," Kotone suggested.

"That's too narrow. A man's love isn't just protection. Any friend could do that. A man's love is about knowing you're valued. It's his passion for you, and his gratitude, and whether he remembers all the special moments we've shared before." Genevieve corrected her.

"But there has to be an element of loyalty," Kotone replied. "Passion could be given to any pretty girl. He could be grateful for how she pleases him too. Where does that get you? No, I'd know if someone loved me if he cared about me more than anything else. If he cared about me more than anything else, I'd know he cared about me more than anyone else too."

"A guy who's only devoted to you, and nothing else, is nothing but a dog—or a slave. What's the appeal in a one-dimensional feeling like that?" Genevieve shot back.

"But what if the man isn't devoted to you? What if he's devoted to what he sees inside you? What if the man loves…your soul? Can a dog love souls? Is it slavish to revere the sacred?" Kotone asked.

"If your boyfriend has been worshipping your soul, I suggest his grabbing your hand is just the start of his intentions." Genevieve smiled kindly.

"He wouldn't say it. You'd just see it in his eyes—that desire to protect and that look that says, 'I will give my life for you,' except it's not for you. I'm not making any sense." Kotone blushed angrily.

"No, I think I've seen that look before. It's like the look of a man staring at a painting in the Louvre. They stare and stare, and they have this sort of tense look about them, like they're about to jump into action, like they finally found what they've been searching for. They finally found something worth preserving at any cost. How strange. I'd completely forgotten that look, until you brought it up." Genevieve thought back to Paris wistfully.

"I know a man who stares at me like that. I'm his painting in the Louvre. He's been alone his whole life. He wanted to protect someone. He wandered down every wing of the museum, but no matter how many paintings he saw, he never tensed up—not until he saw me. When I realized how he was looking at me, I wanted to have his children. Do you think I'm crazy?" Kotone asked.

"No…no…I—" Genevieve broke off, tears welling up in her eyes. "Miguel never looks at me. I just try to help his dream, so he'll think fondly of me. He doesn't love me." Genevieve Desmarais sobbed. "He only loves his own reflection in the mirror."

"I'm sure he loves you as much as he knows how." Kotone comforted her. "I'm sure he means well."

"They all mean well. But look what he's done. I'm in some rotten cave, abandoned, in a fight for my life. How could he? How *could* he?" Genevieve yelled.

Kotone forced back a smile. *How's that, Shiori? How's that, Chiharu? Now I'm a true Choice Giver.* It felt wonderful.

Chiharu and Tien Feng strode into another chamber. This time there was a black man wearing a ton of gold chains, with a gold-plated gun. *I guess that counts as magical weapons and armor.*

"Tien, what's going on? My Wyrd says you're no longer a Dead-Ender. And why is *this* girl still a Choice Giver?" The black man pointed at her.

"Compel him," Chiharu ordered. The man looked shocked then jumped behind a boulder. Chiharu muttered to herself over the missed opportunity.

"Fight him as best you can," Chiharu ordered. Then she sat back and waited for an open shot.

Tien flew over the rock, trying to enslave the man, but she was too slow. After a few shots from his gold-plated gun, she dropped to the ground.

"Little girl, I'm guessing what you did," he told her. "I'm guessing you can turn our own magic against us, but it doesn't look like you can turn our suits against us, can you? I'm guessing I just have to blast you with this gun."

"Unless I blast you with mine," Chiharu answered sweetly. Both of them sat behind rocks in separate corners of the cave.

"I'm guessing you rely on others for everything. I'm guessing you're a one-trick pony. I'm guessing this is the end for you." The man kept talking.

Chiharu thought about it. There was no point to his blather. This man said he wasn't using his magic. But what if he was like Isao? What if he was using his magic right now?

Chiharu pointed into the air between them and invoked Cyan. "Counter." Cyan flashed blue. *That son of a gun.* If he could attack before she noticed, she needed to finish this quickly.

"I'm guessing you can't counter all my airborne drugs. I'm guessing you'll fall to one soon, little girl. I'm guessing you were the weakest of them all." The gangsta kept on ranting.

"It's finally your turn, buddy." Chiharu patted her Mark 7,000 rifle. "Show them what you can do." She imagined the laser in her gun not shooting; she imagined reflecting the laser back and forth, keeping it trapped, just growing the beam and trapping it between so many reflects that it was incredibly pressurized. The laser never touched any of the gun's sides. It just bounced between her walls of magic. *That's right. That's the pace. Next up, amplify the beam. Stronger. Keep bouncing. You can't come out yet. Amplify some more.* The beam was getting hotter. *The "weakest"? I'll show you weak.*

Chiharu stood out from under her rock's cover and shot her laser. It was as bright as a firebird; it was as hot as the sun. The man was huddling safely behind his cover. But there was no such thing as cover against Chiharu. The moment the laser shot above his head, Chiharu yelled out one more time, "*Deflect*!" The beam turned at an impossible angle and vaporized the entire area. *Vectors can do anything, punk.*

"Mastermind!" Shiori shouted. Miyamoto was unconscious in a heap. "It's over! Give it up!"

Mastermind turned and gazed upon her with endless fury. "It was working. It was working. What happened to my box?"

"I guess it just needed some love," Shiori quipped. "Please tell me you're going to put up a fight. I promised to punch you in the face."

"I will rebuild. I'm almost there. I'll extract Miyamoto's magic into another vessel. I will become a Wyrd. Do you know how many times I've tried? You're just one more road bump. After I kill all of you, I will find a way. There's *always* a way," Mastermind insisted.

"Rapidfire," Shiori said. Her boots sprouted jet flames on her heels. She was faster than anyone. She shot toward Mastermind with the fury of a comet, summoning flame into her knuckles. *This whole ordeal will be over in one more punch!* And then she was suddenly on the other side of the room. Shiori spun, her jet boots tracing a wide arc, and then she launched herself at him again.

And then she was back on the far side of the room. Suddenly Mastermind's hand was behind her, blasting into her armor. Shiori pitched to the floor but instinctively rolled out of the attack. Mastermind was still standing in front of her. *What the hell is this?*

"Shiori! Remember back at the box!" Awesome called out. "He always wanted to fold up! His magic is teleportation!"

"That's great!" Shiori shouted back, her jet-ski boots skidding across the floor, as she desperately zigzagged just to stay away from his floating fists. "But you haven't told me the important part. What on Earth can I do about it?"

"I don't know. Why not try a ranged attack?" Awesome asked.

"Firefly!" Shiori shouted. A swarm of fireballs zoomed toward the floating atomic man. And then they were behind her, and only Shiori's diving leap watched them fly overhead.

"Nope!" Shiori reported.

"I saw!" Awesome yelled back.

"I am Mastermind. I am the head of all Dead-Enders. Did you think these cheap tricks would work against *me*?" The man sneered contemptuously.

"I'm the most beautiful girl in the multiverse!" Shiori shouted back. "I'm the brightest light in the stars! I am hope! I am life! I am Shiori Rin! You never stood a chance against me!" Shiori shouted.

Shiori spun to point directly behind her and summoned fire into her fist. "Buuurrrrsssttt Knuckle!" Her punch passed through the air behind her, using the same point to point spatial connection that had teleported her fire flies. She felt a satisfying crunch as it burned right into his face.

Chiharu was carrying Miyamoto on her back when they emerged from the cave. Kotone was escorting a crying woman. Isao had his arms up, pinning his spear against the back of his head. Shiori followed them back out of the cavern and soaked in the noonday summer sun, or perhaps it had a touch of fall to it. It was no matter; fall was a useless season. All she wanted was for it to be Christmas.

"Rei, are you feeling better?" Shiori asked, kneeling down to hold her sister's hand.

"Not really," Rei whispered. "Actually, *all* my injuries still hurt. And now I've lost my voice too."

"If you're healthy enough to complain, you're fine." Shiori beamed down at her. "We won, Rei. It's all over."

"I know, Shiori. Your face already told me everything." Rei stroked Shiori's cheek, and only then did Shiori notice she was crying.

"We won," Shiori repeated. She didn't know what else to say.

"I know, Shiori." Rei couldn't stop smiling.

"Greetings, folded surface dwellers. I am Bubbles." The Wyrd flashed a bright light blue.

Everyone started laughing.

"What, did I already mess up?" Bubbles asked worriedly. "Diplomacy is so hard between species…"

"Please tell me you arrested the dark Wyrds." Chiharu cut to the chase.

"Yes, umm. Yes, precisely. Thanks to your investigations. Well, I was sent here to…to tell you we've arrested them. The dark Wyrds won't be troubling Earth any longer." Bubbles flashed a bright blue. "If you people already knew this, I wish I hadn't taken a one-way mission to tell you—"

"Don't worry, Bubbles," Kotone told him brightly. "One of our kids will be a Choice Giver. Once you're contracted, the Earth is a lot of fun."

"There will still be some Dead-Enders, whomever the dark Wyrds allied with before the spigot was closed. The Wyrd council Onyx used to report back to is still out there. I'm sure they're all plotting our destruction somehow or other," Chiharu said.

"Let them come," Shiori said fiercely. "We'll just beat them too." Then she turned away from the cliff face and helped Rei back to her feet. "Everyone, let's go home. I, for one, am ready for bed."